This book is dedicated to all the caregivers who, after hearing our bizarre list of symptoms, treat us for the underlying problem of chronic Lyme disease even though the CDC denies its existence.

To the plethora of patients who are still seeking a Lyme-literate doctor: May you soon find yourself in a room with a caregiver who listens to you and helps you.

Special Thanks to my husband and our kids. My mom. Friends & family. My editors and blurbers. My caregivers. My guides, angels, and shamen. And to the Massachusetts State Rep from Berkshire County who took a chance on hiring me as his intern in the summer of 1984.

Also to Lyme disease, for giving me back my life while almost taking it away. And for providing the foundation for this book.

I Cannot Play With You

Dana Biscotti Myskowski

Black Rose Writing | Texas

The final approval for this literary material is granted by the author.

First printing

This is a work of fiction. Names, characters, businesses, places, events and incidents are either the products of the author's imagination or used in a fictitious manner. Any resemblance to actual persons, living or dead, or actual events is purely coincidental.

ISBN: 978-1-68433-165-9
PUBLISHED BY BLACK ROSE WRITING
www.blackrosewriting.com

Printed in the United States of America
Suggested Retail Price (SRP) $19.95

I Cannot Play With You is printed in Chaparral Pro

I Cannot Play With You

"Fiction is the lie through which we tell the truth."
— Albert Camus

Chapter One

Clipboard in hand, Anna McGrory greeted the last of their early summer visitors as they disembarked with other vacationers and a few locals from the Casco Bay Lines ferry that serviced the smallest of the year-round Southern Maine islands off the coast of Portland. Since Cliff was the final island down the bay after an hour-long journey of stops at four other islands, Anna greeted their guests with a cooler of water bottles. The champagne would wait till later. Right now she simply wanted to get everyone to the private cove where she and her family had, years earlier, scattered the ashes of their beloved greyhound.

Guests were carted the half-mile stretch down the dirt road in a wooden trailer pulled by an antique tractor with just enough paint left to identify it as having once been green. Luggage belonging to those who would be staying over was carried by the island taxi. It was the only van on the island, driven by a year rounder who was born and raised on Cliff. He'd recently been given the key to Portland during his surprise 80th birthday party held during the winter outside on the state pier. The snow was not enough to force people indoors on the sunny day. Anna loved that about the islanders—that they took care of each other and celebrated milestones together, even outside in the cold.

Ordinarily, Anna would have walked the stretch to the singing rock beach, nicknamed for the rhythmic clickity clacks the stones made as the waves of high tide receded. However, today she accepted an empty seat next to her nephew who drove supplies back and forth in a golf cart—the preferred mode of transportation on the island. She reasoned it was the wise thing to do since she was dressed in a mustard-yellow tea-length taffeta gown that reminded her of something a fifty-year-old Nancy Drew might wear. It certainly wasn't normal attire for her. But her daughter loved it, so Anna caved and purchased it.

"You look so pretty!" Anna's best friend, May, said when she saw her. "I still can't believe Joanie got you into a dress."

"Yeah, yeah. Second time for everything."

"Your own wedding?"

Anna nodded as she walked among the guests, deftly parting them until some semblance of an aisle appeared. Satisfied, she yelled, "Let's have us a wedding!"

A freshly groomed black and brown dog—a rescued hound mix—raced to her, rings bow-tied to his collar. The crowd laughed, enjoying the spectacle. Anna dug a treat out of her beaded pocket-sized purse and he plopped down at her feet.

Dressed in sandals and sundresses and each carrying a sunflower, the bridesmaids promenaded through the crowd to the rocky shore. A moment later her daughter Joanie emerged, accompanied by Tom, Anna's husband and Joanie's father.

That's when she lost it.

May put an arm around Anna and gently tugged the clipboard from her grasp. "I've got this now, Mama."

Joanie and Tom approached. "I refuse to look at you, Mom, because I know you're crying and I don't want to start too."

"Join us," Tom said, offering her his other arm. She took it. As the three of them made their way to the rocky shore, the aisle widened just enough to allow them to pass. The grinning groom waited patiently beside the water. He and Joanie had dated for more than a half dozen years, and, three years earlier, had opened a small, local advertising firm together that was still going strong. Today was both the culmination of their time together and the beginning of the rest of their lives.

After the ceremony, some guests snapped pictures as the father of the bride and the bride's aunt took professional photos. Other guests meandered to the island's center where the reception would be held at the CIA hall, an acronym for Cliff Island Association. Anna always loved being able to say that she was a member of the CIA. It was an added perk to vacationing in the Southern Maine community each summer.

At first, no one noticed the motorboat approaching. Anna had written it off subconsciously as a lobster boat returning to the island. But as it neared, she could see it was a water taxi from Portland.

"I've got this," her best friend said. Anna always could count on her. She admired May's purposeful stride as she marched to the shore. May even looked official, still armed with Anna's clipboard. But as the boat neared, Anna recognized one of its occupants.

Her daughter caught her mom's look. "Everything okay, Mom?" she called from her latest pose.

Anna managed her best smile. "Yes, honey. No worries." And she followed after May.

"This is a closed ceremony," she heard her friend say as she joined her on the dock.

"Anna," Senator Ponema said.

"Thanks, May," Anna said. "I'll take it from here." She waited for May to move out of earshot. "This better be an emergency."

"I'm sorry to barge in on your daughter's big day...."

"But?"

"But yes, it is what you would call an urgent situation."

"Get to it," the senator's companion sneered.

"I'm afraid I can only discuss the nature of this matter with Frank."

"He's gone up to the hall for the reception. You're welcome to join us," Anna said.

Senator Ponema glanced at his companion, who shook his head slightly.

The senator turned to Anna, who did her best to hide her perplexed look. "I'm afraid we can't do that." The senator tried to smile apologetically, but the look was off-putting.

"Fine. I'll tell the senator you were here."

"We need to see him now," said Senator Ponema. "We're not leaving till we do."

Anna surprised both men by stepping onto the boat. "Well, give us a hand," she said, reaching for the stranger. "Anna McGrory," by the way.

"I know who you are," he said, backing away.

It was Senator Ponema who helped her onboard. Off his confused look, Anna said, "If you're not coming ashore, then we'll just have to head to the state pier. It's closer to the hall."

The stranger nodded to the taxi driver, and the boat edged away from the dock.

"I'll be right back!" Anna shouted to the wedding party, though no one could understand her over the engine noise. As Joanie watched her mother disappear on the boat, her father had to remind her to smile for the first time that day.

A few moments later, Anna stood on the state pier where the ferry had docked earlier, leaning on the rail and looking down at the strange meeting taking place between the disagreeable senator, his churlish companion, and Senator Frank Barber, her boss of nearly three decades. The two visitors remained on the water taxi talking heatedly with Frank as he stood on the adjacent floating dock, which was connected to the pier by a lengthy metal gangway. It was a steep climb up at low tide. Anna hoped they wouldn't need her for anything else. She didn't want to try to navigate it again with her new sandals that were cute but impractical for rural island life.

"I've never cared for him." Frank's wife, Margaret, joined Anna at the rail.

"Makes two of us," agreed Anna. "There's always an agenda with him, and it's never good for your husband or his constituents." The two U.S. senators represented Massachusetts, but were from opposite parties. Anna never understood how Senator Ponema, the lone Republican sent to Washington from the Bay State, continued to be reelected year after year by the mostly liberal-leaning voters.

Frank stepped back from the boat as it started up. Margaret let out a sigh of relief. "Oh, thank all that is good, he's not going with them."

Anna smiled. She too had wondered if Senator Barber would have to leave.

The party-crashing senator looked up at Anna and Margaret and waved as the boat pulled away from the dock. Margaret turned her back on him. Anna nodded, not able to bring herself to execute a full wave.

"What did they want?" Margaret asked as her husband approached.

"Nothing that can't wait till the senate is in session again."

"Then why didn't they wait?" Margaret pushed.

"You know how some are. Every little setback is an emergency."

"That brought them all the way to Maine?!"

Senator Barber kissed his wife on the cheek. "Have I mentioned how fetching you look in your straw hat and lavender dress?"

"Oh, you!" Margaret protested.

"Give me a moment with Anna. I'll be right up." He gave her hand an affectionate squeeze. Margaret smiled and headed back to the hall.

"I guess I don't have to tell you that you didn't see anything today," the senator said.

"Didn't I?"

"Nothing noteworthy."

"Who was the strange man with Senator Ponema?"

"The consultant who's been advising the committee members."

"Health, education, labor...?"

"And pensions. Yes. But he was never here."

"Got it."

The senator offered Anna his arm. "Now, shall we go see about that beautiful bride and handsome new son-in-law of yours?"

Anna smiled and took his arm as they walked the dirt lane to the Cliff Island Association hall. But she filed away the consultant's face in her memory for possible future use.

***

Cliff Island is the smallest island serviced by the Casco Bay Lines ferry system, which operates out of Portland, Maine. While summer populations may swell to 200 or more, year-round only about 40 to 50 people reside on the island. There is a public library, small store and take-out eatery, post office, tennis court, swimming cove, ball field, walking trails, beaches, public Wi-Fi, church, and a one-room schoolhouse with a greenhouse and playground. Island fishermen provide visitors and residents with fresh lobster, while one year rounder operates an island taxi.

For more information, visit Anna's "Vacation Spots" board on Pinterest: https://www.pinterest.com/anna_mcgrory/vacation-spots/

Chapter Two

As they drove the winding Mohawk Trail of Western Massachusetts, Tom said, "I miss the Berkshires."

"I know you do, Pad," Anna said, reaching over to touch his arm.

Tom smiled. "You haven't called me that in ages," he said, pausing to punctuate the ending with his own endearment: "Lily."

"We were so young then," Anna said.

Tom laughed.

"What?"

"Think about that statement. We can say it at any age."

"And I'll probably say it again in another decade," Anna said, joining her husband in his laughter, and realizing almost as a surprise that she was more in love with him now than ever. Funny how love endured and grew, she thought as she gazed at Wheeler Brook, which Route 2 hugged through the narrow valley of the Savoy Mountain State Forest. "It is beautiful here."

"You despise the Mohawk Trail."

"Only when we had to rely on it to drive back and forth to Boston regularly. As an occasional trip, it's beautiful. I can certainly see why tourists enjoy it."

That morning, Tom and Anna had driven from Maine to Boston to drop their son, Rob, off at Logan Airport. Rob had flown in from Guatemala for the wedding, having taken a few days off from volunteering at his friend's nonprofit organization that helped rural villages with building, farming, water, and education projects. It was the perfect marriage of Rob's skills, since he had studied building with primitive tools at Vermont's Yestermorrow School and had worked with children and on organic farms in his early twenties. Rob, who was now nearly 30, had joined his friend on a spring break building trip to Guatemala last year and stayed. Anna and Tom visited him after the holidays and witnessed the beauty of the area and of the people that had drawn their son to service.

"Watch out!" Anna yelled, but Tom had already swerved, barely missing a bear cub. "There's the mom." Anna pointed into the woods, but Tom was too busy trying to keep his SUV on the road to look.

Tom glanced in his rear view mirror as he steadied his nerves. "And there's another cub."

Anna turned and saw it out the back window. She noticed all the crates that filled the back. "Good thing we packed carefully."

"Good thing we got the extra rider on our insurance," Tom said. It had been his crowning contribution to the wedding—securing the necessary insurance for the entire event, including the days leading up to and following the weekend. Tom also considered it his duty to pay for his daughter's celebration, something he was pleased and proud he could do.

At the senator's pond-front valley home, Anna carried in a crate as Tom closed his gunmetal metallic Honda CRV and followed behind her with a crate of his own. Margaret had set out four glasses and a pitcher of fresh-squeezed lemonade on the terrace that looked out over Mount Greylock, the highest peak in Massachusetts. She was already seated, fanning herself with the Sunday *Globe's* travel section, when Anna joined her.

"That's the last of the lot," said Anna. "Are you sure I can't put them away?"

"No, no, Sheila and Shep will take care of it." Sheila and Shep were the retirement-age couple who lived in the converted carriage house on the other side of a stand of evergreens from Margaret and Frank's home. After he won his first state election, Frank had the carriage house updated so he could hire someone to watch over and care for the estate while they were in Boston for long stretches of time. Sheila and Shep had been there ever since.

"Thank you again," Anna said. "It was such a treat to use the presidential china at the wedding."

"It was our pleasure. You know how fond we are of Joanie. And of you, of course."

Joanie had fallen in love with the dishes the first time she set her eyes on them when she was little older than a toddler. "Tea party?" She had asked, pointing to the impressive collection. Anna was horrified when Margaret let her daughter pick out three cups and saucers for them to use for afternoon tea, knowing she could never pay to replace any broken pieces. But their tea party was a success, and it became a favorite memory of the three women.

The reproduction presidential china was from the first fifteen administrations. Margaret began her collection with the George Washington set, purchasing service for four to use as their everyday ware in their Arlington, Virginia townhouse. It was pricey, but Margaret thought it was a fitting nod to her husband's accomplishment as he stepped from his role as a state representative into his new position as U.S. senator.

At her first dinner party, Margaret decided to use the china, but as the guest list grew, she needed six more place settings. Instead of staying with one dead president, she chose two settings each from the next three administrations: the John Adams, Thomas Jefferson, and James Madison collections. In the four terms of her husband's service, she either purchased or was given place settings from all the administrations up to Benjamin Harrison's. She had amassed 83, which she now kept at their Berkshire home in the china room where Shep had put his carpentry skills to great use. The built-in drawers and cabinets made from maple harvested from the estate were a work of art.

Tom stepped onto the patio and took a deep breath as he admired the magnificent vista of pond, field, woods, and mountains. "I'll never tire of this view."

"You can have it," said Margaret. Tom and Anna shared a look. It was no secret that Margaret preferred the active life in Washington to the country pace that was the norm on her husband's family's estate. "You know you're always welcome to stay long as you like."

They were on a schedule, much as Tom would have liked to stay over. Anna too, if she were honest, though she preferred to live and work out of the guest cottage when the senator and his wife were away in Arlington. The senator was a known workaholic and demanded the same of his staff whenever they were together. Even his rambles through the woods were walk and talks; the senator was thrilled when the cell tower went up nearby a few years ago. Not that Anna didn't work hard, but she also understood the necessity of taking regular breaks and getting a good night's sleep.

"I try to get him to accompany me when I'm working from here, but—"

"Life of a small-firm practitioner. Can't leave too often," Tom said, referring to his three-attorney practice in Concord, New Hampshire, where he and Anna now lived upstairs from the offices.

Tom looked around. "Where's Frank?"

Margaret said that she had just called for him, but couldn't find him. He hadn't turned up for breakfast either. It wasn't out of the ordinary; Frank liked to walk the property every morning, even in bad weather. "He was on a call with Tre till all hours last night. Got so heated, I had to turn the bedroom fan on high just to drown out the noise."

Tre was Senator Ponema's first name. Anna knew Margaret could use the familiar moniker, but was not comfortable doing so herself. It wouldn't be proper for a staff member, no matter how senior, to call a fellow senator by his Christian name.

"I'll go look for him," said Tom. "Where should I start?"

It was a fair question, given the more than 7,000-square-feet to search in the 1948-modernist home that was a veritable museum of custom furnishings and artwork.

Anna pointed. "You take that wing, I'll take the other."

Tom had exhausted the last room in his wing when he heard a scream. He raced to find Anna. A moment earlier, Anna had stepped into the closed-up garage. She saw Frank slumped awkwardly against the window of his silver Cadillac crossover. She screamed despite herself; she hated being squeamish, though she realized this one time she could excuse herself the knee-jerk reaction. By the time Tom found her, Anna had the car door open and a finger on his neck. "Anna?"

Anna looked at Tom and shook her head. Tom turned just in time to catch and hold Margaret back. She sobbed, knowing instantly what Anna had just confirmed:

Senator Frank Barber was dead.

***

Berkshire County, *located in Western Massachusetts bordering Vermont, New York, and Connecticut, is a bucolic area of rolling hills, rivers, and lakes. It features* *world-class museums, theatre and dance venues, bed-and-breakfasts, resorts, camps, and Tanglewood—the summer home of the Boston Symphony Orchestra (BSO).*

For a glimpse of this rural paradise,

visit Anna's "Northern Berkshire County" board on Pinterest:

https://www.pinterest.com/anna_mcgrory/northern-berkshire-county/

CHAPTER THREE

Anna loved the smell of MASS MoCA's largest gallery. Even on this solemn day, she was able to enjoy the sensation of breathing in the essence of wood and concrete mixed with a satisfying hint of paint. She closed her eyes and enjoyed the stillness of the in-between time—just after the exhibit had been hung and before it opened to visitors.

Today's event was different than any exhibit the contemporary art museum had previously known. While the senator's considerable collection lined one wall and her husband's portraits of the senator over his many years of his service lined two others, the centerpiece was to be the senator himself, in an opulent open casket that was by all measures a work of art. It was carved from an oak tree that had fallen two years earlier on his estate. Frank had commissioned his estate's caretaker, Shep, who was a talented carpenter and furniture maker, to carve two matching coffins for the day that would eventually arrive for his wife and him. Anna wondered if Frank had then harbored notions of suicide. She hadn't realized he'd been so depressed. He'd certainly hidden it from her and the rest of his staff.

The idea to hold the wake in the gallery had been hers. While the funeral director droned on about possible locations large enough to hold the vast crowd certain to pay their respects, Anna gazed out the windows at the giant aluminum letters that spelled out the museum's name above the Route 2 bridge in North Adams. A quick call to the museum's director confirmed what she already knew—the gallery was between exhibits. Indeed, one weekend earlier or later and the booking would not have been possible.

The director was happy to assist, sensing the boon it would be for the museum to host such a formal repose. It was almost as if Senator Frank Barber would be lying in state within the immense art gallery. The building belonged to a conglomerate of 20 that had once been a textile mill turned electronics plant. It was fitting to honor the senator in this manner since he had been one of the earliest champions of the museum and a co-sponsor of the bill providing the original $35 million in seed money from the state. He and his wife were among the museum's first members, having joined before the museum even opened.

The governor had visited before, but this was an opportunity to show state and U.S. members of Congress what a gem MASS MoCA was. Perhaps the president himself would attend. It was a fantastical notion, the museum director knew, but it explained the extra bounce in his step.

The Senate secretary had pressed Anna into service since Margaret wanted the ceremonies to be held near the senator's home. Margaret was too shaken up to participate in the planning. Instead, she trusted Anna to make all the right decisions. Both women had attended these things for other senators and representatives, so Anna intuitively knew what she had to do.

Her toughest assignment was all her own doing. When she realized two walls of the gallery would be bare, she made calls and enlisted the service of the senator's staff to gather as many framed photographs of the senator as possible. The pictures hung from walls in the senator's offices, homes, and in local libraries, public spaces, the Massachusetts State House, and even in the dining room of a former aid. Tom had a small collection hanging in his firm's conference room—part of Frank's 60th birthday party collection, which Tom had been commissioned to print and frame for the festivities. At least those photos had been easy to collect for today.

"Mrs. McGrory?" Anna turned, woken from her brief reverie, and saw a museum staffer. "He's here."

Anna followed the staffer outside the gallery to meet the funeral director, his attendants, and her boss for the past 29 years. A WNYT news chopper from nearby Albany, New York, passed overhead, grabbing footage of the numerous limousines and overflowing parking lots that led to a steadily growing crowd, which was reminiscent in size to the throngs drawn to the museum for the band Wilco's Solid Sound Music and Arts Festival held every other summer at the museum.

Once Frank's coffin was properly installed, Shep tended to the finer details of the arrangement. Anna complimented him on his workmanship, but the praise seemed hollow in the shadow of the day's sober gathering. Anna looked around, trying to think of something else to say to fill the silence as Shep moved a crease of fabric a micro inch this way or that, and removed a stray hair from the ornate carving on the panel near Frank's feet. "Where's Sheila?" she asked.

"She's not feeling well."

"Oh," said Anna. "That's too bad." Anna felt guilty feeling somewhat jealous that Shep's wife could escape having to attend the wake at all. Anna excused herself, turning her attention to her duties directing the numerous workers who tended to the details of the day. She bounced from section to section, making sure there were no last-minute issues that needed her care.

Some time later, the wake well in progress, Anna returned to the front of the reception line, checking that Margaret was being taken care of by one of the senator's senior staff members. Satisfied Margaret was in good hands, Anna headed for her next task. She stopped when she overheard an odd conversation between two men occurring just behind the curtain that served as backdrop to the coffin.

"I'm not waiting in that line!"

"It will look odd if you skip ahead."

"I just need a quick look."

"I don't understand why."

"I need to see him for myself."

"May I help you?" Anna announced herself as she parted the curtain and stepped through it. "Senator Ponema," she said, her breath catching as the hairs on her neck stood on end. He was talking with the mysterious stranger from the boat.

Senator Ponema mopped nervously at his brow. "The doctor's terribly upset by this business."

So he's a doctor, Anna thought, and catalogued one more clue away for future use. She hated thinking of herself as playing Nancy Drew, especially on a day like today, but she couldn't shake the feeling that this stranger was up to something that she'd later need to examine.

Senator Ponema placed an arm around Anna's shoulder and led her a few steps away. "He has anxiety issues—something about his being on the spectrum—and wants to pay his respects, but cannot tolerate crowds."

Anna glanced at the doctor, trying to soften and see things from the autistic—or was it simply rude?—man's perspective. His glare did not help his cause.

"He can be a bit abrasive," the senator acknowledged. "And erratic. Again, the spectrum thing."

"Can he return later?"

"No, I cannot return later!" The doctor stomped his foot in opposition to the very notion.

Anna almost laughed, picturing the similarities of this man and Benedict Cumberbatch's portrayal of Sherlock Holmes. She caught herself and stopped her smile forming by feigning a small cough. She glanced out the curtain. Her eyes bounced down the line that snaked out the gallery's door. This would take hours. She noted the people near the head of the queue and closed the curtain. "I'll be a moment, but I think I can accommodate you."

The senator watched through the curtain as Anna approached a woman and her teen son, who stood a few people from the grieving widow and the casket. After a moment, Anna turned and nodded to the senator. Soon the doctor and Senator Ponema stood ahead of the understanding woman. Anna gave a face that tried to convey "sorry for the inconvenience" to the people behind her in line, and signaled to a waiter who carried bottled water to those who waited.

"Tell Bertie I'd like the staff to serve food to the people in line," she said, knowing it was going against her earlier wishes of simply supplying water to people as they waited, and making food available at the café afterwards to anyone who wanted to pay to eat. "I'll settle up the bill with him later." She cringed that she was only just now thinking this through. Maybe she hadn't been the right choice to run this show after all, she chided herself.

Anna remained with the senator and the strange doctor as they made their way to Margaret. The senator took her hands in his and held them kindly. "I'm so sorry for your loss, Margaret. I feel I've lost a powerful and honorable ally." It almost sounded like he meant it too, Anna thought.

"I believe you mean you've lost a powerful foe," Margaret said. Anna smiled. She was proud of her for standing up to the senator who had brought nothing but grief to Frank during his time in office.

Senator Ponema's face turned crimson as he stammered out a response.

"Well, well, indeed, we both had the best interest of the Commonwealth at heart."

The stranger said nothing to Margaret, instead walking past her to the coffin and gazing in longer than necessary, or so it seemed to Anna. Anna gave Margaret a squeeze and asked for the umpteenth time that day whether she'd prefer to sit. The assistant assigned to her smiled and shook her head no as Margaret said as much.

Anna followed Senator Ponema and the doctor out, wanting to make sure the odd man actually left. "Will there be anything else?" She asked, hoping the answer was no.

The doctor and senator shared a look.

"We understand Frank met with several stakeholders over the past few months, though the committee members specifically asked him not to," Senator Ponema said. "We'd like his notes from those conversations. For the committee, naturally. We've come to realize all input should be considered."

"I'm sorry. Stakeholders of what exactly?"

"Yes, right. Well, it's what the sick are called by government agencies."

Anna made a face that matched her disgust. "That's just wrong."

"Be that as it may, we'd like to include his stake—uh, patient—interviews in our committee findings."

"I will have Charlie forward you whatever is found as he and his staff continue to clean out Senator Barber's Washington office."

The doctor snorted his displeasure.

"What my esteemed colleague is trying to say is that your senator was a bit more casual about the interviews, preferring to conduct them from his home here in the Berkshires."

"Well then, I will be sure to keep an eye out for them and forward copies to you soon as—"

Another perturbed grunt from the doctor set Anna on edge. She spun and faced him. "I'm sorry, but if you have something to say to me, say it already!"

"I have nothing to say to you."

Anna glared at the senator.

"Yes, well, you understand, his being on the—"

"Spectrum," he and Anna said in unison.

"He was trying to convey that we need the originals. And they should be regarded as eyes only. For us, that is."

Anna swallowed the bile that was forming at the thought of obeying the ill-mannered doctor and the contemptible senator. What had Frank called him? Anna tugged at her memory. Ah yes, the varlet. Apparently his dishonesty was legendary among his Senate colleagues. She smiled her best pasted-on smile and agreed to send the originals as soon as she found them. It was an easy promise to make knowing that she would be sure to keep copies.

***

MASS MoCA *is both an extensive art gallery and a performing arts center. The refurbished factory buildings provide an enormous landscape to showcase unusual and evocative art.*

For more information, visit Anna's "Northern Berkshire County" board on Pinterest:

https://www.pinterest.com/anna_mcgrory/northern-berkshire-county/

Chapter Four

At a clearing near the estate's oldest pine stand the next day, Anna and Tom joined the small group gathered to pay their respects. Next to Margaret stood Amy—Margaret's best friend since before grade school. Shep and Sheila flanked Pastor Jay, who hailed from the local Protestant church where Frank and Margaret occasionally attended Sunday services. At a respectful distance stood the funeral home's manager and his assistants. It was Margaret's desire to keep the burial service small and private. Since she and her late husband had no children or any living relatives, it was easy to control the numbers.

"Lord hear our prayer," Pastor Jay said for the last time in a litany of refrains. It was echoed by all except Margaret, who couldn't speak through her grief.

As the group strolled back to the main house, a deer jumped into the clearing ahead of them. They stopped to watch, and the deer did the same, gazing at them as if it somehow understood their grief. Finally it bounded off into the woods.

"Frank loved the deer that live here," Margaret said as she wept anew. It was true. He loved them so much that he went overboard posting no hunting signs around his property's 316-acre perimeter.

Knowing this was difficult for his wife, Tom wound his arm around Anna's shoulders as they continued their stroll. Anna had worked her entire adult life for the senator and would miss him terribly. She began as an intern when Frank was a state representative in Boston. She later volunteered for his campaign for reelection her junior year of college. After she graduated, she went to work for him fulltime. When Frank was asked by his party to run for the vacant U.S. Senate seat, he easily won. Anna accepted his offer to run his Massachusetts offices. She was able to create a work schedule that allowed her to work partly from home, occasionally commuting to his Boston and Lowell spaces to meet with constituents in eastern Massachusetts, while staying over at his Berkshires estate when meeting with constituents in the western part of the state or to oversee events held in the Berkshires.

Later that afternoon, Tom and Anna waved farewell to Margaret and Amy from the front door of the Barber's home. The two of them were off to Paris, where Margaret's friend had an apartment in a perfect neighborhood for "forgetting unpleasantness," as Amy had called the grief Margaret was experiencing. Anna doubted Margaret would forget, but at least she had the love of a good friend in a beautiful and bustling city center to keep her occupied.

Meanwhile, Anna planned to stay on at the estate for as long as it took to go through and catalogue all the senator's papers. As a favor to Margaret—and because, if necessary, she would continue Anna's salary beyond the 60 days the Senate normally covered for staff of deceased senators—she'd also agreed to inventory the home in preparation for Margaret to decide what to keep and what to sell or donate. Anna could not talk her out of selling the Barber's family estate. Margaret had never been fond of the country place, though she didn't harbor a particularly malicious distaste of the place. She simply abhorred anywhere too rural for streetlights, sidewalks, and cafés within a strolling distance.

"Wish we could live here," Anna said to Tom. It was a silly notion. They'd never be able to afford whatever price tag Margaret and her realtor decided upon, nor could they meet the annual utility and tax payments or manage the maintenance.

"Maybe in the cottage, but this place is too…"

"Palatial?"

"Was leaning more toward dated."

Anna laughed. "There are solutions to updating. Hello? Home Depot."

Now Tom laughed too. "I don't think you renovate the modernist features out of a home with a few tools, fresh paint, and new carpet. Plus, it's a bit far from the kids."

"Yeah, I thought of that too."

Their daughter and her new husband lived in the town where Anna and Tom had made their home while their kids were in public school. It was a short drive to the New Hampshire state capital where Anna and Tom now lived. They also had some land on one of the town's ponds where they hoped to build a small cabin one day. Their son had lived about an hour away before he left for his Guatemalan adventure. They remained hopeful he'd eventually return to the states and take up residence nearby.

Tom and Anna had an early supper on the veranda, enjoying the view and a fresh seasonal tomato-basil pizza from their favorite independent shop in Williamstown—Hot Tomatoes. Finally, it came time for Tom to leave. Before he did, he checked for the umpteenth time that Anna would be fine on her own. She wasn't on her own, she reminded him. There were the property caretakers, Sheila and Shep, who'd already invited Anna to supper at their place every night while she remained on the estate.

After waving to him, Anna put on a pot of coffee to brew, and walked each room of the estate with her clipboard, making a quick list of what would need to be done. She knew the senator's office was top priority, but she needed a quick visual assessment of the tasks ahead so she could formulate a plan. She'd never closed out an estate before, nor had she ever owned such expensive artworks, antiques, and custom furniture. Creating notes of each room helped make the undertaking seem more manageable. She could do any job, she reasoned, as long as she was able to break it down to its individual tasks. Well, so long as complicated math or science wasn't involved.

The next morning, Anna woke with a start and looked at the bedside clock: 5:13. She grabbed her abdomen and moaned in pain. Food poisoning? She wondered if Tom was feeling sick too. She made her way to the bathroom, but didn't feel nauseous. Instead, what she saw frightened her to the core. She had voided what appeared to be pure blood.

She called the local physician's office. The doctor on call advised her to go to the emergency room since the office wouldn't open for almost four hours. "Better to err on the safe side," he said. "Do you have someone who can drive you, or do you need us to call an ambulance?" Anna was wondering the same thing when she saw Shep stroll by with his chocolate Labrador, Charlie, headed for the pond and their morning routine of fetching the ball from the water.

Anna called to Shep from the bedroom window.

"Oh, good morning, Anna," Shep said in his characteristic cheerful tone. Moments later, they were on their way to Pittsfield. It would be a 20-minute drive to the nearest hospital.

"I've never seen so much blood in a sample," said the nurse as she approached Anna, who sat up on a bed. The nurse regarded Anna's chart.

"You said you've had a hysterectomy?"

"Four years ago," Anna confirmed.

"Any complications afterward?"

"None." The nurse left, looking perplexed, which didn't make Anna feel any better.

The doctor soon joined Anna. "Your quick labs are negative for infection, but with that much blood in your urine, a UTI is our first suspicion." The physician used the familiar initials for urinary tract infection. "I'll put you on Amoxicillin and have you see a urologist who will run additional tests that should help get you some answers. But to be completely honest, I'm not even sure what the questions are at this point. I've never seen a sample with that much blood in it before."

"That's what the nurse said."

"She and I have been at this a long time."

"You sound worried."

"Cautious, curious, and perplexed. We doctors don't tend to worry. We simply do our best to dig for answers. I would like to follow up with your primary care physician, if you don't mind."

"Why would I mind?"

"Normally I send my notes to the primary. In this case, I'd like to know what your doctors ultimately find."

"I must admit," said Anna, "now you're beginning to worry me."

***

Hot Tomatoes Pizza *is a family-owned pizzeria that opened when Anna lived in the Berkshires with her young family. She and her husband and their children often enjoyed stopping in to place an order and waiting out back where Green River hugs the property line. It was a perfect place to practice hopping from rock to rock without getting too wet.*

For more information, visit Anna's "Northern Berkshire County" board on Pinterest:

https://www.pinterest.com/anna_mcgrory/northern-berkshire-county/

CHAPTER FIVE

The next morning, Anna rolled over and tugged the covers with her. It didn't happen often anymore, though sometimes Tom hogged the covers in his sleep. But did he chase bunnies too? Anna looked over her shoulder and saw Charlie sprawled across a throw-blanket atop the comforter. "Charlie!"

The dog woke instantly. His legs stopped. And his tail thump-thumped. Charlie loved Anna's attention almost as much as he adored sleeping on the bed. Anna rolled over so she could more easily pat the caretaker's Labrador as she fell back asleep.

"Wakey, wakey," May crooned as she threw open the curtains, exposing the mid-day sun.

"May? When did you get here?"

"Yesterday afternoon."

"What time is it?"

"Just about time to get you to the doctor's."

"But I thought I didn't see him till tomorrow."

"It is tomorrow. You've slept through an entire day."

"Am I imagining that Charlie was here with me?"

"He just went home to eat."

"Just like him to abandon me for food."

"I'd abandon you for food."

Anna smiled, enjoying having her friend here with her. She also loved that she could count on Charlie for companionship when she didn't feel well. She had been sick twice before while staying over at the estate. Both times Sheila and Shep's dog had kept her company. They didn't mind lending him to her since they were convinced the dog helped Anna get better sooner. Anna wasn't sure that was true, but she enjoyed the dog's company just the same.

"Chop, chop. I've run you a bath. And I've left a tall glass of water for you on the windowsill. When you're ready, I have a grapefruit cut up downstairs along with your coffee. You have just over an hour before we need to leave." May pulled the covers back and gave Anna a steady hand to the bathroom. "How are you feeling?"

"Would you believe exhausted?"

"Need my help in the bathroom?"

"I think I have it from here," Anna said, breaking free of May and grabbing the wall for support.

May listened outside the door for a moment, uncertain what to do. She wished her daughter who worked in a nursing home were here. She looked around and realized she could at least tidy the place. She stripped the bed and listened for Anna to climb into the tub. Once she knew she was settled in, May went downstairs with the laundry.

A half hour or so later, as May sat and knitted in the living room that overlooked the veranda and the pond beyond, she heard an odd thumping sound. Setting her knitting aside, she followed the noise into the foyer where she found Anna sitting and bumping her way down the stairs slowly, one at a time. "Oh my goodness! Why didn't you call me?"

"Was afraid you might suggest I slide down the banister since we're on a schedule."

May helped her friend stand when she landed at the bottom. "Maybe we should move you to one of the ground-floor guest rooms."

"Or get me a kayak that I can ride down the staircase."

"Nervous?" May asked her friend, knowing that her silly quips were a sure sign that she was anxious.

"It's just that I haven't studied, and I know the doctor's going to have tests for me."

May couldn't get Anna to eat the grapefruit, even though it was one of her favorite foods. She was able to get her to drink two more glasses of water and eat a piece of dry toast, which she dunked in her coffee. Knowing the doctor's staff was likely to take blood, May gave Anna a bottle of water and made her drink it on the way to the office. She thought it made it easier to draw blood if you were hydrated. Was she making that up? May didn't know. She worried she was over thinking everything.

In the waiting room, Anna filled out what seemed like reams of paper. One sheet had her rating her level of pain for various parts of her body. Another had her counting the number of trips to the bathroom in a night, and noting whether she was able to actually void each time. She looked up, thinking.

"Need some help?"

"It's kind of embarrassing," Anna admitted to her friend. "I can't remember coming home from the ER, nor getting into bed." She showed May the paperwork. "And I certainly must have gotten up to go the bathroom, but I don't remember that either."

"Why don't you write that down," May suggested.

"Good idea. I will. Once my hand has a moment to rest."

May took the clipboard from her friend and, despite her protest, completed the rest of the paperwork for her, asking her personal questions as discreetly as possible so as not to be overheard by the other waiting patients. When they were done, May moved to set the clipboard aside. Anna reached out. May misunderstood her gesture, offering the clipboard to Anna.

"No. I'm trying to reach for your hand," Anna said. "Sorry to be so clumsy." Anna and May grasped hands. "I really appreciate your coming here to help me like this."

"Of course, silly."

"At the risk of sounding ungrateful, is there a reason Tom's not here?"

"You don't remember talking to him either, do you? He's in court. Couldn't get out of it. You assured him it was fine."

"No, no. It is fine. I'm just sick. It's not like I'm dying."

"Anna McGrory," a nurse called from the doorway.

Anna stood, though she was a bit shaky. May reached to hand the clipboard to Anna. "Any chance I could persuade you to—"

"Right!" May stood, tucked the clipboard beneath her arm, and helped Anna toward the nurse.

"May my friend join me?" Anna asked the nurse, who nodded her consent and looked confused as Anna and May sniggered at the use of May's name as a verb in the question.

May had been right to ply Anna with water. The nurse was able to find the vein in one try, and to draw the six vials of blood necessary for all the tests the doctor had ordered. Anna was also scheduled for a CT scan the next day. There wasn't much more the doctor could do until all the tests were back. Still, it was good for Anna to meet with someone so calm and knowledgeable. Both women felt like Anna couldn't possibly be in better hands.

On their way out of the office, Anna stopped at the front desk and signed a paper allowing the doctor's office to discuss her medical condition with May in addition to Anna's husband who was already on file. Anna also thought to get copies of all the paperwork that day. It had been May's suggestion since Anna had two sets of doctors—one here in the Berkshires, and her primary care doctor in Concord, New Hampshire. She'd continued to keep in touch with her Berkshires physicians even after she moved out of the area since she'd been ill a couple times while working and staying at the estate. Certainly, with this latest round of illness, her doctors back home would want to follow up with her when she returned. She couldn't help thinking self-indulgently: *if* I return. Anna was beginning to wonder if she had something more serious than her doctor was letting on.

At the estate later, Anna settled into the senator's desk chair ready to dig into his files, making sure that closed constituent matters had been properly catalogued and open files were prepared to be forwarded to his successor. In addition to the interviews with patients—or stakeholders, as Senator Ponema had referred to them—she knew the senator wanted all of Frank's files. But she also knew Frank would have preferred she wait and share them with the senator who would soon be appointed by the governor. The Democratic governor would be appointing a Democratic senator. Frank could at least rest in peace on that matter.

May ducked her head in. "Anything else I can get you?" She didn't wait for an answer as she headed for the blinds. As they raised, she and Anna screamed. The blinds crashed back down. In the window trying to peer inside was the face of a madman. Or at least of a stranger.

A tap-tap-tap at the window made both women jump again. Anna stood, grabbed her phone, and signaled to May to open the blinds again.

"Tell me what you want or I'll call the police," she said to the back of the man's head. He turned to face her. "Martin?" Anna opened the window and spoke to him through the screen. "What are you doing here?"

"Here to help," said the aid to the senator from across the aisle.

"Ever hear of a doorbell?"

"I tried it," he said. "Must not be working."

"Meet me at the front door." Anna closed the window again.

"Want me to meet him and bring him here?" May asked as she watched her friend try to hide the pain in her abdomen.

"No. I don't want him anywhere near this office. I don't trust him."

"I don't either. And I don't even know him."

"You forget the rally on the State House steps—the minimum wage debate. He was the one who took several of our supporters' signs and broke them over his knee."

May remembered that day more than a dozen years earlier, shortly after she and Anna had met. The rally had sounded like an interesting thing to do for a day, and she always enjoyed a trip in to Boston. She joined Anna as a friend, but ended up working the event. That led to her volunteering in the senator's re-election campaign. Campaigns. Plural, she corrected herself. Had she and Anna really been friends for...she counted backwards...14 years next month?

"Did you hear me?" Anna asked May on their walk to the foyer. May shook her head as they stood at the front door. "I'm going to say you're my assistant. Therefore, I don't need his help." May nodded. Anna opened the door. "Martin. Good of you to stop by."

"Anna, how are you feeling? I heard about your trip to the ER."

"I don't know how."

"We have our ways."

Okay, that was a bit creepy, Anna and May both thought as they shared a look.

"Going to invite me in?"

"No need. My assistant and I have everything under control." Anna stood aside so he could see May. "May, Martin, and vice versa."

"Oh, I was under the impression you were here alone."

Anna reached around the doorjamb and pressed the doorbell. Westminster chimes reverberated throughout the house. "And I was under the impression the doorbell wasn't working."

"Must have been stuck."

"Must have been. You tell the senator I said thank you for checking up on me. I'll be in touch." Anna closed the door and leaned against it heavily. Her heart was pounding. She had put on a brave face, but the hairs on her neck were standing on end as her sixth sense kicked into heightened alert.

"You were amazing," May said.

Anna raised her hand to show how much it was shaking. May's hand was almost as bad. "Spidey senses alert too?" Anna asked.

May nodded. They had each taught their daughters to trust their intuition. Spidey sense was the term Joanie had used to describe the first time hers kicked into high gear.

"Is he gone yet?" May asked.

Anna pulled back the gauze curtain covering one of the sidelights that framed the door. "He's standing near his car, talking on the phone. Urgent call to the senator, no doubt. I just wonder what it is they're looking for." She looked at May. "Do you want the job?"

"There's a job now?"

"I could use the help."

"That's why I'm here."

"I know you drove down to help me with my medical needs, but do you want to earn a few dollars too? You could help me with the senator's papers. I can see if the Senate secretary will approve my hiring you. Or, if not, I can split my paycheck with you."

"There's no need. I'm here to help you, not look for a job."

"Well, you've found one. Somehow I'll find a way to pay you for your time too," Anna said. May knew not to object further.

"Let's order a pizza and settle in for as long as it takes to find the patient interviews."

"I can be patient," May said. Anna had to giggle. The two of them enjoyed their puns on occasion, even if no one else did. "Speaking of..." May looked at her phone for the time. "You have a CT scan this afternoon at two forty five."

Anna sighed in exasperation. She also worried: What if Martin returns? What if he's watching the place? Or if he knows I have an appointment? She placed a call as they walked back to the office. "Sheila. Is Shep there?" She knew he would watch the place while she and May were away. She would repay him in pizza this afternoon; it wasn't enough, of course, but it was a start.

***

Dogs *seem to know when their owners are sick. Anna wasn't imagining Charlie's attention to her when she most needed him. After a quick search of the internet, Anna dedicated a board of her Pinterest account to dogs who sense when their owners are ill.*

For more information, visit Anna's "Dogs Comforting Sick People" board on Pinterest:

https://www.pinterest.com/anna_mcgrory/dogs-comforting-sick-people/

Chapter Six

A dinner party was not what Anna had in mind when she thought of quiet ways to spend the weekend. It just sort of happened. Tom and May's husband, Jim, joined the women at the Berkshire estate for the weekend. Because Tom had some estate planning clients in the area, he also made plans to meet with a couple of them. One of his clients had become a friend over the years, so Tom invited him and his wife to the house for dinner...and a party was born.

May was already baking fresh bread while the four of them ate breakfast together and discussed the evening meal. While Anna would have loved to sit and chop vegetables for salad and sides, she knew she was too exhausted to do so. Instead, it was decided that Tom and Jim would pick up freshly made salads from the organic shop in town where they also planned to get the local, grass-fed beef for the grill.

While the men were away, Anna stretched out on the chaise lounge beneath a blanket in the nearly 80-degree sun. She wasn't running a fever, but she was chilled. She struggled to read from her tablet between napping and having to get up to head to the bathroom every twenty minutes.

May joined her, bringing her a fresh-squeezed lemonade. "It looks delicious, but I'm not sure I should drink it. Look at this list," Anna said, handing her tablet to May.

May looked at the website that listed a strict diet for people with something called interstitial cystitis. It was compiled by a woman who had symptoms similar to Anna's. When the woman had discovered the restrictive list of foods in a book about the illness, she decided to follow the diet. Two months after sticking to it, the woman had reduced her pain and her urinary frequency.

"I like how she calls it her 'no-food diet,'" May said, pointing to the headline above the small list. "Do you think you have this inter-what-cha-ma-call-it?"

"You mean should I really be self-diagnosing?"

While neither woman believed they could take the place of a physician, they also knew that it paid to be proactive and educated when it came to their own health. Whether or not Anna had interstitial cystitis, a restrictive diet that excluded acidic food, gluten, soy, artificial sweeteners, and additives couldn't hurt. Though it might be difficult to manage.

"And how exactly did you come to this self diagnosis?"

"I realized I have many of the same symptoms my dad did when he was diagnosed with prostatitis. So I Googled prostatitis for women and found IC." Anna called interstitial cystitis by its easier to pronounce and remember initials—something other websites used as well.

May looked up the website on her own tablet and followed some of the links. "Maybe I should order this cookbook she mentions. I wonder if I can make a gluten-free yeast bread."

"Oh, no." Anna hadn't thought this through entirely. How could she possibly give up May's breads? She was the best baker she knew—even better than most commercial bakeries. "Maybe it's not what I have. I can wait till I see Dr. Matthews on Monday and hear what he thinks the tests reveal."

"Dr. Matthews?" Tom asked.

"You're back," Anna stated the obvious. "Just in time to help me to the bathroom." Whatever was making her sick was taking its toll. She found it difficult to stand and move about. She hoped something as simple as a restrictive diet could help her regain her strength.

"Your doctor is—"

"Dr. Matthews, the urologist."

"Well, maybe you can hear what his thoughts are tonight."

"Dr. Matthews is your client?" Anna was thrilled. She hoped it meant she wouldn't have to wait till Monday to learn what her tests had revealed.

That evening Anna began her restrictive diet, even forgoing May's triple braided bread. Tom had gone out a second time to pick up a few of the bladder-friendly foods and drinks listed on the website. Anna could get used to eating more blueberries, but she wasn't sure she'd ever warm to chamomile tea. She preferred Chai tea or, even better, hot chocolate.

Anna had planned to wait till after dinner to discuss her medical questions with Dr. Matthews, who had insisted she call him by his first name.

She wondered if knowing him as Rory would be uncomfortable. But he was Tom's client, and yet here they were chatting—proof you could be both business clients and friends. She couldn't remember who had first mentioned the interstitial cystitis. The topic had arisen organically since Anna's plate reflected her newfound diet.

"I'm not sure it's interstitial cystitis," Dr. Matthews said. "It can be a diagnosis of exclusion, when we're sure it's not one of the other possibilities. We need to wait until all your tests are run. I have another couple I'd like to do when you come into the office Monday."

"Do you have any ideas about what it is that's making her so sick?" Tom asked.

"Well, I don't want to speculate, or put a damper on the evening," Dr. Matthews paused. He had just gained everyone's rapt attention. "I mean, like I said, there are still tests out, and more tests to run. So nothing is firm yet."

"But you have an idea," May said.

Dr. Matthews turned to Anna and looked her directly in her eyes with an intensity that unnerved her. "I hope I'm wrong, but I'm thinking you might want to make some calls. See people you'd like to see one more time."

"You mean you think I have...?" But Anna couldn't say it.

"What?" Tom asked.

Dr. Matthews' wife reached and touched his leg to give him strength. She'd seen her husband struggle before when he'd suspected the worst for a patient. He patted her hand appreciatively, swallowed, and again gazed at Anna. "I think there's a possibility that what you have is stage four bladder cancer, which means you might only have a few weeks left to live."

***

The highly restrictive **IC diet** *still includes many yummy options such as avocado, potatoes, cooked onions, pears, and gluten-free oatmeal. What it excludes can be categorized as acidic foods and drinks, artificial sweeteners, and bubbly drinks such as seltzer water.*

For more information, visit Anna's "IC" board on Pinterest:
https://www.pinterest.com/anna_mcgrory/ic/

Chapter Seven

The next morning, Anna called Stephen, the senator's top aid in Washington. Together they decided it would be best for another staffer to close up the senator's home office. By the next afternoon, two staffers had arrived.

Anna spent the rest of the week instructing them and going through some of the files herself. She still hadn't located the patient interviews, which is what drove her to remain in place even though Tom was hoping she'd return home right away and see another specialist for a second opinion. Or at least see her regular primary care physician who might have some ideas that weren't cancer.

Under normal conditions, May understood Anna's drive. However, given the prospect that she might soon die, she couldn't understand Anna's insistence on continuing her work. "When are you going to tell your daughter?" May asked over her afternoon coffee and Anna's chamomile tea.

"I'm hoping the doctor is wrong, and I'll never have to."

"I'd be mad if my mom died without telling me she only had a few weeks to live."

"We don't know that for sure."

"Oh, I know for certain I'd be mad at you."

"I mean we don't for sure it's can—"

May held her hand up to signal stop. Anna knew May hated that word. She felt like just saying it invited it into your life. Anna didn't agree with that, but why take a chance?

"Maybe when they get back from their honeymoon," Anna said.

May nodded and released her stressful grip a bit on her mug. She agreed that Anna didn't necessarily have to call Joanie on her three-week trip to Guatemala. For her part, Anna hoped she'd know something more concrete by the time Joanie and her new husband returned home.

It was nearly a month later when Dr. Matthews called Anna. She was home by now, being tended to and fussed over by her own mom, Gail, who had flown in from the West Coast to be with her. Because Anna had also begun to lose her hearing among a plethora of other symptoms, she put the doctor on speakerphone. "I have some good news: It's not cancer."

Tom, Anna, and Gail each released a heavy sigh of relief.

"I also have some not-quite-so-good news: I still don't know what it is."

Anna kept a brave face, but her exhaustion made her feel like she was going to cry. She might have, but another odd symptom she'd been juggling was dry eyes. "Do you have any ideas?" She asked.

"Strictly conjecture at this point, but maybe your interstitial cystitis guess was a good gut instinct."

Anna was glad that she'd pushed to get herself an appointment with the physicians at the Pelvic Health Clinic at Concord Hospital. She was scheduled to see them the following week.

Anna called May to let her know the news while Tom called their daughter at work. Anna and Tom exchanged phones a couple minutes later so they could each talk to the other person at the end of the line. Their last-second shoulder-season trip back to Cliff Island on the upcoming weekend, which was Anna's last wish if she needed such a thing, would be a celebration. Even their son was flying in from South America for it.

The weekend ended up being a blur of laughter and good food—all bladder-friendly fare. Since it was Anna's celebration weekend, they all decided to eat from her regulated list. One benefit was that it cut down on the number of items they needed to cart to the island. Fortunately for everyone, Anna had done some internet sleuthing to find a life hack around the no-coffee rule using a cold-brew coffee maker and low-acid beans. The bonus was that it tasted great.

The next week was a blur of a different sort. It began with her appointment with the gynecologist at the Pelvic Medicine Center. "I know what you have," she said as she entered the exam room. "Interstitial cystitis. Just as you suspected." The urologist entered next and seconded the verdict.

Anna almost cried. She would have if not for the dry eyes.

From that appointment she was referred to a team of caregivers: a physical therapist, nutrition counselor, chiropractor, psychologist, and an acupuncturist. Each saw her within just a day or so of her diagnosis. Whatever was ailing her, she'd be better soon, she was assured. Her medications were either topical or over-the-counter pain meds, only taken as needed, which was another thing she was pleased about.

Within six months, Anna had some of her more painful symptoms under control and was even considering trying to add foods back into her diet as the nutritionist suggested: one at a time for a period of two weeks, beginning with foods that weren't on her strict list, but had been "bladder-approved" by another group that worked with IC patients. She was also able to last almost two hours between bathroom breaks.

But her primary care physician, Dr. Carry, was perplexed by pain points around Anna's body, her ongoing exhaustion, brain fog, and neuropathy in her hands and feet. While additional tests had turned up no new results, Dr. Carry was able to diagnose Anna with fibromyalgia and chronic fatigue syndrome. Those diagnoses added four new caregivers to Anna's expanding list: an aqua therapist, rheumatologist, podiatrist, and neurologist. She also had to see a surgeon since a hernia was suspected. It added up to busy days, weeks, months, and—before she knew it—an additional year had passed.

The year and a half had been a blur for Margaret too. While her best friend was able to stay in Paris with her for six weeks, she had to leave to help her daughter with her adopted newborn. Margaret stayed on another two months before heading back to Arlington in time for the holidays. It wasn't the same, naturally, now that her husband was gone. She quickly found out who her real friends were, and that she didn't have many in the Washington crowd. She soon grew frustrated with the elitists who apparently cared only to entertain those who wielded power. She hadn't realized just how much influence her husband had held as ranking member on the Senate's Committee on Health, Education, Labor and Pensions.

She put her Arlington townhouse on the market and traded it in for a one-story condo in Beacon Hill, Boston. While life would be different in the City on a Hill than it had been when her husband was a state representative over a quarter century earlier, enough time had passed that she could simply move in and enjoy the company of a couple old friends who lived nearby. Her new life quickly filled with museum trips, volunteering, and classical recitals.

After an overnight with friends at the Inn at Castle Hill following a living room recital at the Crane Estate in Ipswich, Massachusetts, Margaret became a member of the Trustees of Reservations, and soon was discussing the possibility of donating her husband's family estate to the nonprofit organization. The Trustees had obviously done a remarkable job maintaining and promoting the Crane property. She believed Frank would have been proud to donate his beloved home to the Trustees. Margaret knew Anna had been struggling with her health, but she also knew how much the estate seemed to mean to her as well. Because of that, and because she felt like she needed a second opinion from someone who had known Frank nearly as well as she did, Margaret picked up the phone and called her.

"I think it's a fantastic idea," Anna said. She knew at once that Frank would be proud to know his estate would not only be preserved, but would be shared with visitors, and she said so. "It fits in perfectly with his selfless dedication to others." Margaret dabbed at her eyes. She hadn't teared up in a while and her reaction surprised her. Anna heard an emotional sniffle on the other end of the line, which prompted her to ask, "Do you need my help?"

"Can you? I mean, are you well enough?"

"I won't be running Boston this Patriot's Day, but I've been getting around a bit better lately." Anna referred to the Boston Marathon, known simply as Boston to runners and New Englanders.

Margaret had hoped Anna might be able to help her with the project. There were still things to be done at the estate. Beyond clearing out the office in the weeks following his death, nothing else had been touched, except that dust covers had been draped over the furniture. Sheila and Shep still watched over and cared for the place, but Margaret hadn't been able to bring herself to sell it, which is why she simply let it sit.

The two women agreed that Anna would take the bus into Boston in a couple days. When they hung up, each felt revived. Margaret realized how much she had missed Anna. For her part, Anna realized how much she not only missed her old job, but that she was more fond of Margaret than she had realized. She had always thought her fondness was for Frank alone since he had been her mentor.

Later on that unusually warm February day, Anna was working in her garden when it happened: a twig split and an enormous splinter of almost six inches lodged in her shin. Why had she pulled out her shorts? She hated wearing shorts. But 60 degrees in February seemed balmy. She couldn't resist getting a head start on cleaning the gardens before spring arrived.

She hobbled inside and pulled the splinter out, dousing the wound with rubbing alcohol. Two days later, Tom had her in the ER since her shin had swollen and the cut was red and oozing. The ER doctor wanted to admit her, but, after Anna objected, he decided she could return home to take some heavy-duty antibiotics—so long as Tom promised to return her to the hospital if she took a turn for the worse.

Anna bounced out of bed the next morning, feeling better than she had in almost two years. When her primary care physician called, Anna was surprised by her reaction. Instead of being happy for her that she felt incredible, she wanted to see Anna right away.

In the office Anna sat and fidgeted. She felt trapped in the small room, given her newfound alertness and strength. She pulled out a pen and paper and drew up an enormous to-do list, something she hadn't done since she'd left the Berkshires. She recalled the stakeholders mentioned by Senator Ponema, and wondered if Steve or his staff had ever found the files from the patient interviews. She texted Steve, though she wasn't sure whether he had the same phone number. "Who's this?" a text replied. She should have realized Steve might not have her in his contacts list any longer. A brief exchange yielded no new information. Finally Anna texted, "Talk?"

As she waited for the reply, Dr. Carry entered. "I think you have Lyme disease," she said.

"How can I have Lyme if I feel great?"

"You shouldn't feel great. Not on the heavy-duty antibiotics you're taking. You should be back on your couch. That's why I think you have Lyme, or more accurately: Chronic Lyme." Her doctor explained that the diagnosis was controversial since the Centers for Disease Control and Prevention, or CDC as it was more commonly called, did not recognize it. Nor did the federal agency condone the use of long-term antibiotics, insisting that a two-week to 28-day regime was all that was ever needed to cure it. Anna learned that the disease and treatment were hotly debated among physicians and patients.

She and Anna decided Anna would again be tested for Lyme, even though two prior tests within the past year and a half had turned up negative. This time, her physician noted, Anna's blood would be sent to a lab not covered by insurance. "As long as you can pay the costs out of pocket?"

Anna confirmed she could cover the hundred-plus dollar fee, but she wasn't yet convinced she needed to.

"Let me ask you this," Dr. Carry said. "Do you have nerve pain in your hands?"

"No. Nor in my feet."

"Are you feeling like you're in a brain fog?"

"Not at all. I'm actually thinking I might be able to work fulltime again," Anna said.

"I really think we'll find that's what's at the heart of all your symptoms—including the autoimmune disorders you have." Dr. Carry wasn't alone. When she heard the energy in Anna's voice earlier that day, she had called a colleague—the area's only Lyme-literate doctor, someone who acted outside the rigid guidelines of the CDC. He agreed with her assessment of Anna's symptoms, and to help her treat Anna until he could fit her into his own busy practice.

"I don't want to see any more doctors," Anna confessed.

"I don't blame you," Dr. Carry said. Yet she was able to convince Anna that this would be her last new physician.

***

The Trustees of Reservations *preserves special properties in Massachusetts for the use and enjoyment of all. Land, history, sustainability, and education are just a few of the things the nonprofit organization cares about, promotes, and protects.*

For more information, visit Anna's "Vacation Spots" board on Pinterest: https://www.pinterest.com/anna_mcgrory/vacation-spots/

CHAPTER EIGHT

By Sunday, Anna and May were back at the estate. Anna had finally spoken with Steve, who said that the staff had not turned up any patient interviews. She poked around the barren office looking for any scraps of paper that might have slipped behind the shelves or been left in any of the file or desk drawers. She had a desk drawer pulled out all the way and was looking into the cavity where it fit when May entered, carrying two steaming mugs of low-acid afternoon coffee.

"Maybe there's a secret drawer," May said, as she set Anna's cup down for her.

"I've never seen one."

"Hence, the word secret."

"I've been looking in all the secret-type places I know of."

"The short drawer with the cubby behind it?"

"Check," Anna said.

"The side panel that's actually a storage space?"

"Nope. Not in the front either," said Anna, as she knocked on each of the decorative panels.

"The lip under the tabletop that's actually a drawer?"

"The what?" Anna asked.

May set her coffee down and started pulling on all the trim. Anna joined her, but nothing happened.

"Maybe we have to push to release it," Anna said as she tried her theory. On her second push, they both heard a click. The trim pulled away and a hidden tray slid out. On the tray was a file folder. It was filled with hand-scrawled papers.

"That must be what Senator Scary Pants wants."

"Hello," said Anna. "He's the Varlet. Remember?"

"Senator Scary Pants is easier to remember."

Anna looked around, half wondering if there were bugs or hidden cameras in Frank's office. She tucked the file folder under her arm, grabbed her coffee, and headed for the door. "We'll need to go buy a big envelope to send this to Senator Ponema," she said in an exaggeratedly loud and clear voice.

"Oh. Okay. Let's do that," May said, imitating her tone, though she wasn't quite sure what Anna was playing at. She followed Anna to the living room, where Anna sat on the dust-covered sofa and began poking through the file.

May finally put two and two together. "You think they may have bugged the office but not the rest of the house?" May pulled the dust cover off the coffee table and set her cup on a coaster there. She folded the cover, and did the same with the cover from a chair before she sat.

"I don't really think they bugged anything. I was just taking precautions." In her exaggerated voice Anna said, "You're right, May, the post office is closing soon. We'll have to send this tomorrow."

"What are you doing, using my name?" May whispered loudly.

"You don't think they know your name?" Anna laughed.

"You're just pretending, right?" May asked, getting nervous.

"What?" Anna looked up from the notes. "Oh, yeah," she said, seeing May's concern. She went through the papers, her face revealing her bafflement. "I can't believe he saved this."

"What is it?"

Anna reached a couple papers toward May, who looked and started to read aloud, "First we'll take control of—"

Anna shushed her. And winked in a "just in case" way. May grimaced, sure Anna was taking this too far. Anna pointed to a sentence in block letters that read, *How we'll rule the world*. The letters were decorated with flowers along a vine—Anna's signature doodle.

May pointed and mouthed, "You?"

Anna nodded. She stretched and yawned exaggeratedly.

"I'm getting kind of tired," she said in the exaggerated voice that she was sure would be picked up by a wire, if there was one planted here. "Let's knock off for today and head into town to get dinner. That way we can hit the hay early, and get started all the earlier tomorrow."

May rolled her eyes, but was already up and sliding into her shoes. You didn't have to tell her twice they were going to eat. That was one of the many things the two women shared in common—their love of good food.

At the restaurant, Anna and May enjoyed locally raised, grass-fed beef burgers, sweet potato fries, and salads. Anna's greens were plain since she still couldn't eat acidic food and many spices. While they ate, Anna told May about the time she, one of the then-state representative's aids, an intern, and Frank traveled from Boston to the estate. They hadn't paid close enough attention to the weather report, so what began as an unusually warm early spring day in Boston turned into heavy fog around Greenfield, and into snow in the ironically named town of Florida. "Up near Whitcomb Summit we slid off the road. Poor Brad, the intern, was driving. I'm sure he thought Frank was going to chew him out."

Anna told May how instead, Frank took a look around, saw something he recognized, and told them to follow him. They ended up trudging for what seemed like forever in the snow, through the woods, to a hunting cabin owned by the family of one of his childhood buddies. Frank hadn't been there since he was a teen. Yet, he remembered everything perfectly—including where to find the key to the front door.

Later that night, while the snow raged outside, they sat around the woodstove eating caviar, smoked meats, and vegetables from cans and jars, with chocolate chip cherry biscotti for dessert. The real treat, though, was a sampler of Taza chocolate, which they mixed with shelf-stable cashew milk to turn into cups of authentic Mexican hot cocoa. That night, as the four of them brainstormed how to rule the world, Anna took notes.

"Wasn't that mean of you to eat all their food?"

"I'm waxing nostalgic and you're worried we ate their food?"

"I'd be hopping mad if I got to my cabin and found all my food gone!"

"Relax there, Laird of the land. We repaid our debt. On the trip back out to Boston at the end of the week, we not only replenished what we had taken, but doubled the amount we had consumed."

"That's more like it," May said. She took a bite of her dinner and chewed, satisfied with her own meal. May nodded at the papers between them. "What did you think happened to your plans?"

"I didn't really think about them. You know me: I never could stay up late." May did know that about Anna, and imagined it was even more difficult for her to stay awake in a warm and cozy cabin with a belly full of delicious food and hot chocolate. "I fell asleep, and in the morning the papers were gone. I had a vague notion that Frank or one of the others had burned them in the stove. They were just silly ramblings, after all."

"Sounds like you had fun."

"I did. It's one of my best memories with the senator. He became more than just my boss that night. I saw him as a real person for the first time. I think it was when I started to think of him as a father figure." May reached out and touched Anna's hand. Anna had choked up, recalling the evening, and how much the senator had meant to her. "I miss him," Anna said.

"I know you do, sweetie."

The next morning, Anna woke with a start. She'd had a nightmare and couldn't shake it. There was rumbling and pounding...and there it was again. Awake, she realized someone was pounding on the front door of the cottage where she and May were staying.

May and Anna met in the hallway, each in their warm flannel pajamas with sweatshirts overtop. The temperature had dropped, which was nothing out of the ordinary for the Berkshires in February.

"Maybe it's Shep," Anna said, though she knew he could let himself in if he wanted to. Of course, he would never do that. He would consider it to be a violation of their privacy. Still, he'd never pound on the door like that. So who could it be?

"What time is it?" May asked. Anna shrugged as she made her way down the staircase and May ducked back into her room to grab her phone. The modernist grandfather clock in the hall read between 5:35 and 5:40. May confirmed, reading the time aloud on her iPhone. "It's 5:37."

The pounding sounded again, making both women jump.

"Who's there?" Anna hollered.

"Oh good, you're here," Senator Ponema said on the other side of the door.

Anna rolled her eyes and made a face at May. Upon opening the door, she smiled as best she could through gritted teeth. "It's 5:37 in the morning."

"Yes, I'm perfectly aware of the time, young lady," Senator Ponema said as he stepped inside, shrugging snow from his coat onto the tile floor and the women's socks.

"We were sleeping," Anna said, trying with difficulty to keep her temper in check.

"I'm sorry, but I was on my way to Washington, and figured I'd look in...in case you happened to find that missing file of Frank's?"

The women exchanged a glance. They were both horrified. Had he actually bugged the place?

"It's just that I ran into Margaret, and she told me you were here to organize the estate." He looked at Anna pointedly.

Anna stared back at him. She was considering her words carefully. May watched silently, determined to follow Anna's lead, whatever she decided to do.

"Would you like some coffee?" Anna finally said.

"No need. You either found the file, in which case I'll take it with me, or you didn't."

"I did find a file, but I'm trying to recall where I put it last night. Lyme fog, you know. I'm always forgetting where I've put things. I can mail it to you once I find it. It's what I'd planned to do this morning anyway."

"I'll wait for your brain to wake up. Save you a trip to the post office."

"I'll go put the kettle on," May said as she scooted off.

"I think I left it in the main house," Anna said. Let me just get some clothes on. She started up the stairs and ignored the senator's "if you must," which he didn't try nearly well enough to conceal under his breath.

At the Barber's house, Anna pretended to look for the file. She started in the living room, moved to the office, and finally to the kitchen.

"The car?" Senator Ponema asked.

"Maybe," Anna lied. She headed for the front door.

Senator Ponema pointed in the opposite direction. "Isn't the garage this way?"

"I can't park in there," Anna said. "Not after finding Frank."

"Of course," the senator said. "Sorry."

Just as Anna was about to open the front door, May entered from the backdoor and called out. "I found it!"

May met them in the foyer, and handed an oversized envelope to the senator. He took it and smiled a creepy, almost maniacal smile. "I see you've found an envelope too."

"Yes, we bought it last night when we went out to eat," May said. She shot a quick look at Anna. They were both thinking the same thing—he couldn't have bugged the place, yet he must have, otherwise why would he make the envelope comment?

The senator headed for the door and grabbed the handle.

"You sure you won't join us for coffee?" Anna said.

"Nope. Got what I came for." He held the envelope up triumphantly. "Long ride to Washington." He started to close the door behind him, but stopped and poked his head in again.

"You didn't look at this, did you?"

"Just a quick glance. I couldn't make it out, but when I saw it was handwritten notes, I figured it was what you were probably looking for," Anna lied again.

"Good girl," the senator said as he left, this time pulling the door closed behind him.

Anna and May looked at each other with huge, saucer eyes. Neither of them could believe his visit was a coincidence. Anna placed a finger to her lips and the two of them headed for the back door and the path to the cottage. They were greeted by Charlie, who wagged his tail at seeing them and stopped for a quick pat on the head before continuing on his way to the frozen pond.

"You two are up early." It was Shep. He was dressed in a warm, snowmobiling-style jumpsuit and wearing snowshoes.

"Not by choice," Anna said.

"I thought I spotted the senator's car."

"He scared the beetle juice out of me."

Shep smiled big. "I haven't heard that saying in a long time. It's nice to have you back." Down near the beginning of the woods path Charlie barked. "Someone wants me to join him for our daily walk."

"Thank Sheila for those muffins yesterday," May called after him as he strode away.

Shep waved his arm without looking back. "Will do."

May started toward the cottage again, but Anna held her arm. "Hang on a minute," Anna said.

"I'm freezing."

"Me too. But...." She waited for Shep to get out of earshot. "I know where they are."

"Who?"

"What," Anna corrected. "Come on." She started toward the cottage again. "You got my text then?"

"Yep," May said. "The copies are in the bottom of your knapsack."

***

*What is it about **secret compartments** that fascinate so many of us? While Frank utilized a desk with a secret drawer to hide a file, many tuck away cash and valuables in unusual spots.*

For more ideas, visit Anna's "Secret Compartments" board on Pinterest: https://www.pinterest.com/anna_mcgrory/secret-compartments/

Chapter Nine

Route 2, or The Mohawk Trail as it was referred to in Western Massachusetts, was slick that morning. But as Anna and May approached the hairpin turn, they passed a bus driving down the mountain, so they knew the road had been well plowed and salted.

At the top, Anna pulled into the lot of the Whitcomb Summit Hotel and parked. She waved back to the attendant who sat behind a giant plate glass window where she watched them pull into the empty lot. Anna withdrew the photocopied papers and shuffled through them. One page stood out from the rest. It was the one original page May had retained, as per Anna's texted instructions. It contained the GPS coordinates to the camp. Anna didn't want the senator knowing about the place that had meant something to her. Now she was glad she let her nostalgia dictate part of her text, for she was sure Frank had concealed these papers in the desk for her to find, knowing that she would go to the camp and find the interviews he had hidden there. She hoped that was his intention anyway.

Anna plugged the GPS coordinates into her phone and handed it to May so she could navigate the rest of the way. Anna pulled back onto the road and drove more slowly so they could find the cabin and the best pull-off place to reach it. She recalled having been near the summit, but not in sight of it yet when they slid into a ditch—how many years ago? But the mostly desolate crossroads all looked the same, which meant Anna couldn't be certain where they had inadvertently parked. May pointed to the area on the road closest to the hunting camp, and Anna looked for a shoulder to pull off onto, which wasn't easy in February since massive snow banks lined either side of the road.

"We could walk from the pull off, near that deer statue south of the hotel," May suggested.

"Do you think the hotel attendant will see us and think it's weird we've parked there?"

"You're afraid she'll call someone?"

"I know. I'm being paranoid, aren't I?" Anna said.

"Yesterday I would have said you were being paranoid. But after this morning's weirdness, I'm thinking you might be right to be cautious."

"Me too." Anna thought a moment as she drove. Finally she said, "The Elk Monument is lower than the office. Maybe if we park as far down as possible, she won't notice us."

Anna found a plowed driveway and turned around. As they neared the pull off, she slowed and prepared for ice. She wasn't sure if the state bothered to salt this area, but someone had at least plowed it. The enormous drift just beyond the Elk statue—a monument to those who died in World War One— was tall enough to block the view of their car.

"If we can't see her window, she can't see us, right?" May said hopefully. Anna was thinking the same thing and told her so.

The women donned ski pants and snowshoes they had found at Frank's. Anna grabbed her phone. May carried a bag she'd tossed together of snacks and drinks—just in case the ritual of leaving a provisions box had been discontinued.

"Looks like we have just under a mile to trudge," Anna said.

"Thank goodness we thought to grab these then," May said as she tightened the straps on the snowshoes.

Slogging through the deep snow was a chore, even with snowshoes. Both women preferred to hike paths made by snowmobiles, but today there were only occasional crisscrossing tracks. While Anna may have appreciated a better-worn path, she was also relieved that it was looking like she and May wouldn't run into anyone at the cottage. Anna hoped the return trip would be a bit easier since they'd be able to retrace their steps back to the car.

By the time they arrived at the hunting camp they were exhausted. Despite the snow pants, their feet, ankles, and legs were wet and nearly numb. Their noses and cheeks glowed bright red. Each silently hoped there would be some dry wood there to start a fire and warm them. Anna had thought to grab a handful of kindling and matches, but she didn't consider that she might need a few sticks of wood too. She hoped she wouldn't regret her decision to hike out here.

As they circled around to the front of the cottage, they were relieved to see that one side of the porch was stacked with dry wood. Both women were also grateful when Anna found the key to the front door in the same place it had been hidden all those years ago. "I hope this means they have the provisions box again too," Anna said.

May removed her backpack as they stepped inside. "You didn't think I would come unprepared, did you? Bladder-friendly fare for us both." Anna smiled. She could always count on May to pack a picnic lunch for any occasion.

Within a half hour, Anna had the wood stove going. Their outer clothes, which hung next to it, had already begun to drip dry. They moved about in their flannel pjs, which they'd worn beneath their snowsuits. May set out breakfast from the food she carried in. They decided they didn't want to make the trek in again to replace the provisions, so they'd leave the cabin's stash for someone else.

They nibbled while they looked everywhere, searching the obvious places first: inside drawers, on shelves, in the one closet, under the sofa and chairs, in the woodbin near the stove, beneath the ancient braided rug, etcetera. Next, they searched all the super-secret hiding places they could think of: inside cushions, in the pockets of the handful of hunting clothes left behind, and in the walls, floor, and cabinets. They knocked, pushed, and pulled on every piece of wood, trying to find a concealed drawer or locate a hidden panel anywhere. Exhausted and frustrated after finding nothing, they sat.

"We've been going about this all wrong," Anna said, as she shuffled through the papers. "Maybe the clue's spelled out for us here in the notes."

May held out her hand. "Let me have a look at some of the pages. After all, two eyes are better than...wait, that's not it."

"Four?" Anna laughed.

"You know what I mean."

Anna jumped up, excited. "May! You're a genius."

"Why, thank you. It was nothing."

"It may have been everything."

"How? I don't even know what 'it' is."

Anna climbed the ladder to the loft and grabbed the antique rolled-up schoolhouse map off the hooks where it hung. It served as a curtain from the balcony to the main area of the cabin.

"I already looked there. It doesn't even seem to have a false layer sandwiching the papers within it," May said.

"No that's not it," Anna said. She pulled at the end cap of the roller, but it didn't budge. "That night we were all being silly." Anna flipped the roller to the other side. "I think it was Brendon who talked about mapping out a plan to rule the world, just as the map snapped shut. He was behind it in his skivvies, trying to change from his still-damp long underwear to his jeans that had finally dried. Someone yelled, 'We see you!' And he pulled the end cap off the tube." Anna popped the end cap off the tube. "He looked through it." Anna looked inside. "And he said, 'No, I see you!' Which, of course, he didn't, because only one end cap was off. We told him so. But he said, 'You know what I mean!' And the rest of night we spent writing our treatise." Anna tipped the tube and out fell a small cardboard tube. Inside were the patient interviews.

Anna and May spent the next hour reading. There were 57 interviews representing just over 90 patients. Some of the interviews were of parents who were infected with Lyme, and who had ill children. One was of a young woman who also described her sick mother.

Anna and May were horrified to read the list of symptoms and how long patients had gone misdiagnosed. Or, when finally diagnosed correctly, how they'd had to fight the insurance carriers or their doctors to get the necessary dosage of antibiotics extended beyond a month.

One patient was told by her doctor that she had passed on the Lyme bacteria to her babies while they were in utero. After her doctor lost his medical license due to a lawsuit that challenged his overprescribing of long-term antibiotics for patients, she never again found a doctor who believed in placental transfer of the bacteria that causes Lyme disease, even though Frank had noted in the margins that there were some scientists whose studies confirmed that it was possible.

Anna and May decided that they would later make a list of all the symptoms and track the irregularities and similarities in the patient stories. Of particular interest: they wondered how many times they had read of physicians losing their licenses, leaving their practices, or being sued. Moreover, they wondered who had brought the suits, since none of the patients seemed to know the answer to that question.

***

The Mohawk Trail is a scenic byway that winds through the Berkshires in the northwest corner of Massachusetts. Often appreciated for its beauty, it is also historically significant as a Native American trade route from ages past.

For more information, visit Anna's "Mohawk Trail" board on Pinterest: https://www.pinterest.com/anna_mcgrory/mohawk-trail/

Chapter 10

Anna pulled into the parking lot of the Golden Eagle restaurant, located at the end of the infamous hairpin turn on an exceptionally steep section of the Mohawk Trail in Clarksburg, Massachusetts. She carefully backed into a spot next to the building and turned the car off. Both women let out heavy sighs of relief. "I hate the hairpin turn," Anna said.

"Especially in the winter," May agreed. "This parking lot is pretty scary too."

"This is what my nightmares consist of—sliding over the edge of the precipice. Though I think the trees might catch us."

"Then how do you get out? It's a long drop whether or not your car has been caught in the trees."

The women looked out to the edge. Despite the brilliant vista that stretched over the Berkshires and Southern Vermont for miles, they saw only danger.

"I'm starving," Anna said. "You?"

"I'm always hungry. You know that."

Inside they were greeted by Glen, who co-owned the restaurant with his wife. "Anna McGrory. I'd heard you were back in town."

"Did you? I've only been back a day." She introduced May as they followed Glen to the gas stove that looked similar to the woodstove they had just relied upon in the cabin. Glen turned it up for them.

"Senator Ponema said so when he stopped by this morning."

"I didn't think you were open for breakfast in the winter. Wasn't sure you'd be open for lunch now."

"Usually aren't open weekdays in the off season, but the senator called last night and asked us to open early for him and his companion. And we have a private party today, so we figured we'd just stay open for any strays who wandered by."

"Well, this stray is glad you're open," said Anna.

"Me too," said May. She inhaled deeply. The aroma of something scrumptious had met them at the door and was teasing her nose still.

"Jo went back to bed for a late morning nap. I'll go get her. She'll want to say hi." Glen stopped two steps later and turned to them. "Sorry. What can I get you both?"

"Whatever you're serving for lunch. Don't want to put you out. Though it has to be low acid. And actually there are a lot of foods I can't eat. Sorry." Anna realized she should have thought this through. But when she saw that the restaurant was open, she wanted to stop in and see her old friends.

May foraged through her purse and pulled out a sheet of paper that had seen better days. "Here's the list of bladder-friendly foods she can eat."

Anna blushed, embarrassed by the reference to the private part of her anatomy. But Glen didn't seem fazed as he read the list. "I can work with this. Mind if I photocopy it?"

"Be my guest," May said.

"Alright, be right back with something good and friendly."

"And coffee?" May asked hopefully.

"Coffee. Absolutely."

Anna made hers just a hot water since she needed the special low-acid coffee that she was able to buy at one of the Concord, New Hampshire, grocers. As Glen left, Anna kicked off her boots and took off her wet snow pants.

"What are you doing?!" May was aghast.

"I have my pajama bottoms underneath, you know that." Anna hung the pants from a hook near the stove.

"But we're in public now."

"There aren't any customers."

"There's the private party that's coming."

Anna looked around the dining room. All the tables were devoid of utensils, placemats, glasses, and decorations. "They're obviously seating them upstairs. They won't even notice us as they duck up the staircase."

"And the owner and his wife?"

"Glen and Jo? They're practically family," said Anna. She and her husband had met the culinary couple shortly after they had purchased the restaurant. Tom and Anna had hiked one of the many trails up Mount Greylock, and were just settling in for a picnic lunch on their favorite rock outcropping when Glen and Jo arrived with their picnic. Turned out the couple had met each other at college, and this had been the spot of their first date. It was Tom and Anna's third date. They combined their picnics and enjoyed their first double date together.

In the near decade that Anna and Tom had made their home in the Berkshires, the couples had enjoyed many more hikes and outings together. Later, Anna introduced the restaurant to Senator Barber, and it became a favorite place for staff lunch meetings, especially as they drove back and forth between Boston and the Berkshires.

"Anna!" Jo said as she carried a tray with a coffee pot, a small teapot, and three cups to their table. "Glad to see you're making yourself comfortable. You're welcome to get down to your skivvies too."

May blushed. "I also have my pajamas on underneath."

"Then what's stopping you?" Jo sat and pulled out a small, travel-size container of almond milk from her pocket. She opened it, poured some in her coffee, and set it on the table.

Anna grabbed it and read the label. "What's this?"

"Can't have dairy," Jo said. "Ever since I got diagnosed with Lyme disease. Apparently the bacteria like dairy. And sugar."

Anna told her about her recent Lyme diagnosis.

"I'm so sorry."

"Me too!" Glen said as he carried a platter to the table and joined them. "It's not fun." He set the platter down and dealt out sandwich plates. "Brought some of everything we're serving for that private party. Crab cakes with gluten-free breadcrumbs, though they do have cracked pepper in them, half-sized, grass-fed Angus burgers on a portabella shell, which should be safe, and veggie rounds, which are our version of a veggie patty—it's Jo's recipe. Think that one's safe too. But I brought some plain gluten-free toast and a couple hard boiled eggs, in case you want to go that route."

"There's so much to choose from," Anna was amazed how far her diet could stretch in the hands of a chef. She made a mental note to make some crab cakes at home without pepper since they looked and smelled so good.

"All Lyme-friendly foods," Jo said. "We're making an effort to offer more delicious items that are gluten and dairy free."

"May makes an incredibly yummy gluten-free yeast bread," Anna said.

"It has milk in it though," May said.

"That can be replaced with one of the nut juices or coconut water," Jo said. "If you're willing to share your recipe, I'd be happy to give it a go here. We haven't yet mastered the gluten-free yeast breads. Anna's toast is store bought, I'm afraid."

As they ate, they learned about Jo's history with Lyme. She had been misdiagnosed for years. First her doctor thought she had MS, or multiple sclerosis, then Lupus. Neither was ruled out entirely, though she was also diagnosed with other autoimmune disorders including chronic fatigue syndrome and fibromyalgia. "Honestly," Jo said, "it seems like the doctors don't have a way to diagnose or verify any of the autoimmune disorders or Lyme. I had three tests—all negative. It took five years before it finally came out positive."

"And that was only because we went with some other lab that wasn't covered by our insurer," Glen said.

Anna relayed her similar experience so far, and took notes on things she might not have otherwise considered, including upping her daily dose of probiotics. She was starting to feel overwhelmed, but she appreciated that she could call Jo for advice.

The private party arrived, sending Glen and Jo to the upstairs dining room to assist their skeletal off-season staff. Glen had brought a small plate of dessert, but Jo warned Anna against feeding sugar to the Borrelia burgdorferi bacteria that her antibiotics were currently battling.

As Anna resisted the temptation, instead helping herself to a second cup of steaming hot water, she wondered if it might be helpful to draw out the bacteria with sugar, and then pummel them with antibiotics. That was something she would ask her Lyme doctor when she saw him the following week.

"Earth to Anna. Come in, Anna." May had been trying to get Anna's attention for a full minute. Anna looked at her. "What are we going to do now?"

"Right," Anna acknowledged. "I think I have a plan. Let's start by returning to the estate and finishing the job Margaret has hired us to do."

"You're kidding. Work among all the bugs?"

"Pretending we know nothing of them."

"I'm not sure I'm comfortable with this plan of yours," May said.

"Neither am I, but I figured out a way we can catalogue the rest of the items in the house in just a couple days."

***

The **Golden Eagle Restaurant** *is located on the Mohawk Trail's infamous hairpin turn. While the turn and the restaurant's parking lot may scare or thrill many visitors, it also provides a scenic vista that stretches out across the Northern Berkshire and Southern Vermont valleys.*

For more information, visit Anna's "Mohawk Trail" board on Pinterest: https://www.pinterest.com/anna_mcgrory/mohawk-trail/

Chapter 11

Anna and May returned to the estate, showered, put a load of laundry in, and started working in the foyer where they removed dust covers, took photos of and made notations for each piece of art, the hand-carved bench, and a small hand-hooked area rug. Then they proceeded to the parlor where it took them three times as long to catalogue the contents.

The photos were uploaded to Anna's laptop. May read any text that was written on each item, such as copyright information, artist's signatures, countries of origin, etcetera, and Anna typed it up as a photo caption in a catalogue she was creating in a desktop publishing program. She planned to send the resulting document to a printer near her home in Concord. After dropping May off at home, Anna would pick up a couple copies and take the bus in to Boston to meet with Margaret to go through it with her. Unless Tom drove, Anna always took the bus to Boston, since the city traffic unnerved her.

Once Margaret had the brochure, she could take her time deciding what to do with each piece—keeping the handful of items she'd forgotten about but that were still special to her, giving some items away as gifts, donating others to charitable organizations she and Frank had supported over the years, and leaving the rest in the residence as part of the estate's donation to the Trustees.

The dish room was easy since it had already been catalogued, as had the hunting room, which wasn't an actual hunting room, but held a collection of waders, fly fishing equipment, snowshoes, outerwear, biodegradable clay pigeons, and two rifles, which had been used exclusively for sport—never on animals. Frank didn't mind hunters working with Fish and Game officials to keep populations under control. He just didn't have a personal desire to shoot anything that could die. As far as Anna knew, he'd been the only one to use the rifles. Frank hadn't purchased them. Probably never would have. Rather, they were gifts from one of the Texan senators, now long since retired.

Frank had tried to teach Anna to shoot, but she was too wary to actually pull the trigger. Instead, she often helped him clean them after a session. It was something she wished she'd been able to do with her father who had preferred sharing such bonding moments with her younger brothers. She wondered if her brothers could take a rifle apart and piece it back together while blindfolded. It was a trick she'd seen in some movie. She had convinced Frank that they should learn to do it too. The last time they had competed, she won by a fraction of a second. It was the only time she ever beat him at their game.

If anyone were still listening in on their conversation they'd likely find it boring. "Chippendale, circa 1765." "Really? I thought everything here was modern." "It was a family piece." "More coffee?" "Yes, please. With that almond milk. You know, it's actually not too bad." "I know; I'm using it now too." "I'm starving." "Me too. Shall we take a break?"

It was at lunch and dinner that they could finally talk. They moved around the county, changing up their eating locations. May enjoyed visiting the area's museums, so they tended toward the in-house cafes, though May always thought to pack her friend a low-acid alternative in case Anna couldn't find anything to order from a menu.

"Aren't you getting tired of looking at so much art?" Anna asked.

May was aghast. "You forget I was an art minor. Renaissance was my favorite."

"All I know of Renaissance is fairs," Anna said. "But I know art I like when I see it."

"That's a fair statement." May giggled despite her best attempt to remain composed as she lobbed her pun. Anna rolled her eyes, but smiled. Quieting down, May asked, "Should we get burners?"

"What does that mean?" Anna pictured wood burners, and wondered if she'd missed that part of the art pieces they'd seen in the many galleries of the Clark where they currently strolled.

"You know. Throw-away phones."

A security guard passed behind them. They stopped talking and regarded the oil painting of a paper bag of groceries as if it were the Mona Lisa. As she gazed at it, Anna realized this was exactly the kind of crisp, clean art that she enjoyed. The groceries returned her to happy memories of buying large orders for her family when the kids were younger—back when paper was the socially responsible, environmentally friendly choice. Now it stressed her out so much when she forgot her cloth bags that anytime she did so she would purchase bags at checkout. She would have amassed a huge collection, but Tom liked to give the kids groceries every time he visited them.

Anna thought about how many times she'd been away when Tom visited Joanie or Rob. Her happy memories dissolved into guilt at being away, and even jealousy over how much time Tom had gotten to spend with their now grown children. Anna shook off her thoughts and returned to the present. After looking around to make sure no one was in earshot of them, Anna asked, "Why would we need burners?"

"Because they can't be bugged."

The women hadn't used their phones for anything more than small talk with their husbands and kids. They were convinced their phones were bugged too.

"Oh, this is ridiculous," Anna said. "I think we're being overly paranoid. I mean, how do we even get these disposable phones?"

"I have no idea. It was something I saw on *The Wire*."

"You mean the phones the drug dealers used? I rest my case. It must be impossible for normal people to get them."

They headed back to the art institute's lobby. While Anna excused herself to talk with one of the curators, an acquaintance from many years of fundraisers at the museum, May poked through the posters. She couldn't decide which to purchase, so instead she picked up a sale copy of *The Clark: The Institute and Its Collections* to poke through and help her choose. She and Anna had already decided they would return tomorrow with snowshoes so they could hike the trail to the top of Stone Hill where the large-scale architectural sculpture "Crystal" by Thomas Schutte stood. Anna was fascinated by architecture, and both women enjoyed snowshoe hikes, especially when an unseasonably warm, sunny day was in the forecast. May loved how the world-class museum also included 140 acres of fields and wooded paths.

As May watched Anna conclude her chat with the curator, she caught the eye of a security guard who seemed to be watching Anna from the opposite side of the lobby. May smiled reflexively, but froze when he raised an eyebrow. Anna finally finished and turned, looking in a circle until she spotted May. She approached her. "What's wrong?" Anna asked. May was transfixed, locked in a stare with the guard. Anna looked in the direction of May's stare, and saw the guard turn away as he approached the curator and talked with her. "You look like you've seen a ghost."

"I don't know what just happened. I think he hexed me or something," May said.

"Hexed you?"

"Or he was flirting with me."

"Wow. You've obviously been out of the game a long time," Anna said as she gently grabbed May's elbow and directed her toward the exit.

"You have too," May said. They'd each been married long enough to have grown kids who were starting their own adult lives.

Anna turned and opened the doors with her back. She glanced over May's shoulder and saw the guard watching them. Once outside, a glance over her shoulder gave her the impression that not only was he still watching them, but that he'd spoken into his cuff. Did museum guards have cuff mics like the secret service agents who had been assigned to protect Frank when he was in Washington?

"What is it?" Now it was May's turn to question her friend.

"I just thought I saw another friend inside."

"Who don't you know in this county?" May was amazed that her friend who hardly knew anyone in the town she'd lived in for 15 years could know so many people in the county where she worked.

"You forget that the life of a senator—and therefore of a senator's assistant—is constantly one of meeting with the public. Now, what do you say we stop at that big box store that we both hate so much and see if we can find burner phones."

"I thought that idea was too paranoid for you."

"I'm finally beginning to realize that a bit more paranoia may be good for us both. I only wish we could take our concerns to someone. See if we're being silly."

"Margaret?"

"No, don't want to worry her. Especially if I'm wrong."

***

The Clark, *established in Williamstown, Massachusetts in the 1950s, features an impressive art collection on a 140-acre campus that is open to visitors. More than a public art museum, it also features research and academic programs.*

For more information, visit Anna's "Northern Berkshire County" board on Pinterest:

https://www.pinterest.com/anna_mcgrory/northern-berkshire-county/

CHAPTER 12

That evening, Anna and May stepped into the lobby of MASS MoCA, the museum where the senator's wake had taken place. Anna hadn't been back since that day and would have preferred not to visit now. It was still too painful for her to remember. She surprised herself yet again at how much she missed Frank. But May had never been to the sprawling contemporary art museum, so when a dinner concert had been advertised, May suggested they buy tickets. In the end, Anna didn't feel right not letting her friend see the amazing facility. Plus, she felt guilty staying away from the museum that had helped her and Margaret so much.

As they shook the new snow from their overcoats in the outer lobby, May pointed. "Isn't that Tom's work?"

It was Anna's husband's photography on a wall of the museum store. Anna beelined it toward the display. A collection of five of his photos were for sale as magnets, on totes and t-shirts, or as prints—framed, unframed, or as metallic pieces that were ready to hang. One featured the senator standing and chatting with a young 4H member who sat upon her pony. In the background, not at once visible, the young girl's grandmother gazed in adoration. It was one of those chance moments that artists are able to capture in such a way that stirs an emotional response in the viewer.

"This one's my favorite," May said, picking up a framed print of lobster boats harbored in a cove at Cliff Island.

"Mine too." Anna had lobbied Tom to get a copy of that print for her home office. When her husband hadn't complied by her next birthday, she ordered a print for herself and had it framed. Tom had thought Anna was only being polite and supportive. He couldn't believe she loved his work that much.

Anna grabbed an assortment of magnets, a t-shirt, and a tote. "Tom didn't get you any?"

It was Keith, the museum's director who had helped Anna with the wake.

"He didn't even tell me these were here."

"The originals are on display just inside the first gallery."

Keith insisted Anna and May take what they wanted of the merchandise, but Anna refused. He countered that they simply pay the cost of each item, but still Anna declined, saying she wanted to support the museum. She finally agreed to accept a doubling of her customary 10-percent member discount.

Keith left them to explore before the dinner show began. Standing in front of Tom's original photographs in the gallery, Anna was proud, but also a little bothered. "I don't know if I should congratulate him, or pretend I don't know these are here."

"I've already texted Jim a photo of Tom's bio, so I'm guessing it won't be too long before he knows you know."

May was correct. If Tom hadn't already heard from Jim, he would hear about May's text when he saw him Friday night at their monthly cribbage tournament at one of the local pubs.

"Should I feel jealous that I didn't know about these?"

"Jealous of who?"

"You're right. It's not like he cheated on me."

May entwined her arm through Anna's, and the two strolled the galleries. In a small, interactive display, May nudged Anna and whispered in her ear. "That guard looks like the one at the Clark today."

Anna managed to resist her knee-jerk reaction. Instead of turning to look at him, she walked a step or two, stopped, turned to gaze at a painting, and looked up into the same eyes she had seen that afternoon. Suddenly she was angry.

She marched right up to him. "Are you following us?!"

"Ma'am?"

"Don't ma'am me, you copper wannabe. I asked you a question: Are. You. Following. us?"

"No, Ma'am. I'm not. Perhaps you have me confused with someone else." He looked at her, and Anna felt as if he'd looked all the way into her head and could read her mind. "If you'd prefer, I can cover a different exhibit."

May watched Anna with concern. She knew her friend to be

confrontational when pressed, but she also knew Anna would be shaking like a leaf in a minute.

In a quieter tone, Anna asked, "Were you at the Clark this afternoon?"

"Yes, ma'am. I actually work for them. MoCA was short staffed tonight, which is why I'm here." He stopped and looked from Anna to May and back to Anna. "Now I remember. You were in the lobby talking with Sandra while your friend browsed the gift shop."

Anna drew in a deep breath. She wasn't sure she was buying this Andy Griffith "aww shucks" routine. A part of her still believed he was following them. "Yes, that's right."

"Well, there you have it," the guard said. "I can see now why you thought I was following you."

"Come on." May grabbed Anna's elbow and led her away. Within seconds of turning a corner, Anna was shaking. "Dessert?"

"Yes, please."

They went straight to the Club, found their table, and ordered dessert. Though Anna was not supposed to eat chocolate, she ordered the chocolate cake with chocolate icing and chocolate ganache—two slices. Her body was already going to be suffering from her fight-or-flight response. What would a couple pieces of triple chocolate cake hurt?

Later, after the show let out, Anna and May walked through the courtyard singing the chorus to one of their favorite tunes from the night's performance. As they passed through the narrow alley to the parking lot, a taxi pulled up behind them and flashed its headlights. Anna and May stood to the side in single file for the car to pass. Instead, it pulled up alongside them. "Anna McGrory?" the driver asked.

"Yes?"

"I was told to give you this." He handed her a folded piece of paper and drove off.

"I was afraid he was going to make me get in," Anna said as she walked to a light and opened the piece of typewriter paper. She saw written by hand: "You were right: I was following you." The women looked at each other in alarm.

"Does it say anything else?" May asked. Anna turned it over, but neither of them saw any other writing on the sheet.

"I don't know if we should go back to the cottage tonight," Anna said, looking around to see if she could spy the odd guard. She pictured him taking aim at her now—either with a camera or a high-powered rifle.

"I don't think he's going to be on the roof, do you?" May asked, following Anna's gaze.

"Never know."

They approached the car, but instead of climbing in, they each took small flashlights from their pockets and shined them like pros under the car, under the neighboring truck, and through the car windows. The flashlights lit up the big box store bags with the unopened pre-paid phones. "Broad safety sweep complete," they said in unison. It was something they'd learned in one of their self-defense classes. They were particularly paranoid by the possibility of a knife-wielding kidnapper hiding beneath a neighboring car or truck who might cut their ankles, then jump out and grab them, stuff them into the trunk, and drive off.

They climbed into the car, but only because they were freezing. They both wanted to talk this through before they drove back to the estate, but couldn't. Not in the Jeep. They were sure it must have been bugged too. Neither of them had any idea how to find a bug, though they had tried looking in some likely places according to a blog post they had read.

"I'm still keyed up," Anna said. "Let's go see if the 24-hour diner is still open." Anna drove the streets from memory, and found that the diner was closed as they pulled up to park out front. "So much for twenty-four hours," May said as they read the sign listing the hours as six a.m. to midnight most days, open till two a.m. on Saturdays. Anna pulled a U-turn and headed back to the mini mart that was open a couple blocks back. Before she got more than a few feet, they heard a police car's siren.

Anna pulled over and sighed. She turned on the interior light and rested her hands on top of the steering wheel, as she'd seen in some video. May rested her hands on the dashboard in clear sight.

"Evening, officer," Anna said as he approached.

"Ma'am, do you know why—Anna McGrory, is that you?"

"Officer Daniels," Anna said.

"Jeffrey, please."

They shook hands through the window.

"I'd heard you were sick."

"I am. But I'm improving."

"What are you doing out at this time of night?"

"My friend, May, and I." Anna sat back so Jeffrey could look through and see May.

"Hi there!" May said.

He nodded as Anna continued. "We were just at the Club at MoCA. We're still wide-awake. Thought Tiny's Diner might still be open twenty-four hours."

"His son runs it now. Hardly anyone misses the overnight hours."

"Except us," Anna said.

"Me too when I work this shift." He suggested a couple of the lounges at the area's larger hotels, noting they might at least be able to get some munchies or dessert, and sent them away with a warning for the illegal U-turn.

As Anna drove away, she turned to May. "Not so bad, my knowing everyone in the county now is it?"

A few miles later, Anna pulled into The Orchards, a larger, yet still boutique-feeling hotel on Route 2 in Williamstown. May presumed Anna was going for that snack she had mentioned to the officer. Instead, Anna requested a room. Once they were safely tucked inside it, they could finally talk.

"I've been thinking about the note," said May. "You don't suppose he used invisible ink, do you?"

"I wouldn't be surprised by anything at this point."

"If it is, we'll have to heat it up to make the ink appear," May said.

"Whatever you say, Dr. Watson."

"You presume you're Sherlock?"

"Sorry, Sherlock," Anna said as she watched May pull out the complimentary iron and board from the closet and plug in the iron. "How do you even know these things?"

"Elementary, my dear Watson." Anna rolled her eyes as May continued. "Was a member of the Dick Tracy Detective Club as a kid."

"Of course you were," Anna said as she helped herself to a candy bar and a bottle of water from the mini fridge, and motioned for May to do the same.

"We should have stopped at the mini mart," May said. "Probably could have bought a case of candy bars for what this will cost us tomorrow."

"I might ordinarily worry over the cost, but not at this point." Anna pulled the note out of her jacket pocket and handed it to May, who flattened it out on the ironing board.

"Oh no. I hope he used lemon juice or vinegar," May said as she headed into the bathroom to wash her hands.

"You mean instead of..." Anna trailed off, unable to bring herself to say what else he might have used, if he did indeed leave an invisible message for them. As Anna washed her hands, she tried to shake the idea from her consciousness. He wouldn't have used bodily fluids, would he?

The iron beeped. "You want me to do the honors?" May asked.

"You know if I do it, I'm likely to burn it, like I do with toast."

"And eggs. Cookies. Pies."

"Okay, okay. So, I'm not the best cook." Anna had been improving though. When she got sick, she suddenly needed to control every ingredient she ate. Gone were the frozen Newman's pizza nights, the store-rotisserie chickens, and now that she couldn't eat dairy products, the Blake's gluten-free potpies. She had even begun making bone soup from the Sunday supper chicken carcass. Anna was turning into May, which Anna had to admit was a pretty good thing.

May wished she had rubber gloves, but decided she could wash her hands again. Carefully, she held an edge as she set the iron onto the paper. She let it sit a few seconds and raised it up again. "Do you see anything?" Anna didn't, so May tried again, this time holding it for 15 seconds, which Anna timed via her phone.

This time, they began to see letters form. May moved the iron over and set it on the paper. Anna timed it. They proceeded in this manner until the entire eight and a half by eleven-inch paper had been ironed. Finally they could read it. Or could they? It was gibberish. "Is it just a design or a watermark left by the paper's manufacturer?" Anna asked as she raised it up. May pointed. "No, it's written on the other side."

Anna flipped it over and read it aloud: "I am retired Secret Service. Worked for Frank. Meet me Friday. 10 am. Brown Bag Deli. Concord. I can help."

"Stop." May said.

Anna looked up at her.

"It sounded like an old telegram. I was just adding the stop at the end."

"He knows I'm going to Concord Copy Friday morning."

"He's been listening in."

"It's creepy." Anna sat as she sank deep in thought.

May watched her. Finally, she couldn't take it anymore. "Do you believe him?"

"Not really. You?"

May shook her head.

"Doesn't mean I won't meet with him though."

***

*As home to so many world-class arts and cultural attractions, **Berkshire County** also offers a number of beautiful places for visitors to stay. The Orchards Hotel in Williamstown, Massachusetts, is among the many quaint, modern places for a traveler to rest.*

For more information, visit Anna's "Vacation Spots" board on Pinterest: https://www.pinterest.com/anna_mcgrory/vacation-spots/

CHAPTER 13

The next morning, May found Anna curled up in a ball on the bathroom floor with a blanket wrapped around her. She hurried to her, kneeling and touching her arm.

"Morning," Anna said. It was an exhausted voice, no louder than a whisper.

"What's wrong?"

"The chocolate was a bad idea. My bladder pain is through the roof. Having trouble moving."

"Did you take anything for it?"

"Don't have that medicine with me. Haven't needed it in a while."

"You need a prescription called in?"

"No, there's an over-the-counter version available."

"I'll get dressed and go get it. You should have woken me sooner."

"The drug store wouldn't have been open anyway."

May helped Anna onto her bed, and got her to help with the exact name of the bladder pain medicine: Phenazopyridine Hydrochloride.

After May returned and Anna took the medicine, it took about a half hour before Anna could uncoil herself. Another 30 minutes passed before they were finally leaving the room. As May drove, Anna nibbled on what was left of a plain gluten-free donut May had brought her from a nearby bakery. The aroma of May's coffee from the donut shop was driving Anna crazy with anticipation for her own low-acid coffee she would brew once they arrived back at the cottage.

While their work was slowed by Anna's return to her painful symptoms, the duo managed to finish cataloguing the estate's contents. Anna sent the file to the printer a day early. She loved that they'd somehow gotten ahead of schedule, and knew the owner Ken would be thankful for the additional time to print, collate, and bind the brochure.

Before they headed home to New Hampshire, May stopped at the end of the driveway and carried in an empty plate to Sheila. "I meant to bake something in return, but we got so busy that I didn't have time. I'm sorry," May said.

"Please, don't be. I know you were working. I was happy to bake for you both."

"Still, my mother would be disappointed to know I returned an empty plate." It was how May and Anna had both been raised, which meant the two of them frequently ate well since they were always passing full plates back and forth. When Anna got sick, May put her foot down and forbade Anna from doing anything but eating her goodies. It took a few weeks before Anna overcame her perceived shame at receiving without giving back. She only truly felt better after May's husband Jim told her that an empty plate made May feel useful.

Sheila slipped on her boots, hat, and coat and walked out to the car with May. May knocked on Anna's window as she walked to the driver's side. Anna's pain had returned, so even reaching to power down the passenger window took obvious effort.

"Oh, dear," said Sheila. "Are you all right to ride all the way home?"

"I'm in good hands."

"We'll look forward to your next trip." Sheila said the words, but Anna wasn't sure she meant them. One item that had yet to be determined was how Sheila and Shep's years-long arrangement might figure into the donation process of the estate to the Trustees. It was one of the reasons Margaret was okay with dragging her feet for so long before making a decision. Eventually, though, that too would have to be addressed. Anna hoped Sheila and Shep could stay on in residence until the pair of them left of their own accord. She wondered if it was too morbid to stipulate till their death, and decided to let Margaret's estate-planning attorney worry about the wording.

May powered up Anna's window for her from the driver's controls, and waved back to Sheila as they pulled out. A late morning squall had coated the trees that lined the lane. The sun's rays cascaded through the clouds, causing the branches to sparkle. "It's beautiful here."

"It is," Anna said. "Wish we could afford to buy the place?"

"Maybe if it was on the ocean."

"Oh yes, then we would find a way to at least write ourselves in as permanent caretakers." Anna smiled at the thought as she fell asleep against the cool window. It was a welcome feeling as her body warmed with the onset of a low-grade fever—yet another symptom she had grown accustomed to over the past several months of battling chronic illness.

***

Later, Anna was in bed watching her latest favorite BBC detective series on her iPad when Tom climbed the stairs from his office to their home.

"You're not going to meet this guy," he said.

"Hello to you too."

"You're not."

"I am."

"Then I'm going with you."

"Good. I prefer that."

"Good. It's settled then."

"How was your day?"

Tom blinked. Was Anna mocking him by changing the subject? But as she closed her iPad and sat up, he decided she was genuinely curious. "Fine. It was fine." Off her look, which he knew meant that she liked to hear more than just "fine," he sat next to her and told her about an odd occurrence involving a confused elderly woman who mistook the law firm for her physician's office, refusing to believe that it wasn't a doctor's office.

His office administrator was about to call the police to help identify the woman, who they were certain was missing from one of the area's senior residential facilities. Before they could, the woman's adult daughter arrived. Turned out the woman had been talking about going to see Dr. Walker for a few weeks. He had run his practice from the offices that now served as the small law firm. After the visiting nurse had arrived at the woman's house that morning and found the backdoor open, a neighborhood search was conducted, which yielded nothing. The daughter recalled the conversations, and stopped by on a hunch.

Tom was surprised to see that his story elicited sadness from Anna. "What's wrong?"

"It reminds me of the times I got so confused I couldn't remember where I was or where I was going—like that day when it was really bad." Anna and Tom recalled the day almost a year ago when Anna pulled into the driveway of the house where they used to live, in another town about a half hour away. When her key didn't work in the lock, she panicked. Fortunately, one of the neighbors who had lived there when she and Tom and the kids were there walked by with her dog and saw her. She invited Anna in for tea while she called Tom at work.

"I was that woman."

***

Cold brew coffee is not only good for the IC diet, but it also tastes great. It's easy to make at home with one of the cold brew systems available on the market, with a French press, or with whatever you have on hand.

For more information, visit Anna's "IC" board on Pinterest:

https://www.pinterest.com/anna_mcgrory/ic/

Chapter 14

As it turned out, Tom was right: Anna was not going to meet the super-secret spy guy. She was in so much pain that she couldn't even walk to the bathroom. She berated herself for eating chocolate and vowed to stick to the bladder-friendly list for the rest of her life if necessary.

Tom said he would go, but Anna didn't know how to describe the man beyond 50s, about Tom's height, broad shoulders, close-cropped salt-and-pepper hair, and eyes that could peer into your soul. Tom wanted to know what color these soul-piercing eyes were, but Anna could only remember blackness. Did anyone actually have black eyes? Tom had a logical explanation though. He always did. It was probably dark in the gallery and his pupils were enlarged. Anna tried to remember if May's eyes had appeared black.

"May!" Anna called after Tom as he was about to leave. Anna had her phone out and was dialing when Tom returned to the bedroom. "She can identify him. May? Any chance you can go to the shop with Tom this morning?"

Tom watched as Anna's hopefulness vanished.

"No. Of course. I understand completely." Anna hung up and flung the covers aside.

"What are you doing?" Tom hurried to help her.

Anna shrugged him off. "I'm going. This is ridiculous. I'm going to be in pain whether or not I go with you. I might as well go and meet this creep."

"May's busy?"

"Jim doesn't want her involved any longer. He's afraid it's gotten too dangerous."

"I agree with him."

"I know you do. And maybe I do too a little, but I want to figure out what's going on. I think I should at least get enough information to share with Margaret." Anna moaned in pain as she tried to get her pants on.

Tom helped her. "I'm taking you to the doctor afterward."

This time he got no argument from his wife. Anna finished getting dressed and grabbed her newest tote bag—the one she had purchased at MASS MoCA. As Tom helped her down the stairs, he noticed it. "Nice bag."

"Why didn't you tell me you had an exhibit there?"

"Must have slipped my mind."

"Really?"

"No."

"No kidding," Anna said.

"You were really sick when Keith called me to arrange it."

"That sounds more like an excuse than a reason."

"We need to get going. Should we discuss this later?" He waited till Anna nodded.

Even though they lived less than two blocks from the coffee shop, Tom and Anna were five minutes late. Try as she may, she could not walk anywhere close to her normal pace. Anna looked around as soon as they entered. "He's not here. Maybe we missed him. Oh, I should have let you just come alone."

"Relax. Let's just order and wait." Tom helped Anna to a chair, and stood in line for his coffee and her cup of hot water.

Anna watched the door, blinking back the scant tears that sometimes formed despite her dry eyes. They were brought on by a new pain in her abdomen. It was more than just the chocolate cake and candy bar; it was an ache she'd never experienced, and so far her over-the-counter remedies were not helping. A group of schoolgirls pushed through the door with their coffees, giggling and chattering nonstop. Anna's phone chimed. She glanced. It was a message from May: "Did you meet him?"

She typed a quick, "No," and resumed her study of the door.

"A hot water for you, my dear," Tom said as he approached with their cups, setting hers in front of her. "Just need to doctor mine."

She watched as he walked back toward the counter where the sugar and milks were and was shocked to see the super-secret agent guy at the counter stirring his coffee. She texted May: "He's here! I'm calling you now. Put it on mute and listen in." May answered on the first ring. Anna set the phone on the chair next to her, where her coat rested in a heap.

The former secret service agent approached. But he kept walking, right out the door.

Anna grabbed her coat and her phone and hobbled after him. "Tom! He's leaving."

Tom had just placed his coffee cup lid on, turning in time to see the agent push through the door and drop his phone as he did so. "Hey! Buddy! Your phone." But the agent kept walking as the door closed behind him.

Anna grabbed the phone and stepped out the door, looking up and down the street. He was nowhere to be seen.

Tom joined her. "Where is he?"

May asked the same thing via Anna's phone. "May, I'll call you back." Anna hung up and looked at the dropped phone—an old school flip phone. She opened it and found a sticky note that read: "Don't make a habit of being late." Anna moaned in frustration. She tried the phone, but the screen was locked. "What do we do now?"

"Get you to the doctor's office," said Tom.

Tom helped Anna back home and into his car, returning to Capitol Copy to pay them to overnight the brochure to Margaret. On their 20-minute drive to the doctor's office, the dropped phone rang. Anna opened the phone on the second ring and put it to her ear.

"Your friend was right—you should be using burner phones."

"Who are you?"

"Throw this phone away at the doctor's office. Hope you feel better soon." The connection went dead. Anna looked for a number, but it was blocked.

"Who is he?"

"He didn't say."

"We should call the police," said Tom.

"And tell them what?"

"Someone's stalking you. How else would he know about the doctor's?"

"Do you think that's what he's doing—stalking me?"

"I don't know, but this has gone way beyond weird."

At her family physician's office, Anna was met by a nurse who ushered her into an exam room. As Anna walked by her into the room, the nurse hissed almost under her breath, "You don't have Lyme!" Anna was so surprised that she said nothing in return as the door closed behind her, leaving her to wait alone for her doctor.

The quick check-in with Dr. Carry resulted in a change to Anna's antibiotics regime. The two women decided Anna would stop taking one of the three prescriptions, and see if that helped minimize her pain. She was also advised to increase the probiotics, something she had just started taking thanks to her discussion with Glen and Jo. Dr. Carry gave Anna a hug on her way out the door. "Thank you," Anna said, surprised by her kind gesture. It was the first time any of Anna's physicians had offered a hug, though her physical therapist and she hugged every time they saw each other.

"You've been through a lot with this disease," Dr. Carry said. "And I have too. I'm learning so much from your experience and through conversations with your Lyme-literate doctor. Anyway, I hope you don't mind a hug. I just don't like seeing you in pain."

They hugged again, and Anna realized she felt a little less lonely on her Lyme journey. She knew she had May and Tom with her, but Dr. Carry had been a godsend. When Anna had first fallen ill, Tom suggested Anna get a nurse to meet with her once a week—someone to keep an eye on all her medical charts since she was seeing so many different doctors. When Anna asked Dr. Carry what she thought of the idea, she was pleasantly surprised that not only did Dr. Carry think it was a great plan, but that she wanted to be the weekly person in charge of her coordinated care. Fortunately the insurance company approved, though Anna and Tom paid one hundred percent of each visit until Anna finally hit the year's deductible at the end of the third quarter. It had been an expensive illness.

It took a couple days of resting on the sofa over the weekend to help her feel better. By Monday, Anna was up and ready to go again. She was eager to visit with Margaret, but first she needed to meet her Lyme doctor—her newest and last doctor she would ever need to add to her impossibly long list of care providers. Or so she hoped.

***

*There are a number of organizations that offer a physician referral service, helping to put Lyme patients in touch with **Lyme-literate doctors** who treat the disease outside the rigid CDC guidelines. Some patients credit their Lyme-literate physicians with saving their lives*

For more information, visit Anna's "Lyme" board on Pinterest:

https://www.pinterest.com/anna_mcgrory/lyme/

Chapter 15

May drove Anna to the Lyme specialist's office. Jim was comfortable with May's being a friend to Anna, but just not a fan of their amateur sleuthing. Still, May wasn't ready to give up. She pored over her own copies of the patient interviews and built charts tracking similar symptoms, timelines, medications, and insurance company shenanigans, a term she decided was apt since insurers seemed so determined to make sure patients did not get compensated for the treatments they needed.

They arrived at the doctor's office 20 minutes early, which gave them time to compare notes with each other. Anna had already submitted her new patient papers to Dr. Flynn, so there was nothing to do at check-in but present her insurance card and cover her copayment. She'd been working with Dr. Carry to treat her Lyme until the impossibly busy Lyme-literate doctor had an opening in his schedule. Anna had waited months to see him.

Anna's charts looked similar to May's, except May's were more beautiful. They had decided not to use their computers, which they were sure could be tracked by whoever might want to do so—like Senator Ponema and his staff who seemed so determined to get the patient files. Instead, they did everything by hand. While May had spent more time color-coding and writing in an elaborate script to present her findings, Anna had grabbed her old school calculator and recorded averages.

Of the patients interviewed, 93 percent were diagnosed after five point two years with symptoms. Only 22 percent of patients had a positive Lyme test by CDC standards. Seven percent of the total patients interviewed had a positive test on the first try, which is why they received antibiotic treatment immediately. However, not all of those testing positive had a noticeable bulls-eye rash. Instead, only two-thirds of them presented with the classic symptom.

Nearly 100 percent of patients—97 percent of them to be precise—reported family members within the same house having been diagnosed with Lyme disease. All the patients reported knowing of other Lyme patients, which then broke down into categories, including patients in the same neighborhood, in extended family, in coworkers, and in friends.

All the patients reported that their primary care physicians had told them that chronic Lyme didn't officially exist, which was in line with the philosophy of the CDC. Yet, 75 percent were told that they definitely had chronic Lyme by other doctors, and the other 25 percent were told that they had Post-Treatment Lyme disease syndrome...even those who had never before received Lyme treatments.

"Anna McGrory?"

Anna looked up into the eyes of a nurse.

May gathered all the papers and tucked them back in her bag as Anna followed the nurse. Their discussion would be continued over lunch, which Anna had promised in exchange for May's driving her. Not that Anna had to buy lunch in order to get May's help. But May appreciated the gesture as she settled in to knit her latest project: a baby blanket for her fourth grandchild—her youngest daughter's first baby.

In the exam room, the nurse took Anna's vitals. She was quiet, so Anna didn't disturb her concentration as she sat on the exam table. "Okay," she said at last, "the doctor will be right in to see you."

Within five seconds of her leaving, the door opened and in walked a man in a white lab coat. He looked like a doctor, but Anna recognized his eyes immediately and noted that they were black, even in the brightly lit exam room.

"What do you think you're doing?!"

"Take this." He tried to hand her a burner phone, but Anna crossed her arms across her chest.

"I'm done with this cloak and dagger routine."

"It's for your own safety."

"I don't believe you."

"No kidding." It was a standoff. They stared at each other until he finally relaxed and let his arm drop to his side. "I'm just trying to help."

"I'm Anna. Good to meet you, Just Trying to Help."

"James."

"You're kidding, right? Last name Bond?"

"Smith."

"You couldn't even be bothered to come up with a better fake name than that?"

"It's my real name. The one that's on my birth certificate. I promise."

"What is it you're trying to protect me from?"

"Not what. Who."

"You mean the sneaky senator and his kooky doctor friend? I think I can take either one of them. Both of them at the same time even."

"There are others. They believe you have the patient interviews and that you've been studying them yourself. Do you have them?"

"I gave the folder to the senator."

"It wasn't the material he was looking for."

"And how would you know that?"

"It's in your best interest that I know that."

A knock on the door startled them both. The door opened slowly as the real doctor poked his head in. "Are you decent?"

"Yes," Anna answered as she looked in his direction. By the time Dr. Flynn stepped into the room, James Smith had disappeared out another door. The burner phone rested next to Anna.

"Was I supposed to change into a hospital gown?" Anna asked as she stood and slipped the phone into a pocket of her coat.

"What? No."

"It's just that you asked if I was decent."

"Right. Sorry. Old habit," Dr. Flynn said. "I began as a general practitioner before focusing solely on Lyme."

Dr. Flynn was kind and soft spoken. He put Anna at ease almost immediately. If not for her visitor, she would have been completely calm and may have even enjoyed her appointment.

"I went back through your medical records," Dr. Flynn said. With a wave of his hand, he invited her to join him at his desk where he turned the computer screen so they could both look on together. "I believe your symptoms began about five years ago when you presented with a rash that was diagnosed as ringworm."

"I wondered the same thing," Anna said. She told him about the rash beneath her right breast that looked like a bulls-eye, with one red ring around a red circle. She'd been given a topical cream, and the rash went away about two weeks later. She hadn't thought about it until she and her primary care physician went back through her records a few weeks ago. "There's a nurse at Dr. Carry's office who thinks the cream cleared up the rash."

"Hard to say," Dr. Flynn said. "The Lyme rash would have disappeared in roughly the same time frame. Either theory can be supported, but your medical history that follows the incident indicates Lyme."

Since the ringworm diagnosis, Anna had suffered several recurring bouts of bronchitis and pneumonia. She had also twice experienced poison ivy rashes so severe that they spread to nearly every inch of her body, even crawling inside her ears and dangerously close to her eyes. Her body could not seem to fight off infections on its own anymore, which indicated her immune system had been compromised.

She also recalled having been more depressed, anxious, and exhausted during this time, and having an increase of complaints about sore joints and nerve pain. When taken individually, it didn't raise any significant red flags. But bundled together, it was apparent to Dr. Flynn that Anna had chronic Lyme. Anna was fortunate she had Dr. Flynn in her corner. He told Anna what it meant to be a Lyme-literate doctor, or LLMD. It was a term used by Lyme patient advocacy and support groups that had sprung up in reaction to the CDC and the establishment in the medical community who continued to ignore the needs of sick patients. LLMDs were the only physicians actually treating Lyme patients.

"So, what do we do now?"

"Your primary care's prescriptions are working now that they've been tweaked, right?" Anna nodded. "Let's continue that until you're symptom free."

"How long do you think that might be?"

"It's tricky. Different for every patient. Best-case scenario is you're on them for three or four months, but that might run to half a year, or even a full year. You'll need to call my office if you notice any new symptoms, which could be a sign we need to change your antibiotics or check for co-infections."

That was something Anna only had a cursory knowledge of through her readings in the patient files. Dr. Flynn listed off the possible co-infections of Babesia, Bartonella and others, and gave Anna literature to read about them and about her Lyme. Because she seemed so interested in the history of Lyme disease, and the controversy surrounding its diagnosis and treatment, he recommended she read a book by Pamela Weintraub. Anna pulled out her cell phone and ordered a copy of *Cure Unknown: Inside the Lyme Epidemic* before leaving. She didn't care if Senator Ponema would know that she had done so, if he was indeed monitoring her phone. Anna was beginning to get angry about this entire Lyme debate and she didn't care who knew that about her.

Back in the waiting area, as Anna scheduled a series of follow-up appointments with the receptionist and received a copy of her standing order for blood work every two months, May bagged up her knitting, placing it atop the photocopied patient interviews and her colorful charts. Afterward, Anna wound her arm through May's as they strolled toward the exit. "Where to?"

It was May's turn to pick the lunch place since Anna was treating. May didn't hesitate: "Angelina's." It was a cozy, ground floor, quasi basement-level Italian restaurant that seated maybe two dozen patrons at a time. It was a favorite spot of both women. More importantly, the chef knew Anna, so it was easy for her to order a bladder-friendly, Lyme-healthy meal.

Anna hung her coat as they entered. She and May sat and ordered the day's special. Once Nick the waiter had left, Anna leaned over to May and whispered loudly, "You'll never guess who stopped in at the doctor's office."

"You mean besides the doctor and the nurse?"

May had the same thought about what James' last name should have been. Bond really did suit him and their situation better than Smith did.

"He gave me another burner."

"If he can just pop in to see you wherever you are, why bother?"

"I thought the same thing," Anna said. "That's why I left it in my coat by the front door."

"I don't follow."

"In one of the Canadian broadcasting shows I like to watch—you know, the one from Newfoundland?" May looked perplexed. Turned out she wasn't familiar with *The Republic of Doyle*, which Anna had started watching since some of Tom's relatives were from St. John's. A few episodes in, she was hooked. "The cops use cell phones to listen in on people's conversations."

"So don't use it to call anyone," May said.

"I mean all the time. Anytime you talk. Like our conversation right now. Which is why I didn't say anything about him until I could get rid of the phone."

"What about our regular phones?" May took hers out of her bag. Anna did the same. They shared a look of defeat before Anna remembered grabbing an extra foldable bag. She grabbed it, opened it up, and they placed their phones inside. Anna carried it to the entrance and hung it on a peg next to her coat.

"I feel like such an idiot," Anna said as she sat again.

"I feel like I'm in a crime novel or something," said May. "This can't possibly be real life, can it?"

"I'm not sure."

"You think he's listening to us now? Or would be if the phone were closer?"

"He asked me if I had the patient files."

"Is he working for Senator Scary Pants?"

"I wondered the same thing. But I don't know how to check," Anna said. "I do know he's giving me the creeps."

"Spidey senses alerted?"

"Not really. But I'm still not sure I should trust him."

"I don't know who you can trust anymore."

"Well, I hope I can trust you!"

The women toasted to their mutual trust of each other with water as Nick delivered their meals, and cracked pepper over May's serving. It was one of the spices that Anna missed, but which set off her flares of bladder pain instantly. They began eating, but Anna was troubled by all the unwanted attention brought on by the interviews. She couldn't stop and simply enjoy the fresh haddock cooked in an olive oil and garlic sauce just for her. May's was steeped in a fresh piccata sauce—Anna's favorite, which she hoped she'd get to enjoy again in the future.

"What are you going to do now?" May asked.

"I don't honestly know. Though I have been daydreaming about getting away for a few days. Someplace they wouldn't think to bug, where I can pore over the files. Maybe I could trade cars with Joanie, under pretense of having her husband drive it for a while to see if the clutch is slipping."

"You think the clutch is slipping already?"

"No, but I want to drive a car that is less likely to be bugged."

"Thinking of heading to Cliff Island?"

"It's my favorite place in the world."

"I know."

"So do they."

"You're afraid they've bugged the entire island?"

"You have a point," Anna said. "Maybe I could just rent a different cottage. But I'd be afraid they'd pull up to the dock. Then what would I do?" The women ate the rest of their lunch in silence as they thought about what they should do next.

After lunch, Anna grabbed the bags with their phones, but left her jacket accidentally on purpose hanging near the door. While she didn't know what else she would do, she did know that she refused to be played by James Smith. If that even was his real name.

***

*Anna was raised on central Italian cuisine prepared by her grandmother. Though she occasionally tried her own hand at making homemade pasta and meatballs, she found the most authentic home-cooked Italian dishes could be found at her favorite restaurant: **Angelina's Ristorante Italiano** on Depot Street in Concord, New Hampshire.*

For more information, visit Anna's "Restaurants" board on Pinterest: https://www.pinterest.com/anna_mcgrory/restaurants/

Chapter 16

Tom's receptionist knocked on the door at the top of the stairs as she opened it. "Anna? You here?"

Anna stepped out of the bathroom in her jeans and t-shirt as she towel dried her hair. "Celia. What's up?"

Celia handed Anna a pink message slip. "Margaret's been trying to get a hold of you all morning. Apparently you weren't answering your cell phone so she called the office. I told her you were at the doctor's. Hope you're okay."

"The good news is: I'll live." Anna still had no control over her bouts of exhaustion or her memory lapses due to something patients commonly referred to as Lyme fog, but at least she could joke about it. "Thanks. I'll give her a call now."

Celia returned to the law firm's office downstairs as Anna grabbed her cell phone from where it had been plugged in since she'd been home. She turned the ringer on and saw she had seven missed calls from Margaret. There were no texts from her since Margaret didn't know how to do that sort of thing. She called Margaret, knowing their conversation would be overheard. But she also suspected whoever was listening in had also just heard Celia tell Anna to make the call.

"Hello?"

"Margaret, it's Anna." Anna marveled that Margaret preferred to use the landline to her cell phone. Anna and Tom didn't even bother to have a landline installed in their new home when they'd moved in, though the cable company insisted on charging them for one. Something about bundling and saving money. Anna wasn't sure about the details, but she knew it was more expensive not to have a cable-assigned landline even if there was no physical phone attached to it.

"Anna, yes. How are you?"

"I'll be fine. Sorry I didn't have my phone with me at the doctor's." Anna cringed at the lie. But it was easier than explaining that she thought her phone might be bugged. "Is everything all right?"

"It is, but I'm hoping to see you before I leave."

"I didn't realize you were traveling."

"It's a last-minute arrangement. I don't know how long I'll be gone, but I'd like to get the estate sorted prior to my departure."

"I'm so sorry. I had meant to be there by now. Was planning to get on a bus directly after my appointment, but I was feeling sick afterwards." Anna lied again. She hoped it wouldn't become a habit. Truth was she was so shaken up by the comings and goings of James Smith and his gifts of burner phones, that she'd forgotten to pack a bag before her morning's appointment with her new Lyme-literate doctor. She knew she couldn't tell Margaret about her super-secret stalker guy over the phone.

Anna opened her laptop and looked up the bus schedule. There were still four more buses to Boston leaving almost every hour. If she hurried, she could even make the first one, though she told Margaret she'd be on the four o'clock bus. If someone was listening in, she wanted them to miss the three o'clock bus where she'd be. "Would you mind if May joins me?"

"Oh, that would be grand!" Margaret said. "I have symphony tickets tonight, and my usual companions are both away. I was going to skip it, but I'd love to take you both."

Anna knew May would enjoy that, but she wasn't sure if she could stay awake during it. Fortunately, the lobby had comfortable furniture. If May could join her, then at least she wouldn't be leaving Margaret alone if she needed to sneak out for a moment and get comfy enough for a short nap. Good grief, Anna thought, I'm turning into my Uncle Morty. Into the phone, Anna said, "Thank you. I'll see if May can get away this evening. Either way, one or both of us will be at your door by six o'clock."

An hour later, Anna and May were on the three o'clock bus to Boston. They'd surveyed the rest of the riders and decided they probably weren't spies for the senator. They also noted with a certain amount of glee that James Smith was nowhere to be seen.

"I can't believe Jim let you go with me," Anna said as they settled into their seats.

"He didn't have much of a choice once he heard we were going to the symphony." Anna knew May loved the symphony almost as much as she loved museums. Actually, she loved just about any kind of live performance, so she was always up for a last-second trip if it included an evening out on the town.

The two women glanced around again and, deciding the coast was clear, they pulled out their charts and pored through their findings. They made a new list of commonalities that included frequently reported symptoms, local municipalities, similar hobbies and professions, pets, habits, and physicians. They noticed that of the 90 patients either interviewed or mentioned during an interview in the file, three Lyme-literate doctors were mentioned with surprising frequency. "Are there really that few Lyme doctors?" May asked.

"I'm beginning to think so," Anna said. "I thought it was a New Hampshire thing—my doctor's the only one for miles."

"How often are these doctors mentioned?"

They went through the files again, this time listing the names of the patients beneath the doctors. Two doctors saw more than two-dozen patients, while three others had seen about a dozen, and one had seen seven. Only one patient was unaccounted for; she had sought treatment in Canada near the town where she had grown up.

"I still don't understand why Senator Scary Pants wants this file so bad," Anna said.

"Hey, I thought you weren't using my nickname for him, preferring the Varlet."

"My brain fog's gotten so bad I can never recall that name. Besides, Senator Scary Pants has a certain ring to it, even if it is a bit juvenile."

"You mean like your 'scared the beetle juice' out of me?"

"I've been working on removing that silly saying from my vernacular. Came in handy when the kids were little though," Anna said. As they shuffled through the papers again, organizing them to put back away, Anna pointed to one of May's charts. "You noted the frequency of the doctors here."

"Yes, but I wanted to double check my accuracy with you."

Anna realized she must have seen the chart earlier that day in the waiting room of the doctor's office. She wondered if somewhere deep in her brain's recesses she could recall it. She decided she better start keeping a journal if she wanted to have a shot at remembering all the things she hoped to summon up later. One of those things was a nagging suspicion growing inside her. She couldn't help wondering if her Lyme had been caused by an accidental tick bite or if it were deliberate, almost like someone had poisoned her. She shook her head at the obvious absurdity of such a notion, certain she was being far too paranoid even for her.

At Margaret's building, the doorman greeted the women with a huge smile. The sun was out and had warmed the city to unseasonable temperatures, which seemed to make everyone happy. Anna's breath caught as she and May approached the elevators. Anna stopped and eyeballed the magnificent staircase that wound inside the building.

Recognizing her friend's inner dilemma, May said, "I can take the bags with me on the elevator if you want to take the stairs."

"It's seven floors," Anna said.

"If you get too tired partway up, you can always jump on the elevator from there."

Anna nodded. She actually hadn't thought of that. For her it was an all-or-nothing issue: either she could ride inside the tiny box with only one way out and the horrific possibility it might break down, or she could climb up all those flights with knees that ached from Lyme-induced arthritic pain. Lately, the antibiotics had reduced that pain to an occasional bother, but she was worried the stairs might be too taxing for her sensitive joints. However, the medicine had given her some of her energy back. Telling herself she could do this, she left her bags with May and took to the stairs.

Three floors up, Anna heard the elevator swoop skyward. She was tired, but not tempted to push the call button. Floor five, she wished Margaret lived in a shorter building. Floor six, she knew she could push through her exhaustion and do this.

By the time Anna arrived on the top floor of the ancient building, May and Margaret were waiting for her in the hall. Margaret gave Anna a big hug, despite Anna's insistence that she was a sweaty mess. "My girl, you'll wear yourself out if you insist on taking the stairs each time you come and go," Margaret said. "Your cheeks and nose look like a bright red butterfly."

Anna grabbed two of the bags and followed Margaret and May to a door where Margaret used a key to let them in. The foyer was covered in white

Italian marble that reflected the late afternoon sun. "I love your place!" May said.

The condo actually belonged to Margaret's neighbor who was still at her winter place in the Florida Keys. Anna admired the warm and welcoming cottage-style blue and white furnishings and the bright pops of colorful, original, nautical-themed artwork. Her favorite was an oil painting of five vibrant dories in the harbor that reminded her of Cliff Island summers.

Though both condos featured three bedrooms, Margaret had turned one room into her studio since she'd taken up watercolor painting—a hobby she hadn't partaken of since before she'd met Frank. Her friend, however, still had two fully functional guest rooms. Margaret thought the women would be more comfortable in their own space for the couple days they'd be in Boston.

"As a matter of fact," Anna said as she eyed May, "this works out better for another reason too." Anna told Margaret about her suspicions of bugs being planted in her phone, in the car, at her home, and at the estate, telling her about the odd early-morning appearance of Senator Ponema. She added that she wouldn't be surprised if Margaret's condo was bugged too.

"Oh, that's just conjecture. Wouldn't you agree, May?" Margaret asked.

"I was skeptical too," May said. "But when the senator showed up at 5:17 in the morning—after we'd only discovered the file he wanted the night before—I began to have my suspicions."

"Can we at least agree to discuss the estate and any plans from this condo?" Anna asked.

"I do think you're being paranoid," said Margaret. "But I'm willing to meet in here tomorrow." They would discuss the plans in the morning. Margaret had invited her estate-planning attorney to join them, and she wanted to wait for him. Plus the women needed time to shower and change, and to get to Symphony Hall to eat at the café before the Boston Symphony Orchestra, or BSO as it was known, took the stage. Because of Margaret's connections and ongoing support of the BSO, she had been able to get last-minute reservations for dinner.

After Margaret left to get ready, Anna took out one of the burner phones she and May had purchased at the box store and texted her husband. "We are here. Please tell Jim. Love, Lily."

A moment later Tom's reply sounded. Anna looked and laughed. She showed the phone to May who read the text aloud. "Roger that. Secret protocol confirmed. Love, Pad."

"I think he thinks I'm nuts."

"I think you're nuts," May said.

***

Lyme fog *can be a very real problem for many patients struggling with the effects of Lyme disease. It might hinder decision-making, confuse the patient, or make the person forgetful.*

For more information, visit Anna's "Lyme" board on Pinterest: https://www.pinterest.com/anna_mcgrory/lyme/

CHAPTER 17

An hour later, the well-dressed trio took a taxi to Boston's Symphony Hall, a National Historic Landmark that was completed in 1900 and serves as home to the Boston Symphony Orchestra, which owns and operates the building. The setting sun reflected a spectrum of crimson against the red brick building with its marble columns that line the south entrance. Daylight savings time had gone into effect the week before, and while none of the three of them had quite yet adjusted to the loss of the hour, they appreciated the extra light this evening.

They checked their coats upon entry and went straight up to the narrow, rectangular, modernist Cabot-Cahners room on the second floor to claim their meals from one of the bartenders who handled the dinner reservations. Anna declined the chocolate cake dessert plate. She might have risked it had she not paid so dearly for her earlier brush with chocolate. May and Anna sat at one of the handful of round tables with seating for four and ate every morsel of their dinners while Margaret nibbled a bite or two and spent the rest of the time standing and catching up with friends. She clearly enjoyed her evenings out among people she was beginning to think of as her extended family.

The BSO was brilliant, as Anna knew it would be. But the day was catching up with her. Between movements in Mahler's Ninth Symphony, she made her way to the ladies room. After washing her hands, she turned to reach for a towel and gasped at the stranger who walked toward her. It was the odd doctor who consulted with the senate committee and who had insisted on cutting the line at the wake to see Senator Barber. Anna felt her cheeks flush as her heart picked up its rhythm. "This is the ladies," Anna said.

"We need the file."

"I gave it to the senator."

"It's the wrong one."

"It's the only one I found."

"I sincerely doubt that," the doctor said as he kept moving toward Anna. For every step back she took, he took two forward. Afraid he was going to hurt her, she managed to turn herself so that she was backing toward the door.

"If you touch me, I'll scream."

"I don't want to touch you." The doctor seemed repulsed by the mere idea.

"I'm warning you," Anna said as the doctor continued his march toward her. "I know self defense."

"I'm not going to hurt you! I just want the file! I know you have it."

"Even if I did have it, why on earth would I bring it to the symphony?"

"I don't think you brought it here. But I do think you have it."

"Well, I don't!" Anna punctuated her statement with a quick exit through the swinging door. She ran into the first of several women making a beeline for the washroom now that intermission had begun. As her heart rate began to return to normal among the safety of all these people, she turned and watched the door waiting for the strange doctor to emerge, but he never did. Was there another way into the room? Or was he hiding in a stall, embarrassed to be discovered inside the women's room?

Anna jumped at a hand on her shoulder. "Anna, it's me," May said. "What's wrong?"

Anna told her. Curious, May entered the ladies room to have a look for herself.

Anna waited and watched the door nervously. A steady stream of women entering and exiting trickled to just a few. Finally, May emerged. "Well?" Anna asked.

"I checked every stall. He's not in there, unless he's standing on a toilet seat."

"You didn't open every door?"

"It was bad enough I was looking under doors. I didn't see another way out. You're sure he was there?"

"I may be losing my mind, but I didn't imagine seeing him." Anna continued to watch the door. Her fight-or-flight response had pumped so much adrenaline into her body, Anna realized she was going to crash hard later.

"Maybe he followed you out and you just didn't see him since you were hurrying to get away from him." Anna had thought the same thing, though she still wondered how she could have missed him. May looked around to make sure she wouldn't be overheard and asked Anna in almost a whisper, "Do you think he *knows* or does he just suspect?"

"I think he simply suspects," Anna said. "But that doesn't mean we're safe."

"What's this we stuff?" May joked as the lights flashed, signaling the end of intermission. "Want me to stay with you?"

"You don't have to," Anna said. "Actually, I think I might just grab a cab and head back early if that's okay."

May nodded, but she wasn't sure she should let Anna go by herself. Anna insisted she'd be fine since Margaret's building had a doorman who saw to it that no strangers entered. Still, she recognized the conflict in May's face. Knowing how much May loved the BSO, Anna insisted she stay to make sure Margaret got home safely. They said their goodbyes, and Anna headed for the coat check. Even though her glances confirmed she was alone beyond a couple BSO staffers, she couldn't shake the feeling that the creepy doctor was watching her.

The young woman working the coat check brought Anna two coats. "I only had one," Anna said. She was ready to turn one away, sure that it belonged to someone else and was hung with hers by accident, but stopped when she recognized the second as the one she had left hanging at Angelina's restaurant earlier in the day. She grabbed it and looked around, trying to see who had brought it here. "Do you know who dropped this off for me?"

"I presumed you did, ma'am," the young woman replied. She watched Anna's furtive looks around the lobby. "Are you okay?"

"No. I'm not." Anna left a larger tip than she meant to since she wasn't paying attention to the denomination of the bill she placed in the jar. She staggered toward the front doors. Upon reaching them though, she couldn't summon the courage to push through. Instead, she turned and found a seat against a wall. She decided to sit and wait for May and Margaret since she was no longer keen to return to the condo alone. She even vowed to take the elevator up with them. Her fear of confinement in small spaces had just been trumped by her fear of the men who seemed eager to track her movements.

***

The next morning Anna sat in the window seat in her room soaking up the first rays of sunshine. She loved her early mornings alone. She had just completed her nine repetitions of the Five Tibetans and was now settling in for her daily meditation. She was getting better at setting aside a minimum of 20 minutes to meditate, and was even occasionally sitting for double that amount of time. Today, however, she found it impossible to quiet her brain.

Each time she tried to focus on her breath, her head reminded her of the previous night. Had it really only been eight and a half hours since the creepy doctor had confronted her in the women's room? That wasn't what most troubled her though. She wondered if he had brought her the coat, or if James had brought it himself. If it was the former, then wouldn't it stand to reason that James and the senator and the strange doctor were all working together? And if it was the latter, did that mean James was lurking somewhere nearby? She wished she had a photo of the mysterious retired secret service agent to show Margaret.

Anna tried again to focus on her breath, thinking almost out loud, "Breathe in, breathe out, breathe in, breathe out." She wondered if the burner phone James had given her was still in the coat pocket. Why hadn't she checked last night? She knew why. She had been so scared she was practically paralyzed. She'd found a chair and sat upright, scanning the room as she waited for the concert to finish, and for Margaret and May to emerge. She'd actually fallen asleep waiting, though she still couldn't believe she'd been able to relax that much. Fortunately, May saw Anna on her way out the door. Anna wasn't sure how she would have coped had Margaret and May gone home without her.

The chimes of her meditation app signaled she'd reached the end of her session, though Anna wasn't sure she could count this sit as true practice. She stretched out her kinks and headed to the bathroom for the rest of her morning routine. She was looking forward to losing herself in a long, hot shower.

Later, Anna headed into the living area to make the morning coffee and was greeted by the aroma of a fresh pot. That was the advantage of traveling with May, who also rose in the morning. "Good morning," she said as she poured herself a cup of the low-acid concoction that she and May now made a habit of drinking each morning.

May looked up from her book. "You have about a half-dozen missed calls on that phone James left for you."

"Did you answer it?"

"I'm not touching it."

"I don't want to either," Anna said. Anna grabbed her coat off the chair where she had dumped it when they returned home the previous night. She bit her lip and started to reach into the pocket. BRINNNNGGGG! The phone rang like an old-time house phone. Anna screamed and tossed the jacket over the sofa. May jumped, but kept herself from making any noises.

They looked at each other and burst out laughing. "Nervous much, are we?" May asked.

"Using 'are we' now, are we?" Anna answered. It was a phrase from their favorite Britcom, *Miranda*, which they had recently discovered.

A muffled train whistle sounded from her coat pocket.

"That's the first time I've heard that sound," May said. "Maybe that's his first message."

"I'm going to have my coffee first." Anna doctored her cup with cashew milk and sat with May.

"Don't forget to take your morning pills," May reminded her.

"Already took the empty-stomach ones. I'm not hungry enough to eat and take the others yet. Thank you."

May returned to her book as Anna looked around the condo. She carried her coffee around the room, surveying each painting and sculpture. She really fancied the painting of the five dories, and wondered if she could order a print. She couldn't quite make out the artist's signature, so she set her coffee down and took the painting off the wall. She turned it over and was pleased to find the name of the gallery. She looked around the room again, and noticed a pad of paper resting on an antique desk that was set between two enormous glassed-in bookcases. The paper was from an inn on Martha's Vineyard—the same island the painting had come from.

"Have you ever been to Martha's Vineyard?" Anna asked May.

"No. You?"

"Nope. Closest I've been is Cuttyhunk."

"Cutty what?"

"Hunk," said Anna. "It's the last of the Elizabeth Islands, south of the Cape."

"I hate the traffic on the Cape," said May.

"Me too, which is part of the appeal of Cuttyhunk. You take the ferry out of New Bedford, which isn't on the Cape."

"What are you doing with the picture?" May had finally looked up from her reading.

"I like it. Going to look into ordering a print." Anna tried to hang the picture again, but had trouble finding the nail.

"Oh! Order me one too, will you?" May watched Anna struggle. "Want some help?"

Too late. Both women heard the tear of paper. Anna cringed as she turned the painting over. She let out a sigh of relief at seeing that it was only the back layer of paper that ripped. She went through the drawers until she found some tape. She taped up the back, which wasn't as easy as she thought it would be since there was at least an inch of airspace between the canvas and the paper backing. "That's it!" Anna said.

"What's it?" May was standing near her, ready to help in the repair and the second attempt to hang the painting.

"Hold this." Anna handed May the painting, and held a finger to her lips indicating the universal symbol for silence. Anna grabbed her coat with the burner phone, opened the slider to the cold outside deck, dropped the coat on a table, closed the door, and walked back to May. She flipped the painting over and pointed. "You could hide papers inside here."

"What do you mean?"

"I have an idea about how we can double check that the estate is bugged and prove to Margaret that Senator Ponema is behind it."

"You want to give him the file?"

"Not the whole thing. A paper or two. Make it look like Frank split the file up. Maybe we find a paper or two in the desk—someplace we didn't already check."

"Which pages?" May grabbed her file from the hidden pocket at the bottom of her knitting bag and sorted through it.

Anna took a moment to answer as another thought occurred to her. "Of course! That's what we'll do."

May looked at her, wondering what was so obvious. She watched as Anna paced, trying to fully form the idea. Finally, Anna stopped and pivoted toward her.

"Let's pick two or three pages that all correspond in some way—same doctor or clinic or location. Then we'll monitor and see if anything happens after the senator gets the papers."

"What do you think will happen?"

"I don't know, but from the reading I've been doing in the book my doctor suggested, I'm thinking we might see a doctor suddenly close his practice or have a lawsuit filed against him or something." Anna was referring to *Cure Unknown: Inside the Lyme Epidemic* by Pamela Weintraub, though she could never recall the title or the author's name. Her brain fog tended to scramble her memory.

"And we monitor how?"

Anna heard May's skepticism, which might ordinarily have irked her since Anna could be a tad bit impatient, especially before her illness. But the Lyme had slowed her down, brought her to a world where daily meditation and yoga was her new normal. Consequently, she was fully able to stop and consider what May was asking. She knew she didn't have an answer, and admitted as much.

"Maybe I can help," a man's voice said as he entered the condo.

***

*The **Boston Symphony Orchestra,** or BSO as it is known, performs at Symphony Hall in Boston in autumn, winter, and spring. Summers find the orchestra at Tanglewood, where patrons may choose to sit inside the Shed or the Seiji Ozawa Music Hall, or out on the lawn. Many bring elaborate picnic suppers to enjoy before and during the concerts.*

For more information, visit Anna's "BSO" board on Pinterest:
https://www.pinterest.com/anna_mcgrory/bso/

CHAPTER 18

Tom walked to Anna and reached to hug her. But she was too surprised to hug back. "What's wrong?" he asked.

"Why are you here?"

"I asked him to join us," Margaret said as she entered.

"I don't understand," Anna said.

"I told you I was expecting my estate-planning attorney to join us today," Margaret said. "Don't tell me you didn't know I was referring to your husband."

"I had no idea," Anna said.

"Client confidentiality," Tom said.

"So I guess you don't know that he's Jim's and my attorney too?" May asked.

"Is there anyone I know that you don't represent?" Anna asked Tom.

"Probably," Tom said. "Is that coffee I smell?"

May brought the pot to the table, along with the cups, cashew milk, honey, and organic raw sugar.

The doorbell rang. "Must be the organic breakfast bread I ordered," Margaret said as she went to answer it.

Anna watched Tom as he doctored his coffee. She never understood why he put the milk in first. It seemed more logical to lead with the sugar, mixing it into the hot coffee so it could melt, and then add the milk. She'd said so once. He asked her to let him fix his own damn coffee his way. That was a couple years ago. Two or three months before Frank died and Anna got sick. And the day Anna had moved out.

Watching him now brought back the negative emotions and memories of that time. That summer, he had told her that he was no longer in love with her—that he had felt left out of her life for years. She did travel quite a bit for the senator, but mostly during the week. The occasional weekend trips were for social events that the Barbers wanted both she and Tom to attend. She had thought that those were occasions Tom had looked forward to since they mostly happened in the Berkshires—the place that he so dearly loved. But that day—the day he'd broken her heart—she'd learned of the years of resentment that had built up. He'd never said anything before then. She spent the next month wondering how she didn't know, and blaming herself for obviously having been so selfish.

He was so secretive. Anna knew this was a good thing for his legal practice. But it wasn't good for their marriage. Their reconciliation had been just days before their daughter's wedding, which was followed quickly by the senator's death, the wake, the funeral, and her illness. It was a whirlwind that never allowed them a chance to talk and to properly process all that had occurred between them. She wondered if Tom was happy now. And if he loved her.

The foursome went through the brochure Anna had created, noting what artwork and furniture would stay with the donated property, what would be liquidated for expenses, and the couple items that would find their way next door to Margaret's condo.

"Do you want anything?" Margaret surprised Anna with the question.

"I hadn't really thought about it." Anna stole a glance at May who knew that was a lie.

"We don't need anything, Margaret," Tom said.

"Except there is one item." Anna could feel Tom's eyes boring into her. He didn't like to be upstaged or corrected. Anna suspected he felt more intense about this since Margaret was a client. She wondered if he would deduct the value of the piece from his legal bill.

"The replica of the *Little Dancer* statue?" Margaret did know her.

"I can always order one from the museum," Anna said. "It's just that—"

"You'll need to wear the same patina into another bronze." Margaret referred to the left foot of the dancer, which Anna had rubbed for good luck over the years. Anna purposely avoided the outstretched right foot, preferring the stability of the left foot, which she thought held the dancer up. "I should have realized. I'm sorry I didn't."

"No apologies necessary. I appreciate your thinking of it now."

"I'll deduct the value of the statue from your bill," Tom said. Anna rolled her eyes, though only May noticed.

"You'll do no such thing," Margaret said. "It's a gift. And as I now recall, I left it to Anna in my own will, didn't I?"

"I don't remember the particulars," Tom said, "but that does sound familiar, yes."

Anna looked at Tom, but he avoided her gaze. She was sure now that the gulf between them had reappeared. She wondered what might have happened to them had she not gotten sick. She couldn't help thinking that they would no longer be together if Tom hadn't felt some sort of obligation to care for his ill wife.

At the conclusion of their meeting, it was decided that Anna would drive out to the estate to meet the assessor the next day. May wasn't sure if she'd join her or return home since one of her daughters was vying for a girl's day out together. Outwardly, Anna encouraged her friend to go home with Tom and visit with her daughter; inwardly, though, Anna hoped May would join her for this last trip to the estate.

Finished with the meeting, Margaret went next door to prepare for an afternoon appointment and May went to her room to organize her things, leaving Tom and Anna alone.

"I could go with you if you're nervous about being there alone," Tom offered, sensing Anna's hesitation.

"No, that's silly," Anna said. "I know you have work to do and clients to meet."

"Nothing I can't reschedule. And I can do much of my work from there."

"Sensing a divide growing between us?"

"No," Tom lied. "Just thought I'd offer to be there with you—especially given the odd things that you say have been happening to you."

"The odd things that *are* happening to me."

"That's what I said."

"No. You made it sound like I was making it up."

"You do have a tendency toward the overly dramatic," Tom said.

"So you've pointed out on numerous occasions before. But in this case my concerns are real." Tom didn't seem to begin to believe her until she told him about her visitor in the ladies' room at Symphony Hall.

"I'm going with you. End of story," Tom said.

Anna was both relieved and frustrated. She didn't like being a burden to anyone. She wanted to be able to take care of herself. With May, she felt like they were in it together. But with Tom, Anna wasn't so sure.

On the way to the Berkshires the next day, Anna stumbled upon a podcast that tackled the controversy over Chronic Lyme. She and Tom listened to the Lyme-literate doctor explain the benefits of antibiotics, the possibility of co-infections, and the controversy over the 40-year-old tests that were still being administered to find out if a patient had Lyme or not. He and the show's host were joined by a singer-songwriter who had seen about 20 doctors before finding her way to him...and to a diagnosis that saved her life.

"Is this how you feel about your experience?" Tom asked at the conclusion of the recording.

Anna sniffed. She was tearing up a bit and couldn't help it.

"Are you crying?" He couldn't look at her to see for himself since his eyes were glued to the twists and turns of Route 9 as they took the road that brought them from Concord, NH, through the forests of Vermont's Green Mountains to Bennington and eventually into the Berkshires of western Massachusetts.

"As much as I can with these stupid dry eyes of mine."

"Why?"

She swallowed and tried to get a handle on her emotions. Tom let her have the time she needed to find her words. "I just—" The tears poured forth. It was like a dam burst, leading to an undercurrent of deep sobs that swelled up from within her. It actually felt good to finally have a proper cry, though she was a bit embarrassed.

Tom reached over and patted her hand. He was driving through the worst section of the road, though, and following a logging truck of all things. He needed both his hands on the wheel. "One moment. I'm looking for a place to pull over now."

They rode in silence for another few minutes. Finally, Tom saw a pull off and eased his SUV onto the dirt. The view of the mountains from their southern Vermont vantage point was glorious, though not nearly as majestic as the vista they would soon enjoy driving over Hogback Mountain. Not that either of them noticed at this moment. Tom put the car in park and turned off the key. He reached over the central console and touched Anna's shoulder. Awkward as the seating was, Anna dove into Tom's embrace and cried anew.

"What I wouldn't do for a bench seat right now," Tom said.

"I still have almost no recollection of three months of my life before being diagnosed with Lyme." Anna managed to blurt it out through her after-gasps.

"I'm sorry," Tom said. Anna knew he meant it.

"I'm thankful you were there for me. That you're here with me now. All I remember from that time is crawling from the sofa to the bathroom and back again."

"It was awful seeing you like that," Tom said. He fought back his own tears as he recalled seeing her then. "You were in so much pain, and the doctors had zero answers. You didn't even have the interstitial cystitis diagnosis yet."

"That's right," Anna remembered.

"Thank goodness you self-diagnosed that part of your symptoms at least. I still believe you healed yourself back to walking with that ridiculously restrictive bladder-friendly diet of yours."

Anna straightened herself and sat up again, stretching out the kinks that were quickly forming. She looked Tom in the eyes. "Listening to that podcast brought back my journey, and reminded me that it's not over yet."

"It's not, but you're doing incredibly well. Especially compared to where you were."

Anna had daily proof of that in both the things she could manage to do now, and in the still-occurring Herxheimer reactions that instantly reminded her of the violent bacteria she was fighting. The short-term reactions occurred when the bacteria died off; it was a detoxifying effect on the body, resulting in a spike of random symptoms. Eventually those side effects wore off as Anna's body healed.

Her latest herx from a few days ago sent tremors down each of her arms and ended with tingling sensations alternating with the pins and needles experienced after a body part falls asleep. There was some nerve pain too, but it was minor compared to the pain that had sent her to consult with a neurologist before she had been diagnosed with Lyme.

"I'm better now," Anna said, reengaging her seatbelt.

"Maybe I should choose what we listen to next?" Tom said as he started the car up again and consulted his phone, pairing it with his car. Soon an indie artist they both liked—Patrick Watson from Montreal—crooned over the speakers. Tom turned on his blinker, looked around at the empty road, and pulled back onto the main thoroughfare. "Well, at least we've managed to shrug off the nasty diesel fumes of the logging truck."

"That was really my intent all along," Anna said. "The tears were just for show."

***

*The podcast Anna and Tom listened to was **Jill Blakeway's "Grow, Cook, Heal"** Ep. # 22 with Singer/Songwriter and Lyme Patient/Advocate Dana Parish and Dr. Steven Phillips, LLMD.*

For more information, visit Anna's "Lyme" board on Pinterest: https://www.pinterest.com/anna_mcgrory/lyme/

CHAPTER 19

It was an unusually balmy first weekend in April—the kind that is perfect for lying out on the deck, if only the estate's outdoor furniture had been set up. It was in the barn where it wintered, and where it would remain until all possibility had passed of spring snowstorms, which weren't unheard of in the Berkshires.

It would have been a great weekend for walking the property too, as long as you wore tall, waterproof boots. Had Frank been alive, he would have hiked through the muck without a second thought. Anna could picture him walking by as she threw open the windows even though they had no screens. It was worth it to let the warm breeze freshen the main house. Besides, she reasoned, there shouldn't be any black flies or mosquitoes this early in the season.

She did a double take when she spotted Tom out on the muddy lawn. She knew how much he loved the outdoors, but he hadn't brought a change of shoes. "What are you doing?" she called to him.

"Taking pictures of the outdoor sculptures for the appraiser," he said. As he waddled by, Anna giggled. He was wearing a pair of boots that were at least three sizes too large for him. "Don't like my fashion statement?" Tom winked as he lifted his legs in an exaggerated show of his odd walk.

Anna realized this was her chance to test her theory and hide a few of the pages of patient interviews that she and May had identified as the best ones. They had done so while riding back to Concord with Tom from Margaret's without Tom realizing what they were doing. It wasn't that they wanted to keep Tom out of the loop. However, Anna wasn't sure that he was completely buying the idea that she was being followed and bugged. She didn't care to be called overly dramatic again.

As Anna looked around at the paintings, trying to choose the best one to use, she realized that she and May still didn't see the connection of all the patients yet—only noting some similarities among smaller patient groups. Yet, they were sure there was a reason Frank had singled out this group to interview. If Anna could figure out why, she thought she might be able to begin to understand why Senator Ponema and that odd doctor were so eager to get the file.

Anna chose a painting that had no monetary value but a ton of sentimental worth. It was one that her son had created in his three semesters at art school. Knowing the students were selling their work during the annual end-of-the-year student exhibit, the senator and Margaret had called the college and asked for information on Rob's work. He had three pieces entered that year. Anna and her mom had already spoken for two of them. Without even seeing the work, the Barber's bought the last remaining piece anonymously. They had it professionally framed and added it to their collection without a word to Anna. It was the first thing she noticed the next time she visited the estate. She was beyond moved by their generous and loving gesture.

She took the painting down, flipped it over, and carefully pried part of the backing off. She slipped in the two original sheets of paper from the file that she and May agreed on, resealed the backing as best as possible, and hung the painting again. She surmised that if the senator had wanted to leave pages of the file for Anna to find, it would stand to reason that this painting would be the one he would have chosen.

Anna had one more page to hide. She walked into the nearly empty office, pulled one of the desk drawers all the way out, stuffed the paper in the back, and replaced the drawer. This might look less like a clue being left and more like an accidental sheet of paper falling out of the original file. It didn't matter to Anna, who was sure it would be enough to get Senator Ponema or his underlings to make an offer on the desk. She was also certain that after he was finished looking through the desk, the wood would be worth little more than kindling. It was an unfortunate side effect to what she considered a necessary experiment.

Anna scrunched her nose. Did she smell smoke now? She did! She hurried from the office and ran to the family room. Outside, she saw Tom and Shep burning brush near the pond. Tom was in his element now. Anna giggled for the second time today as she watched him move about like a schoolboy, jumping here and there, gathering sticks and adding them to the fire or tossing one for Charlie. It was fun to see him so happy. Anna wondered for about the thousandth time in their 30 years of marriage if she had ruined his life almost two decades ago when she insisted they move to New Hampshire for a better legal job for him and more opportunities for their kids to make a living in that area as adults.

Gravel crunched outside as a car approached. Anna went to the front door, anticipating the arrival of the appraiser. She opened the door before the guest could knock and gasped.

"You forgot your coat again," said James, holding out the coat Anna had left on the balcony of the Boston condo. "Perhaps it's the Lyme that's made you so absentminded?"

"What are you doing here?"

"You're welcome," James said, though Anna just stared at him. "It's quite nice. I'm surprised you'd let it out of your sight so often."

"I didn't want your phone."

"I figured that out."

"I don't like being spied on. Or followed." Anna tried to close the door, but James stuck his boot in the way.

"Perhaps the Lyme has made you forget your manners too?"

"Perhaps you're the one with the bad manners. Please leave."

"I don't intend to do any such thing. Your life is in danger. I made a promise to your former boss that I would keep an eye on both you and his wife."

"Then why aren't you in Boston with her?"

"She's not the one in danger."

"How do I know I can trust you?"

"You don't."

"Frank would have left me some sign so I would know what you said was true..." Anna trailed off as James handed her a red laminated raffle ticket with Keep This Coupon printed on one side. "How did you get this?"

"How do you think?"

"I don't know what to think anymore." Anna recalled the two days and nights she and Frank had spent in the hospital waiting room worrying over Margaret, who had been rushed in for an emergency appendectomy. She suffered complications from the surgery and didn't wake up right away. When she did, it took her almost half a day to recognize her husband.

At some point during her long wait with Frank, Anna overheard some volunteers talking about the hospital raffle. She bought two tickets, and handed one of the Keep This Coupon stubs to Frank, who absentmindedly pocketed it. Within minutes, Margaret awoke.

A year later Frank showed Anna that he still had the raffle ticket. "How could I possibly throw it away?" He said. "It brought Margaret back to me. Besides, it says to keep it."

"That's not meant to be taken literally." Anna and Frank had laughed about it. At the time, Anna noticed that the corner had ripped off and the sides were tattered. Without Frank realizing, she lifted the ticket from his wallet, had it laminated, and returned it. Frank was surprised and grateful. It became a thing that only the two of them knew about. Or so Anna had thought. Of course, there was no reason he wouldn't have told Margaret. And perhaps she had told someone else. Who knew how many people actually knew about the ticket. Looking at the stub James had just given her, with its tattered sides and torn corner, Anna wondered if it was the actual coupon or a fake. It certainly would have been simple enough to make a copy.

"It's not a fake," James said, seemingly reading her mind. "Frank said you'd recognize it."

Anna turned the ticket over in her hand and examined it. Something caught her eye: the faint penciled-in initials of the volunteer who had sold it to her. She remembered them because they were the same initials as her mom when using her maiden name. She clutched it, closed her eyes for a moment, and sent up a silent thank you to Frank, convinced for now that the ticket was real.

"Going to let me in now?"

"Why should she?" It was Tom. He smelled of smoke from the brush burning.

"It's okay," Anna said, pocketing the ticket. "I think he really is here to help." She looked James in the eye. "You better be. You have one chance to earn my trust. And right now, you're teetering on the edge of being a creepy stalker guy."

"I promise I'm only watching out for you like Frank asked." He withdrew his foot from the doorframe and raised his eyebrows in question.

Anna stood aside and let him enter.

Tom evil eyed him.

"I don't expect you to trust me yet," James told Tom.

"Just so we're clear," Tom said.

As Anna closed the door, the gravel crunched again under the weight of another car. Tom recognized the SUV and grinned bigger than Anna had seen him smile in some time. He trotted out to greet the appraiser, a woman he'd been working with for years.

Anna tried to suppress her jealous feelings that surfaced as soon as Jessica Aroosta arrived. It was worse as the four of them walked from room to room so Jessica could examine each item. Her high heels click-clicked on the tiles. Anna wondered how she walked around on what she estimated to be at least five-inch stilettos. For her part, a foot injury in high school—a result of a skiing accident—had left her in flats for life. Her broken sesamoid bones had never healed properly, nor were they expected to, according to her doctor at the time.

In the office, Jessica examined the antique desk Frank had inherited from his father, who had inherited it from his father before him. Tom helped Jessica pull out the drawers, eager to be of assistance. Anna did not do a good job concealing her growing jealousy. She caught the eye of James, who shook his head "no" almost imperceptibly. Anna shot him a look that clearly meant "What are you talking about?" as she tried to remain innocent. James raised an eyebrow. He knew what she was thinking.

"There's something stuck back inside here," Jessica said, looking inside the cavity where a drawer had been. She made a feeble attempt to reach in, obviously not wanting to soil her silk blazer or break a manicured nail.

"Let me help!" Tom reached in as Jessica watched him with a satisfaction that didn't sit right with Anna. Anna shot a look at James. This time he made a face that said he could see what she meant as he nodded slightly.

"What is it?" Anna asked, though she knew very well what it was.

"Patient 13: Mason Stevens, age 57," Tom read.

"Could it be one of the patient interviews Senator Ponema is still looking for?" Anna asked.

James reached a hand toward Tom. "May I?"

Tom held the paper fast. He didn't trust this James person.

"It's okay," said Anna. "I trust him."

"You do?" Tom and James asked in unison.

"More than some," Anna said, trying not to look at Jessica. James' eyes flashed recognition of her meaning, but he hid it from Tom and Jessica.

Finally Tom gave it to James. As James read the paper over silently, Anna and Tom looked more carefully into each drawer cavity. Tom used a penlight as he searched. "I don't see any more, do you?" Anna asked.

"No, but that doesn't mean they're not in there somewhere," Tom said, clicking off his penlight.

James handed the paper to Anna. "This is definitely one of the senator's patient interviews. Senator Ponema will want to see this."

"I'll drop it in the post first thing tomorrow," Anna said. She wished May had been on hand to see how perfectly their scenario had played out. Senator Ponema was probably right this moment calling Margaret and making an offer to purchase Frank's desk.

"How soon till we have values on things like Frank's desk and the rest of the contents?" Anna asked.

Jessica chuckled in a condescending manner.

"Amateurs," Tom agreed.

Anna felt like she was slapped across the face. "Sorry. It's obviously my first rodeo," she said.

"Mine too," James agreed. Anna appreciated his support, even if she would have preferred to be backed up by her husband.

"I'll compare my notes with the certificate of provenance for each item, and with prior insurance appraisals. You have all of those for me, right?"

Her question was for Tom. "Naturally," he replied.

"It will take a while to estimate the value of the entire contents, but I'll start with the more obvious objects first and get those figures to Tom on a daily basis. Some of the art will take the longest since I need to do some research. But I have a very good assistant who has been apprenticing with me for the past three years as she completes her doctoral program in art history. That will help speed the process up."

"Do you have a doctorate?" Anna was surprised by Jessica's assistant's credentials.

"Two, as a matter of fact. Archaeology and art history. And I'm certified by the American Society of Appraisers. So yes, I am perfectly qualified to estimate the fair market value for each piece in the estate. Any other questions?"

"I wasn't questioning your qualifications. I was just surprised at the amount of education needed for the field."

"I hear you have an MFA in creative writing." Jessica fairly scoffed at the notion of such a degree as she click-clicked out of the office.

Tom audibly swallowed, finally realizing the rivalry between the women. "I'm sorry, Anna." He stood in the doorway, torn between the need to follow Jessica so he could give her the copies of all the necessary paperwork and staying to comfort his wife.

"Go. It's fine." Anna tried to put on a brave face, but she was feeling suddenly vulnerable and put down. Her MFA was a source of pride for her. It was something she'd always wanted to pursue. She only had to mention it once to Frank. On her 20th work anniversary, he gave her a hefty bonus and encouraged her to use it to finally pursue her creative writing passion. She was able to balance her work schedule, family demands, and the low-residency program with only a few minor hiccups. During the difficult moments, Anna learned just how little Tom thought of her studies. A couple years after graduating, he'd once referred to her degree as a waste of paper. Anna let out a huge sigh. She fought the urge to cry, but just barely. She was finally thankful for her stupid dry eyes.

"I don't have a creative bone in my body," James said. Anna snapped her head toward him, almost having forgotten he was there. She couldn't figure out what he was getting at. "My mom was the creative one in our family. I think it killed her that neither her husband nor her kids could share in her love of colorful word play."

They locked eyes. Anna nodded, appreciating the compliment he was trying to give her as he left the office. Anna turned to the empty room and tried to swallow away the lump in her throat. "Why did you have to die? You could have talked to Margaret or me. You didn't have to take your own life, you know." Anna knew it was silly talking as if Frank were here with her. But what if it wasn't crazy? Anna pulled out the laminated ticket as a tear streamed down her face. "I miss you, Frank."

She looked up and caught James' eye watching her through the window. He glanced away quickly. Instead of being creeped out by his voyeurism, somehow Anna appreciated being looked after. She sincerely hoped she could really trust him.

***

*Why do we keep items like raffle ticket stubs, pins, and fortunes from cookies? It's sometimes **the little stuff** that most intrigues us and makes us human.*

To see more unique finds, visit Anna's "Interesting Items" board on Pinterest:

https://www.pinterest.com/anna_mcgrory/interesting-items/

CHAPTER 20

It was another early morning rap-rap-rap at the front door of the cottage. Anna was already awake. She hadn't written in years, but hearing the meanness in Jessica's voice when she put Anna down for her creative writing master's degree sparked a desire in Anna to write again. She wasn't sure what she would pen, so this morning she merely jotted some thoughts for possible essays, a couple lines of a poem, and the start of a character who could carry a short story.

The knocking persisted and, as last time, the caller woke the entire house. Tom and James emerged, each dressed quickly in yesterday's clothes.

"Who is it?" Tom asked as he descended the stairs.

Anna had just arrived at the front door. She was still in her pajamas since she'd woken so early and didn't want to disturb Tom by fumbling to get dressed in their dark bedroom. She looked through the peephole. "I'll give you one guess." Anna pulled open the door. "Senator. You really should learn to read a clock."

"I want Frank's desk."

"Hello to you too." It was Tom.

"It's not been formally appraised yet," Anna said.

"Margaret and I agreed upon a price," Senator Ponema said.

It was true. Less than an hour after the information on Patient 13 had been discovered, Margaret called Anna to say Senator Ponema had called and was interested in buying Frank's desk. Anna grabbed one of the burner phones and headed for the field, far from the bugs planted in the house, and placed a quick call to Jessica, who had only left a few minutes earlier. An hour later they had an approximate price for the antique. Anna tripled the quote when she relayed the number to Margaret. As expected, Senator Ponema didn't counter. Maybe she should have quadrupled it.

"You two, give us a hand loading it." The senator looked pointedly at Tom and James.

Tom and James followed the senator to the main house where Martin, the senator's aid, waited for them at the front door. The four of them struggled with the solid mahogany desk, but finally had it loaded into the senator's SUV. They bumped the desk against a doorjamb once, to which Anna warned them to be careful with the priceless piece of furniture. Senator Ponema scoffed. "You know very well what this piece is worth, and how much more than that you've charged me for it."

"And yet here you are first thing to collect it. I wonder why this desk and nothing else."

Senator Ponema raised a side of his top lip in a silent snarl. He did not like Anna any more than she liked him.

"Do you want to tell my husband and my..." She trailed off, looking at James, not sure what to call him.

"Colleague." James filled in the blank for her.

"Right. Do you want to tell them why it is you want the desk so badly, or shall I?"

"I've always admired Frank's desk. Margaret knows this," Senator Ponema said.

"So you deny having bugs in place to listen in on our conversations in the estate?" Anna put her hands on her hips as she challenged him.

Senator Ponema's face turned scarlet. But he denied any such devices existed. Or if they did, that he had anything to do with them.

"But I'm sure you'll be wanting Frank's notes on Patient 16 that we found stuffed in the back of the desk," Anna said.

Tom and James watched the two of them with increasing interest. While his wife's tendencies toward the melodramatic annoyed him in their everyday life, Tom knew it was what made her such a great writer, when she had the time to devote to her art. Or when she wasn't battling brain fog. Still, in this instance, he'd thought she'd been letting her imagination get the better of her.

For his part, James knew the senator's reputation from secret service colleagues who had served the senator over the years. He was not a man to be trusted.

"You found notes on Patient 16 too?" Senator Ponema asked.

Anna waited. She'd set the trap, but she wanted the senator to trip it himself. It was a standoff. Silence ensued. She hoped Tom and James would keep quiet.

"I mean, Margaret told me about the notes on Patient 13, but not on 16," said Senator Ponema.

Drat. Anna hadn't foreseen his ability to navigate the discussion by pretending Margaret was the source of his information. "Oh, that's right," said Anna. "Patient 13. Not 16. The brain fog from my Lyme often confuses me."

"Well, at least you've found notes on one of the stakeholders." Senator Ponema could be a cool actor. "I am so pleased to hear it. Yes, I'd love to get that from you, as you know."

"It's in the cottage," Anna said. "Why don't we all go have some coffee and I'll get it for you."

"Let's not do coffee. Though that reminds me. My wife made some blueberry jelly for you knowing it's one of the few fruits you can eat on that special diet of yours. I'll grab it while you fetch the patient interview."

Anna headed for the cottage. Inside, she watched through the window as the senator handed a small bag to James. Martin climbed into the driver's side and started the car as the senator waited. Anna grabbed the paper and joined the men, handing the patient interview off to Senator Ponema, who was positively giddy.

"You let me know if you find more!" he said as he climbed in. Gravel flew from the back wheels as Martin peeled out.

"Not a snow ball's chance in Hello Kitty."

"You can stop using that ridiculous phrase now that the kids are grown," Tom said.

"Some habits are difficult to kick."

Tom turned to James. "You trust the senator?"

"Not at all," James said.

"Me neither," said Anna.

The three headed back to the cottage. Anna nodded to the bag of jam James carried. "I'm not going to eat that."

"I wasn't going to let you."

Inside the cottage, Anna put the percolator on for coffee.

"I need to get back to Concord today," Tom said. He was checking his phone for about the fifth time that morning. Anna had grown to hate his phone, her phone, and all phones. They took people out of the face-to-face conversational zone. Especially her husband. Over the years she'd grown to resent his phone as if it were his mistress.

"I'll stay and organize things here and pack up the paintings for the auction house."

"How will you get back to Concord when you're done?"

"I'll drive her."

Tom looked at James as if he'd forgotten he was there. He had the annoying ability to blend into the background. Anna had begun to forget his presence too. It reminded her of the couple times she traveled to Washington while the Senate was in session to visit Frank. She'd forgotten that Frank had been assigned a secret service agent when he was there. She tried to remember the faces of Frank's secret service detail, but as hard as she tried, she could not recall having seen James.

"Will you excuse us a moment?" Tom asked James as he gently grabbed Anna's arm and guided her out of the kitchen.

"Keep an ear open for the coffee to pop up, and turn off the burner when it does—but keep the pot on it," Anna instructed over her shoulder.

In the foyer, Tom whispered. "I don't trust him."

"I didn't either, which is why I contacted Stephen." Tom looked confused. "You know, Frank's right-hand man in D.C. Well, former right-hand man. You met him when we attended the inaugural ball."

"You went with May to that."

"Oh, right." Anna smiled as she recalled May's excitement. They had taken the train down from Boston together and visited the area for a week. May had never been to D.C. and she wanted to see every national monument, museum, and gallery there was. While Anna ordinarily avoided crowds and cities, she didn't get quite as nervous when she was with May. Nor when she and Tom had taken the kids to D.C. when he was sworn into the bar of the Supreme Court. But it was more fun traveling with just your best friend. May didn't need diaper changes. Nor did she get cranky when she was hungry.

Well, not *that* cranky. "Stephen verified that James worked Frank's detail when he was in Washington."

"So he's telling the truth about that. Still doesn't mean I trust him."

"I texted his picture to Margaret yesterday. She remembered him fondly. Apparently he joined them for dinner occasionally during his nights off."

Tom paced till he could peek into the kitchen. He continued his loop ending up back near Anna.

"Well?" Anna prompted.

"I don't like it. Leaving you alone here with him."

"Is it me you don't trust?"

"No. That's not it. Of course I trust you."

"Then what?"

"Just because you tell me he worked for Frank, you can't expect me to fully trust him."

"Maybe if you talk to Margaret about him you'll feel better."

"Doubt it."

James called out that the coffee was ready. Tom headed upstairs to shower and change. Anna headed straight for the caffeine.

"Thank you," she said as she doctored her coffee with a healthy splash of cashew milk.

"All I did was turn the stove off. Thank you for making the coffee."

They sat in silence for a few minutes as they watched a pair of birds flit in and out of a lobster buoy that doubled as a birdhouse. Normally Anna enjoyed the quiet, but her discussion with Tom had unnerved her. She still wasn't sure if Tom's distrust was of James or of her. She tried to think of something to say, finally blurting out, "Can you imagine if we had to rebuild our house every spring? All that work! Most of us of would be homeless."

"I like building things."

"Okay. Tom and I, and my friend May—well, actually her husband likes tinkering and building things too. My daughter and her boyfriend, uh, I mean husband—they like to build things. My son builds homes for South American families. Hmm, I guess it's just Tom and me who would be homeless."

"We're homeless now?"

"That was fast." Anna couldn't believe he was already showered, dressed, and ready to leave.

"There aren't any travel mugs here by chance?"

"Already thought of it." Anna had rinsed a travel mug when she was doctoring her own coffee. She filled it and let Tom put in his milk first the way he liked to, then the sugar. She carefully situated the lid and snapped it into place. Once, years ago, her mug had slid out from under the lid before it was attached and she ended up wearing her coffee. She was extra careful ever since.

"Text when you get there," she said as she handed Tom his mug.

"Is your phone on?"

"No, but I'll have it on by the time you arrive." She wondered if he got annoyed with her for not using the phone enough. "I'll walk out with you." She suggested it not because she wanted particularly to go outside yet again in her pajamas, but because she hated public displays of affection, and she wanted to kiss her husband goodbye.

"Thanks for offering to drive her back," Tom said. It sounded strangled to Anna. She was sure Tom struggled to say the words.

"You're welcome," James said. Anna was relieved he hadn't said, "my pleasure," which she was sure Tom might have read more meaning into than necessary.

Outside, Tom loaded up his briefcase, overnight bag, and phone. Anna handed him his coffee, and he slipped it inside his SUV. Anna spread her arms wide. Over the last couple years she had grown keenly aware that hugs and kisses did not happen unless she prompted them. She hoped it was just a phase, and not something that would last the rest of their marriage. Tom stepped into her embrace and hugged her like he meant it. Anna believed he did, which took some of the sting out of yesterday's stiletto woman. They shared a quick peck on the lips. She wasn't sure if she should ask if they would ever kiss passionately again. She was afraid his response would be a firm no.

"You take care of yourself." Tom climbed in. "I still don't trust him."

"You forget: I took self-defense."

"You forget: I've seen some of your moves."

"Call Margaret. She'll tell you she's fond of James and she trusts him."

"I intend to." He backed the car up.

"Love you!" Anna called.

"You too!" Tom said as he drove off.

Anna watched after his car a moment. Turning back toward the cottage, she noticed the curtain in the guest room sliding into place in front of the window. Had James watched them? This time Anna thought his voyeurism was creepy. She vowed to watch her back twice as carefully as she'd originally planned.

***

Washington, D.C., is full of national monuments, museums, parks, restaurants, hotels, and even a zoo. It's a great place to visit, even if you don't happen to work for a senator.

To learn more about D.C., visit Anna's "Vacation Spots" board on Pinterest:

https://www.pinterest.com/anna_mcgrory/vacation-spots/

Chapter 21

Anna woke with the worst case of night sweats in her life. Her clothes were so damp, for a moment she wondered if she'd wet the bed. She fussed, trying to get free from the covers as she struggled to climb out. She stood, but teetered until she fell back onto the bed. Charlie stood inside her bedroom door and whined as if calling for help.

James opened the door partway. "Anna? Are you alright?"

Charlie whined again.

"I'm coming in, okay?" James took a tentative step in, but when he saw her, he hurried to her side. Charlie joined him, licking Anna's hand that hung limp over the side of the bed.

James felt Anna's forehead. She was burning up. He tried to prop her body in what he thought was a more comfortable position, but he realized she and her bed were soaked with sweat. With just a moment's hesitation as he worried over any improprieties, he swept her into his arms and carried her to his room where at least the bed was dry.

He folded the covers so that they would be easy to pull up should she wake chilled. He momentarily toyed with the thought of changing her into dry clothes, but he was afraid that would be a step too far. If May were here, she could do that for her friend, he thought. Instead, he grabbed a change of comfortable clothes from her room and set them on the bed next to her.

He returned to her bedroom and stripped the bed. The least he could do was wash the sheets while he looked for a thermometer. He wished he had the nifty forehead thermometer his sister had used on her youngest child the last time he visited. It was quick and easy. It had the added advantage of making his niece giggle since she claimed it tickled.

A call to Margaret confirmed what he already suspected: there were no thermometers at the estate. Nor did Sheila or Shep have one. If you didn't have kids, it seemed you didn't much care what your temperature might be. James was frustrated, but realized he didn't have a thermometer at his home either.

James checked in on Anna for the third time that morning. Her breathing was less labored, but she hadn't woken. He decided to make a quick trip to the pharmacy.

Forty minutes later, James returned to the cottage with his prize. Sheila was just leaving the room where Anna was as he walked up the stairs. "How is she?" He asked.

"Same," she said. "Though I hope I made her more comfortable." Sheila had changed Anna out of her soaked-through clothes and into the dry yoga pants and long-sleeve t-shirt James had left out for her. "Have you called the doctor yet?"

James nodded. "They want to know her actual temperature."

Sheila followed James back into the room and watched as he ran the thermometer across Anna's forehead. "One hundred three point two," he said.

"Oh!" Sheila was alarmed. "That sounds high."

"It is, but according to her doctor, it's within the acceptable limits for a herx reaction."

"A what reaction?"

"I asked the same thing. The doctor said it's what happens when the Lyme bacteria die off in significant numbers, releasing toxins into the body for the immune system to tackle. He thinks her fever is just her body doing its job." Anna had started a new antibiotic prescription, replacing one of her others. James explained to Sheila that the new meds often prompt such a reaction.

"I hope so. I've got chicken stock simmering downstairs when she wakes."

"Thank you."

Sheila and James left Charlie curled up on the bed with Anna. He was her loyal companion when she was ill, for which they were both thankful. James left the bedroom door open so he could hear if Charlie whined or if Anna called out while he was in the cottage.

Sheila headed back home while James tended the laundry in the cottage and got started sorting the artwork in the main house for distribution or storage. The Trustees had directed Anna and her team to catalogue the contents remaining with the estate and to store them in an environmentally controlled unit until a building inspector could go through the home carefully and a crew made any necessary repairs. James had contacted the storage facility and arranged for them to pick up the items in a couple weeks. He hoped everything would be ready in time.

James labeled three rooms in the main house with painters tape. One was for items destined for storage, a smaller room was for the few items headed to Margaret's condo, and the last was items for auction. As he worked, he arrived at the room where the Degas' replica of *The Little Dancer* stood. He knew from the list he was working from that Margaret was giving it to Anna, so he decided to move it to the cottage. He wanted to check on her again anyway and it gave him the perfect excuse.

James stuck his head into the bedroom and saw that Anna was still asleep. He padded across the carpet and placed the statue on the dresser near the end of the bed.

"What are you doing?"

"You're awake! How are you feeling?"

"Crummy." Anna looked around. "What am I doing in your room?"

"It's your room now. You sweated through your clothes and the covers, so I brought you in here, thinking you'd be more comfortable. And so I could wash the sheets."

"And my clothes?"

"Sheila changed you. I was out. Getting this." He grabbed the thermometer and held it up. "Do you mind if I check?" Anna shook her head no, and James ran it across her forehead. "One hundred one point three."

"That's warm."

"It's coming down." He told her what her earlier temp had been and that the doctor expected this was a Herxheimer reaction.

"I feel worse than I ever have," Anna said.

"Are you hungry? Thirsty?"

"Tired. I think I'll just try to get some sleep."

As Anna turned over and settled in again, James tried to squelch his sudden desire to kiss her forehead. She was not his daughter. He never made room for kids in his life. Even if she looked young enough to be his daughter,

James knew the seven years difference between them made that scenario impossible. Besides, who was he kidding? He definitely did not think of Anna as a daughter. That was another thought he'd have to bury.

Anna woke later and reached for Charlie. Not finding him, she fumbled for the bedside clock. Ten thirty-three a.m. Had she really slept through an entire day? She was post-fever achy and her joints were sore with Lyme arthritis. She looked around the room for her things. It took a few seconds to recall that James had moved her to his room where the bed was dry.

She padded into the hall and to the door of what was ordinarily her bedroom. It was open a couple inches. She knocked lightly, in case James had slept here and was still inside. The door swung open and she saw the bed was still stripped. The clean sheets were folded and stacked on a chair. None of her personal things had been moved. What a gentleman, she thought, realizing he must have slept on the sofa downstairs or in one of the guest rooms in the main house. Anna closed the door and headed for the shower.

Feeling refreshed with her wet hair pulled back in a simple bun, Anna warmed her special coffee on the stove, poured herself a cup, and went looking for James in the main house of the estate. She found him in the parlor sitting on the sofa, straddling an expensive painting by Georgia O'Keefe, and prying at the backing with a butter knife. "What are you doing?!"

He dropped the knife and looked up at her. "Looking for patient interviews like the ones I found in your son's painting."

"Really? How did you find them there?"

"There was a small tear in the paper backing. I took a peek in and found them." He picked up the two patient interviews from the coffee table and handed them to Anna. As she read, he returned to prying the backing off the painting.

Anna bit her tongue and resisted telling him he didn't need to check any other paintings. Instead, she acted as surprised as she could muster. "I didn't know Frank liked hide-and-go seek so much." It was such a silly thing to say. She wondered if her ridiculous statement would give her away.

"It was smart of him. Especially if he thought the stakeholders might come to harm if the interviews got into the wrong hands."

"Patients." Off his look, Anna said, "They are patients, not stakeholders.

I hate that the committee calls them that."

"It's what the government calls them."

"It's not right. It's such an impersonal label. These are real people with difficult problems. Juggling an illness that doesn't officially exist and trying to pay for it when the insurance companies deny coverage."

"You've certainly done your homework."

"I'm dealing with it now myself. Remember?"

"Of course. Sorry. How are you feeling?"

"Better. Thanks. For taking care of me, I mean."

"My pleasure." He peered into the space of the painting. Seeing nothing, he flipped it over and shook. Nothing fell out.

Anna pretended to read the patient interviews as she kept an eye on his progress. He set the painting down and moved to the next. "What can I do?"

"You can reseal the backings with the framer's tape, if you want. Or you can do the prying and I'll do that part. Your choice, since I'm the one who's here to help you."

Anna looked around at the room with all the paintings leaning against the walls on the floor. "Is this everything from the house?"

"The main house, yes."

"You're thinking we should check the cottage too?"

"Don't you?"

It had been decided that the cottage would remain as it was. It would also be accessible to Margaret, Anna, and Tom for as long as they each lived. Anna and Tom had the further option of extending the cottage's use to Joanie and Rob for their lives, but there was a fee payable to the Trustees if they exercised that option. Following the death of the last person the cottage was entrusted to, the building would become the property of the Trustees.

Given the arrangement and the fact that the artwork and furniture contained within the cottage weren't considered of extraordinary value, it had been decided that only the estate would be divvied up and organized. But with Frank's apparent penchant for hiding patient interviews, Anna could see why James would think to go through it too. "And Sheila and Shep's place?" She asked, knowing that provisions had been made for the caretakers to live there the rest of their lives, and that the contents belonged to the two of them.

"Was going to ask your opinion, but I'm inclined to think at least a cursory search might be smart."

Anna was regretting her genius idea. Why had she ever thought hiding some of the papers was smart? What had she hoped to gain from doing so? She tried to recall all the reasons, but her brain fog was making it impossible. Should she tell James she had the file? Did she trust him?

"Penny for your thoughts." James was watching her as he stood and stretched out his kinks.

Anna looked at him before realizing what he meant. She wondered if she was still running a temperature.

"You okay?" James approached and reached the back of his hand toward her forehead. His hand felt cool. "You feel a bit warm still. Maybe we better take your temperature."

Anna stumbled backwards, suddenly weak. James caught her. He guided her to a chair. "I'm more tired than I thought," Anna said.

"I wouldn't wonder. You haven't eaten anything since two nights ago." James got her a pillow off the sofa and tucked it in behind her head. "Are you hungry now?"

As if in answer, Anna's stomach rumbled.

"Stay here and I'll get you something."

"No, take me with you." She looked around the room. "It's too unsettling in here. I don't want to be alone."

James helped her up and Anna leaned on him as they headed back to the cottage. What would she have done without him these past couple days, Anna wondered. She was beginning to trust him, but that didn't mean she should divulge May's and her plan.

Thinking of May, Anna suddenly realized how much she missed her best friend. She made a mental note to call her once she felt good enough to walk outside with one of the burner phones the two of them had purchased. She hoped that would be soon after she ate something. She was beginning to fear she'd never be well enough to do anything alone again.

***

A **Herxheimer reaction** *can cause the patient to relive many of the most painful and exhausting symptoms of Lyme. However, some patients feel relieved when they experience a herx in reaction to a new antibiotic, believing that it means the newest treatment is working.*

To learn more about herxing, visit Anna's "Lyme" board on Pinterest: https://www.pinterest.com/anna_mcgrory/lyme/

CHAPTER 22

A few days later, Anna felt like she would burst with all her conflicting feelings and opinions of James. Anna walked into the pantry, hands on her hips, and confronted him. "Are you working with them?" Her face was red. She was trying to control the tremble in her voice. Including the days she had slept through, it had taken her about a week to work up to this question. "Are you here to spy on me or to help me?"

James set down the cans of soup he was preparing to open for their lunch and pointed toward the mudroom at the far end of the kitchen. Anna was confused. James pointed at the ceiling and then made what he must have considered a universal sign for creepy crawler bugs by shaping his hands into claws and moving his fingers as if they were legs.

Anna turned and headed for the mudroom. She followed James' lead and grabbed her hat, coat, and boots.

Outside, James offered her his arm. Anna couldn't believe it. After she'd just basically accused him of being a spy for Senator Scary Pants. "Or you could eat something instead, get some strength back." He offered her a banana.

"Thanks." Anna took it, peeled it, and bit in. She ate it in less than thirty seconds; she hadn't realized how hungry she was.

"I should have grabbed two." James smiled as he watched her. "You okay to walk a little way?"

Surprisingly, she was. The herx reactions had abated and her strength was returning. Anna nodded as she chewed her last bite. James turned and headed for a muddy path through the field. They walked in silence for what seemed like ages in Anna's state. They came to a clearing surrounded on three sides by woods. Anna knew this part of the path well. Taking it would eventually lead around the backside of the pond. James stopped and looked around. Anna watched him, uncertain if she should have trusted him to lead her out here. Was she too far from Sheila and Shep's place to scream for help? She tried to shake away the thought. Tom was right: she really could be melodramatic at times.

James pointed high up in a tree. "A woodpecker just landed there." As if on cue, the bird drilled at the tree for a moment before flying off again.

"Beautiful," Anna said. She meant it, but she didn't like having the subject changed—she had asked him a question and she expected an answer. What he was doing now was a tactic often utilized by her children, especially when they were teens. She could hear Joanie and Rob sniggering in the back seat, sure they had bamboozled their mother into forgetting what it was that had made her so upset. She could hear her own voice warning them not to change the subject. And their echoing refrain of "oh, Mom" uttered in a way that always made the situation worse. Why did they insist on pushing her buttons? She'd happily forgotten those times, and was not pleased that memories of those parental-children arguments surfaced now.

James seemed to sense Anna's frustration. "If by 'them' you mean Senator Ponema and the doctor, the answer is no, I am not working for them," he said.

Anna wondered how she could trust that he was telling the truth. Either way, he'd have to say that. It's not like he would drag her out here and confess, "Okay, you caught me. What was it exactly that gave me away?"

"Of course, you can't know for certain that I'm telling the truth, because either way I'd say that." James looked Anna in the eye. "But you've already thought of that."

Anna was feeling stupid now. "I should have thought of that before I asked the question."

"What do you want to do now?"

"I don't know. All I do know is that I have so many questions, but I can't ask them because...I don't trust you."

"The ticket wasn't enough."

"It was a nice touch, but no. It wasn't enough."

"Is there a way I can earn your trust?"

"I don't know."

James watched Anna as she scanned the trees. She was searching for some kind of outward sign, while she inwardly mustered the courage to say what she was thinking. "There's really only one person in the world I trust."

"May." They said her name at the same time.

Anna smiled at him. "Yes." His knowing that somehow made her want to trust him. But she realized that anyone would know that. Especially Senator Scary Pants and his minions.

"You want me to leave, and have May join you."

Anna nodded.

"If anything happened to you—"

"It would be my own fault."

"It's not something I could live with."

"And this—you here with me now—it's not something I can live with." Anna wondered if she would push him too far. If he was working with the sneaky senator, there might be a breaking point. Should she fear for her safety now?

"What if May joins you and I stay?"

"I'm not sure that would work."

"I could stay in the main house."

Finally it came to her: "May joins me." If Jim will let her, Anna suddenly realized. She hoped he would. "And you take the latest patient interviews you found to Senator Scary Pants."

"Senator Scary Pants?" James was laughing.

"It's easier to remember than—"

"The varlet? You didn't think I knew that, did you? Senator Barber regularly used his nickname for his colleague across the aisle."

"Or you could have been listening in and heard me telling May that." James looked chastised. "Don't tell me you haven't listened in on our conversations?"

"Some of them, yes. But only to protect you!"

The last bit was lost on Anna, who grew instantly angered. "You were the one who bugged us?!"

"No! I was only piggy backing on their bugs." He squeezed his eyes together realizing there was no way on earth to make that sound like a good thing.

"Get out! Now! Go away and leave me alone!"

"Not until May gets here."

"No. You don't get to decide things anymore. You ever want a chance at earning my trust, you will leave now!"

"But—"

Anna held her hand up in the universal sign of stop. "I don't want to hear any more of your lies."

"They're not lies, Anna. I really am here to help you."

"How can you possibly expect me to trust you now that you've admitted you've been listening in on my conversations?"

"At least I told you."

Anna could feel James' eyes on her face, but she refused to look at him. She heard him turn and walk away.

Anna took a deep breath, and walked into the woods. Around a bend she reached the bench Margaret had purchased for Frank less than a year before he died, insisting he stop and sit during his daily rambles to gather his strength. She'd had it inscribed with his favorite quote from one of his most beloved authors, Joseph Conrad: "We can never cease to be ourselves."

Anna loved that quote too. But seeing it now she realized the book it was from: *The Secret Agent*. Anna didn't know if she should laugh or cry at the irony, so she did what any normal woman in her situation would do and did both.

***

*Joseph Conrad's quote from **The Secret Agent** inspired Frank, while the book has served as inspiration to more than one production by the BBC.*

To learn more, visit Anna's "Quotables" board on Pinterest:
https://www.pinterest.com/anna_mcgrory/quotables/

CHAPTER 23

It was rainbows and unicorns in Anna's world again. May was with her. She'd driven down as soon as James had called. "No, this isn't a trap," James said. "You can wait and talk to Anna when she gets back." May packed immediately. Still, she talked to Anna before she actually left her house.

The two of them were again working together well. While one wrapped items, the other catalogued them. As one wearied or grew bored with her task, the other stepped in and they switched jobs. When one was hungry, the other suggested a place to eat. They were also back to practicing their fake conversations at the house and in the car. Even though it was May's car this time, they couldn't be sure it wasn't bugged. At lunch they often lingered, wondering whether James worked for his old boss as a guard dog, or his new one as a spy. They had a list of evidence for each.

They boxed up most of the books and drove them around the county to donate to public and school libraries. It wasn't entirely a gesture of charity on their part. They wanted access to public computers where they could scan the news without fear of being watched by Senator Ponema and the creepy doctor. They were looking for any scrap of news on the patients they had leaked from the file, of the doctors who treated them, or of the medical centers where they received treatment. In actuality, neither Anna nor May knew exactly what it was they were looking for, but they figured they might know it when they saw it.

At the historic and vastly renovated Houghton Memorial Building, an enormous old Victorian that served as the public library for the city of North Adams, Anna sat in a tiny chair at a miniature desk in the empty children's section. It was ordinarily quiet here during school hours and Anna found that she liked this library best of all the county's public institutions. She was heading for an available computer when the buzzing in her ears got so loud she thought she heard cicadas. Almost instantly a headache followed, which forced her to sit in the first available seat.

May entered the bright room and saw Anna cradling her head. "How bad is it?"

"What's that? I can't hear you above the roar of the crickets."

"Again? That's it. I'm calling Dr. Flynn." May pulled out her cell phone and dialed. As the ring at the other end of the line sounded over the speaker, a librarian cleared her throat loudly. May looked. The librarian pointed to a sign that read: This is a no cell phone area. May's shoulders sagged. "Sorry. But my friend's sick."

"Shh," the librarian scolded.

"I'll be right back," May told Anna, though Anna heard little of what went on. May disappeared down the stairs and out the front door to make the call. She returned a few minutes later. "He wants to talk to you. Come on. We can't talk here."

"She can talk here," the librarian said. "I mean, if she's really sick."

"No, it's okay. Seeing as she is so sick, I'll just be taking her with me anyway, won't I?" May was not happy with the librarian's insistence on rules in the empty section of the library one minute, and her willingness to bend them the next. She hoped Anna would let her pick the library they donated books to next time. She'd been wanting to try the small one that was open two days a week across the border in Stamford, Vermont.

Anna let May hold onto her arm as they descended the stairs. "I'm exhausted," she said.

"Yes, I know, hon," May said. "We'll talk to the doctor."

"Hope your partner feels better soon," the librarian said as she passed them on the stairs.

It took May a moment to realize what she meant. Even Anna's head snapped up at the statement. They looked at each other and smiled. It wasn't the first time they'd been confused as a couple. Why couldn't best friends say "I love you" in public or help steady a sick friend in need without being mistaken for being romantically entwined?

"Well, I guess I could do worse than you," Anna said as they exited the building. It was loud enough that the librarian could have heard if she was listening.

"Don't encourage her!" But May laughed.

The sun was warm and the breeze just enough to keep any annoying black flies at bay. They sat on the library steps as May dialed Dr. Flynn's office again. After a circus of handing the phone off on either end of the line, Anna finally spoke with Dr. Flynn and explained her symptoms.

"Don't forget your anxiety," May reminded Anna. Anna had thought her anxiety was simply due to the threat of being bugged and spied on, but after a few internet searches, May was sure it was caused by her Lyme, especially since Anna's anxiety was often coupled with prolonged bouts of a tight chest.

Dr. Flynn told Anna that her recent symptoms pointed to co-infection. "Apparently I have Bartonella," Anna said as she hung up the phone. "There will be a new prescription waiting for me at the pharmacy."

"Then let's get thee to the pharmacy."

Anna's anxiety was rapidly spiraling into depression. "Here we go down the rabbit hole again," she said.

"I know the cure." After picking up her new meds, May drove them up to the hairpin turn restaurant where Anna could commiserate with her friends for the afternoon as they plied her with all her favorite gluten-free, dairy-free, and bladder-friendly goodies. Jo had even texted a week or so ago that she thought she found the perfect dairy substitute for the gluten-free yeast bread. Anna was looking forward to that. May was too since it was a modification of her invented recipe.

"Anna, are you okay?" Glen asked, running to meet her as she leaned on May.

Anna grunted in the affirmative.

"I shouldn't have brought her here," said May. "But once I suggested it, she wanted to come." May told Glen how they'd just picked up Anna's meds for a newly diagnosed co-infection.

"I'm glad you did. Let's take her upstairs and tuck her in with Jo. They can convalesce together. She's fighting a co-infection too."

They helped Anna up the stairs to a small one-bedroom apartment. It was space Glen and Jo had carved out of the restaurant so Jo could lie down anytime during the day, and so the two of them could stay over when she wasn't feeling up to the 20-minute commute to the small hunting camp community in Southern Vermont where they rented a cabin. Within a couple months of building the space, they sold most of their furniture and left their two-bedroom rental behind. The money they were saving in living expenses helped pay for Jo's out-of-pocket treatment costs not covered by insurance.

"Jo, look who's here." Glen did his best to sound upbeat as Jo tried to turn and look. "She's going to rest with you a while."

He pulled back the covers so he and May could lower Anna onto the bed. May removed her shoes and they guided her under the covers. Anna pulled the covers up over her eyes.

"The light's hurting her head," May told Glen.

"I have just the thing." Glen grabbed a home-knit hat from a drawer in the closet and placed it on Anna, pulling the brim over her eyes. He pulled the covers down to her chin. "This way you can breathe, okay?"

"Umm, this is nice," Anna cooed.

Glen walked around the other side of the bed and brushed the hair out of his wife's face. "Can I get you anything?"

"No, thank you." It was so faint that he had to lean in to hear her.

"Okay. Anna's here now too, fighting a similar bug. You guys can herx together, and Anna's friend and I will make something for when you feel like eating again." May and Glen tiptoed out of the room, leaving the door ajar so they could hear either of them if they called out.

It was dark outside when Anna woke. She struggled to recall where she was. She looked about thinking she might see the moon shining through the leaded-glass windows of the cottage. As her eyes adjusted to the sliver of nightlight emanating from the bathroom, she thought for a moment that she was back in the Boston condo. That wasn't it either. Realizing she had a slumbering companion, she wondered if she were home, next to the ordinarily snoring Tom.

She climbed from the covers and teetered to a standing position. Her stomach rumbled. She was ravenous. She shuffled toward the light and found a bathroom she'd never seen before. She looked about the dark room and seeing another door handle, she wobbled toward it.

Outside the room, she heard faint voices and laughter. She gained her balance and strode through the strange living room into someplace she recognized at last: the upstairs dining room of The Golden Eagle restaurant.

That's right, she thought as she recalled May mentioning something about cheering her up with a stop at her friends' place. As she wove her way through the bare tables, she heard May and Glen's chatter.

"What's a woman got to do to get waited on around here?" Anna said as she stepped into the commercial kitchen.

"Anna, you're up!"

"Is Jo awake?" Glen asked.

Anna shook her head. "Sleeping like a hibernating bear." Glen pulled out a stool for her at the counter and helped her onto it. "Something smells good."

"Good timing. Dinner's about five minutes from being ready. Baked haddock with gluten-free bread crumbs, broccoli, baked sweet potato planks, and for dessert, your favorite."

"I can't eat cheesecake anymore."

"Your second favorite."

"Nor ice cream."

"Third favorite?"

"I give. What is it?"

"Cashew-honey pie. It's a recipe May and I collaborated on."

"With a pie shell?" Anna wondered if it would be rude to begin with dessert. Maybe skip the fish course all together.

"We were able to make it elastic with just a dash of guar gum," May said.

"I'm so thankful you brought me here." Anna looked back and forth between them, and then around the kitchen.

"Looking for the pie, are we?" May asked. "No doubt, wondering if we can start with dessert, are we?"

"Using 'are we' again, are we?"

"Why are you using 'are we'?" Glen asked. Off the stare from both women, he added, "Are we?"

"Well done," Anna said. And she and May told him about the Britcom show *Miranda*, created by and starring Miranda Hart, which had become their favorite comedy show. While Glen knew nothing of the show, he was familiar with Hart's character Chummy in the BBC drama his wife enjoyed, *Call the Midwife*.

"A comedian?" he asked. "I don't see that in her character."

"And a good actress," May said.

While Glen served up plates of dinner, May cut a piece of pie for Anna and added a dollop of Cocowhip, an organic non-dairy whipped topping. Anna loved it, however, because of the sugar, she worried about eating any of it. "Should I?" She said, her fork dangling above it.

"Test your theory," May said. She was referring to Anna's belief that the best way to kill the Lyme bacteria might be to first draw them out with sugar, and then to pound them with antibiotics.

"Okay," Anna said. "As long as it's in the name of science."

The pie was beyond spectacular. She sounded a satisfied moan with each bite.

"I don't think she likes it," Glen said, as Anna finished it in record time.

"Hankering for another piece, are we?" May served up another slice to the grinning Anna.

Anna eyed Glen and May as she ate her second slice. She sensed there was something going on between them, but she couldn't be sure. "What is it?"

May and Glen exchanged a look before May looked Anna in the eye and said, "I told him about the file."

"You what?!"

"You trust him. And I thought we could use some help. Goodness knows neither of our husbands want to talk through all that we suspect."

"This is beyond suspicion," Glen said. "It sounds to me like you've stumbled into a conspiracy of some sort."

"A Lyme conspiracy," Anna said. "Yes, I'm starting to think this runs deeper than a scary senator and his sidekick Dr. Frankenstein wanting a few pieces of paper that Frank wrote out. But I think we need more proof."

***

*While many Lyme-literate doctors and practitioners will caution against eating any **sugar or dairy** since the Lyme bacteria feed on both, sometimes a treat just can't be avoided. Fortunately, So Delicious Dairy Free makes some delicious organic, non-GMO, dairy-free goodies.*

To learn more, visit Anna's "Deliciousness" board on Pinterest: https://www.pinterest.com/anna_mcgrory/deliciousness/

CHAPTER 24

"Could this be our proof?" Anna got up from her seat in front of Jo's computer and let each of them take a look. It was the next day and, though Anna and Jo were exhausted, they were both up and about and eating Glen's excellent cooking.

"It's a suicide," Jo said.

"It's Doctor Brack from the patient files." May thumbed through her photocopied file and double-checked. She was right.

"Not only that, but he was found dead in his car in his closed-up garage," Anna said. "And read the quote from his wife."

"There's no way Jeb would have taken his life. He had too much to live for, including our first grandbaby due any day now and the wedding of our youngest child in less than a month," Jo read aloud.

"The article also states there was no letter left behind," Anna said, pointing to the screen over Jo's shoulder.

"Just like Frank," May said.

"Exactly." Anna strode to the window and looked out across the valley. "Did you pack anything black by chance, May?"

"No. Why?"

"I think we should pay our respects at the wake tomorrow."

Glen took out his phone and looked up the address in Google maps. "It's only an hour and twenty minutes away. I could join you if you want. You too, Jo, if you're feeling up to the drive."

"I don't want to drag you into this, but thank you," Anna said. "Besides, it would seem natural for Margaret to send me as her representative on Frank's behalf. And I can explain one friend, but two or three seems like we're having a party at their expense."

"It does seem like it might be perceived as rather crass," Jo agreed. "Anyway, I'm not up to the trip and would rather not be alone if you don't mind, hon."

"Of course." Glen gave his wife an affectionate squeeze. "Now, what say you all to some lunch? I have your favorite—"

"Dairy-free cheesecake?" Anna asked.

"If only," Jo agreed. "Though that cashew-honey pie was fabulous."

"If you're done daydreaming about eating nothing but dessert for meals, by all means feel free to join me in the kitchen."

Jo reached for Glen as he walked by, stopping him and getting him to help her up.

As the door closed behind them, May turned to Anna. "Do you think it's a coincidence? This suicide by car?"

"No. Do you?"

May shook her head. "I must admit that I'm frightened by it all."

"Oh, May, I'm so sorry. I didn't mean to assume you'd just come along with me. If you want, I can absolutely go on my own."

"No, you absolutely cannot. I won't let you. Just wondering if this scares you too."

"Out of my wits," Anna agreed. "But at least it's a good excuse for a therapeutic shopping trip for something smart in black."

"You hate shopping," May said.

"But you love it."

May had to admit she did enjoy shopping for new outfits every now and again. She'd spent years trying to find a way for Anna to enjoy the process too, but that was just one of those areas the two of them were vastly different from each other and always would be.

"Should you call your super-secret agent spy guy?" Glen asked as May and Anna stepped into the kitchen. Anna gulped, uncertain whether or not she should trust James, but admitted that she had considered it.

"Does he know you have the file?" Jo asked.

"I'd guess he suspects, but he's been good enough not to ask directly," Anna said. "And as far as I can tell, he hasn't looked through any of our stuff."

"I agree," May said.

"Then again, he's probably so good at covering his tracks after rifling through personal items, you'd never notice."

"Glen!" Jo said. "You shouldn't scare them like that."

"It's okay," Anna said. "I've thought of that too. Wouldn't know where we could get one of those dye packs they put with money during a bank robbery, would you?"

"I don't think it works how you're thinking it does," Glen said. "It's radio controlled, so you'd have to know when he was rifling through your stuff in order to mark him."

"Maybe just a mouse trap among our papers?" May suggested.

"I can see us at the hospital emergency room trying to explain how we each have a broken finger," Anna said. "Or don't they actually break your fingers?"

"Think that's a rat trap," Glen said.

"Anyone have any actual ideas of how to catch him if he is spying on us?"

"So you don't trust him," Glen said. "Maybe it's best you don't call him."

It was an easy decision to reach. In fact, May and Anna both decided they wouldn't bother their husbands with this wake business either. Didn't want to upset them, after all.

At a downtown boutique, they found outfits from the current-former season they could get away with from the fifty-percent-off rack. "Why do stores insist on bringing in the new season so far in advance?" Anna wondered. "It's like seeing Christmas decorations in October."

"I'll take it," May said. "I love a sale."

Anna's body was growing accustomed to the new prescriptions, which meant she was only experiencing mild herxes now. When she did herx, it was generally for short, though sometimes intense, amounts of time. She found she was finally able to return to the chores awaiting her at the estate. She and May drove straight there after shopping. Glen had packed them a couple days of meals, so they had no reason to stop at a restaurant.

At the estate, Anna wondered at some of the lights left on inside. "Did we do that?" She asked May as they approached the main house.

"I doubt it." They had left during the day, so it didn't make sense that so many lights were glowing. "Maybe Sheila or Shep stopped in and turned them on?"

"I doubt that too."

"Should we worry?" May asked.

"Maybe."

May reached into the back seat where her husband had placed a crowbar and a bat for their protection. "Which one do you want?"

"I'm not sure I'll be any good with either."

May pointed to the glove box. "Check in there."

Anna opened it and took out a small canister. "Pepper spray?"

"Body spray. Legal in more places. And still as potent," May said.

"Remember our instructor's warning about weapons being turned on those who are trying to defend themselves?"

"How could I forget? Though I wish I could," May said.

"We did well in those classes. We've got this."

"Now I'm feeling like we should maybe call the police?"

"Let's take a peek through the windows and then decide." Anna heard herself say the words, but truth was she wasn't nearly as confident as she sounded. She didn't want to involve the police since she was sure they would think she was crazy or being overly dramatic.

Anna traded May the fake mace for the crowbar after all, and the two of them went window to window peering inside. Nothing seemed out of the ordinary except the lights. They realized it had been cloudy when they left two days ago with their book donations for the North Adams library. "Maybe we did leave the lights on," Anna said.

"Lost your keys?" James nodded at the crowbar in Anna's hand as he walked up the driveway.

Anna and May jumped. "What are you doing here?!" Anna asked.

"I took the latest patient interviews to Senator Ponema like you wanted me to. Now I'm back to do my job. Where have you young ladies been?"

"That's none of your business," May said as she stomped back to the car. "I'll pull it around to the cottage. Do you want to ride with me, Anna?"

"No. Thanks. I'm okay."

May hit the gas harder than necessary, her fight-or-flight reaction to James was feeding adrenaline into her right foot. Rocks spun behind her as she sped away.

"I didn't mean to frighten either of you." James seemed sincere. Anna wanted to believe that he was, but she was wary of his presence. "I returned yesterday. Was surprised when you weren't here by evening."

"I find it difficult to believe you didn't know where we were."

"I knew you were at the library, and after the call to your doctor, that you went to the pharmacy."

"But you lost us after that? How can that possibly be true?"

"The trail went cold."

So did Anna's blood.

"Trust me: it's better that I know where you are. I'm here for you. To protect you. Per—"

"Frank's orders. You said. That doesn't mean I trust you."

Anna marched past him and entered the main house, slamming the door behind her. She leaned against it, breathing deeply. She turned around and reached for the bolt lock. She began to slide it across, but realized it wouldn't keep him out. There were too many doors into the place. She peered out the side window and saw James study his phone, scrolling through some information. He pocketed it and started toward the door.

Anna jumped and scurried out of the foyer, through the parlor, and out the patio door. She jogged to the cottage, glancing once behind her, though she didn't spy him. As she rounded the corner where May parked next to James' car, she saw May struggling to carry all the food and the dresses in at the same time. "Let me help," Anna said.

"I thought you'd never ask."

Anna put the crowbar in the back seat and closed the door. She had forgotten she still had it. Her knuckles had turned white from her tight grip. Anna stretched her hand out as she approached May and grabbed the dresses.

"How'd it go back there?" May asked.

"I don't trust him."

"I'm not sure I do either, but you haven't answered the question."

"I'm afraid of him," Anna said.

The cottage door opened and James appeared from behind it. "Can I help?"

Both women jumped again. "You have to stop doing that!" Anna said.

"Opening doors for you when your hands are full?" James asked. He closed the door behind them as they entered and eyed the see-through plastic bags that protected the black outfits. "Planning to attend the wake tomorrow?"

"We had considered it," Anna said as she climbed the stairs. "And no, you're not invited."

***

Wondering what Frank's estate looks like? **The Trustees Field Farm** *property in Williamstown, Massachusetts, is the basis for the estate. It offers an interesting day hike, and the bed and breakfast provides a wonderful place to stay overnight.*

To learn more, visit Anna's "Vacation Spots" board on Pinterest: https://www.pinterest.com/anna_mcgrory/vacation-spots/

CHAPTER 25

Anna and May rode in the back seat as James drove. Anna hoped making him their chauffeur would get under his skin. It was the only thing she could think to do to him to let him know how unhappy she was that he was accompanying them.

The previous night, while Anna and May ate Glen's incredible cooking, James, who had eaten with Sheila and Shep before they arrived, dialed Margaret and told her his concerns over Anna and May's plans to attend the wake alone. Margaret agreed, and asked to speak with Anna. When James brought her his phone, Anna felt like a teen being told to speak to her mother. Margaret, for her part, tried to understand Anna's fears, but she insisted James accompany them. Once again, she assured Anna that she remembered James from Frank's days as a senator in Washington.

Margaret had even called the secret service to check that James had been honorably retired or discharged or whatever they called it. Anna couldn't recall her exact words now as she sat and stewed over the previous night's conversation. By the time she finally agreed to Margaret's request, Anna could hear the exasperation in the older woman's voice. Margaret hung up before Anna pulled the phone from her ear to hand it back to James.

Anna felt his stare. She looked up into the rearview mirror where their eyes met. James looked like he was sad. Or was Anna imagining that? She looked over at May, who knitted steadily. Anna envied May's ability and desire to knit. Anna hated all that domestic stuff. She'd only ever knitted one slipper in her life. It was for a 4-H assignment. She couldn't recall now, but she was sure she hadn't earned her badge or whatever it was her 4-H leader bestowed upon those who successfully completed their crafts.

James dropped Anna and May at the front of the funeral home. Anna watched him drive up the block searching for a place to park. "I'm tempted to ditch the wake just to get away from him."

"He's not so bad," May said.

Anna's head snapped as she turned to glare at her friend. "I thought you didn't trust him. That's what you said earlier."

"I said I wasn't sure if I trusted him. I do now."

Anna folded her arms in front of her chest. She was too upset for words, feeling somehow betrayed by her best friend.

"All I'm saying is give him a chance. It's not like you have to marry him." May turned and marched toward the front door.

Anna stood and stewed. She could taste her venom. The thought made her pause and assess her physical condition. She had more energy today, and was actually able to find her words for once, but she suspected it wouldn't last for long. She wondered if anger had a healing effect upon the body.

"Thanks for waiting." James approached Anna. "Where's May?"

Anna did not want to be his chum. She strode toward the front door without a word or a glance in his direction.

"Rude," James uttered not quite under his breath as he followed her.

In the hall, Anna added her name to the guest book below May's signature. She added "on behalf of Margaret Barber" and continued inside to join May in the snaking line.

"That was nice of you to wait for him," May said.

"I'm not talking to you."

May glanced over Anna's shoulder and watched James turn the pages of the guest book. "Who is he looking for, do you suppose?"

Anna turned and looked just as James glanced up and met her eyes. He set the book down and headed for another room.

"Maybe he's waiting for others to arrive so he doesn't have to stand with you."

"With us."

"No. It's you. I love you, sweetie. You know that. But sometimes you can be kind of...." May searched for the right word.

"Beautiful? Enigmatic? Charming?" Anna batted her hair, playing the role of a starlet.

"Puerile and insolent."

"Studying a thesaurus in our free time, are we?"

"Adding 'are we' to the end of an observation, are we? Guessing that means the not-talking-to-your-best-friend moratorium is over."

"I'll not talk to you on the ride home instead."

"See? Puerile," May said.

Anna folded her arms in front of her and tried her best to keep her anger at bay as they followed the slowly moving line into a large room made to look like a comfortable and opulent sitting room. To Anna it had the look of the original *House of Wax* film starring Vincent Price. She realized what an apt association that was considering how people in coffins usually appeared.

"What are you doing here?" It was more sneer than question.

Anna recognized the voice immediately. She turned and faced Senator Ponema. "Margaret asked me to come. You remember my friend May?"

He ignored May's uttered greeting. "Why?"

"She and the doctor's wife were school friends, or co-campers or something, in the Berkshires. An all-girl's place. Quite posh apparently."

"If it was the Berkshires, my guess would be it was a camp," May said.

"Camp. School. It doesn't matter. How did she know her friend's husband died? And why didn't she just come herself? It all seems quite suspect to me," said the senator.

"Finally," Anna said. "Something we can agree on."

Senator Ponema stared at her. Behind him, the next person in line cleared his throat loudly. The senator glared at him. Anna stared. May looked around and realized the line had moved again. "Sorry," May said. She grabbed Anna's arm and pulled her till they had closed the gap.

Anna stared ahead. May looked at her. "Is he still there?" Anna asked.

"Yes."

"What's he doing?"

"Watching you."

"I don't like him."

"I don't either," May said. "What's he doing here anyway?"

"Come to pay his respects, I suppose."

"But how does he know him?"

Anna's eyes bulged. May turned to look in the same direction as Anna. They stared at the odd doctor as he cut the line, walking to the casket and peering inside. The people he had cut off did not look pleased, but kept quiet given the sorrowful circumstances.

"Who is he?" May asked.

"I don't exactly know." Anna and May watched as Senator Ponema joined him.

"Is that the peculiar doctor you told me about from Frank's wake?"

"You mean you haven't had the pleasure?" Anna kept forgetting that May hadn't attended that event.

Senator Ponema whispered in the strange man's ear, causing him to turn and stare at Anna. "You?!" He pointed at her as he marched straight at her. "Why are you here?"

The entire line stopped as everyone stared at them.

"I could ask you the same thing!" Anna stood her ground. After all, what would he possibly do to her here in front of all these people?

"How did you know to come here?" He might have jabbed Anna with his finger, but out of nowhere James stepped between them.

"You've exhausted your welcome here, Doctor," James said. "It's time for you and the senator to leave." James looked pointedly at Senator Ponema.

As the senator reached for the doctor's arm to usher him away, the widow strode over. "Who are any of you? I don't know a single one of you."

"Sorry for your loss, Mrs. Brack." Anna stepped from behind James to reach a hand out toward her.

"Why are you sorry for my loss? Are you a patient of my husband's? Is that it?"

"I'm an assistant to the late Senator Frank Barber, here representing his—"

"Frank Barber? The Frank Barber who tried to take my husband's medical license away?!"

"Sorry, I don't know anything about that," Anna said.

May looked nervously about, noticing the murmurs in the crowd. It was beginning to appear a lynching might be next.

"Get out! All of you! Now!" The widow's yell yielded a fresh crop of tears.

Three large, well-dressed gentlemen approached the group. "If you'll come with us," one of them said. The group was escorted to the applause of the mourners. The trio of funeral home workers didn't stop until they were outside where a half-dozen policemen and their cruisers waited for them.

"How did they get here so quickly?" Anna asked May.

"I called them," James said as he walked ahead of them and met one of the officers.

***

Anna and May love the British Sitcom (or "BritCom") **Miranda** *so much that they've seen it together three times. Their habit of quoting Miranda's "Are we?" line has prompted others to watch the seriously fun and addictive show.*

To learn more, visit Anna's "BritComs" board on Pinterest: https://www.pinterest.com/anna_mcgrory/britcoms/

CHAPTER 26

Anna sat on the front steps of the funeral home and watched the scene continue as a policewoman stood at the bottom of the stairs, ready to pounce if Anna moved. May sat and knitted on a bus stop bench across the street with her assigned officer. Anna didn't understand her friend's compulsion to knit so much. Observing her now, Anna wondered if it was helpful in reducing stress.

Beyond the first police car, two patrolmen watched and listened to the senator, who gestured wildly as he appeared to be jabbering away. Meanwhile, the odd doctor paced in a tight circle, poking at his own face and neck with the extended middle finger of his left hand. His nervous tic made Anna wonder if the doctor was headed to a dark place, or if he was already there. Perhaps he needed his meds, if there was a medication for such behavior. As for the senator, Anna wondered if he was more concerned for his friend or his reputation.

"We can go now." James approached from the opposite end of the street as the officer he had been meeting with veered off across the street to where May and her officer sat.

Anna stood and followed James across the street to May.

"Sorry for the confusion," one of the officers said.

"No worries," said James. "We appreciate your service."

The officers left.

"Kissing up now, are we?" Anna said.

"Using 'are we' on me now, are we?"

Anna was taken aback. She had done so. It was a sign of friendship. Or maybe it was just a force of habit. But what if she had weakened? Or was she beginning to actually trust him? She was momentarily blinded in her confusion. That didn't stop her from seeing the unmistakable look of camaraderie that passed between May and James. She stood so long pondering her words, actions, thoughts, and feelings that when she finally realized May and James had begun walking, she had to hurry to close the half-block distance between them.

As they drove out of town, May sat in the passenger seat up front and knitted, James drove, and Anna sat behind her friend and pouted.

"Everyone okay?" James asked.

May nodded her head and made an affirmative humming sound.

"Can we not talk?"

James glanced back at Anna. She looked away. "Whatever you want," he said.

"That's what I want."

"Maybe some music?" May asked.

"If you must." Anna knew she was being rude, but she couldn't help herself. She was angry, and she wasn't entirely sure why. To add to her burdens, she could feel the crushing wave of depression approach. Her Lyme doctor explained that these were symptoms of her BB and Bart—the acronyms he'd introduced to her that represented Borrelia burgdorferi and Bartonella.

May consulted quietly with James. Apparently she was going through his CDs and showing some to him. Anna tried not to become further upset by their budding rapport, but it bothered her to no end. She looked out the window and silently thanked the heavens that she was unable to produce tears. If she could, she knew she'd be a sniveling idiot by now.

A moment later, Yo-Yo Ma's cello music filled the car. Anna closed her eyes in reverence. She loved the cello, especially anything recorded by the master himself. She recognized it almost immediately and was pleased. She couldn't ordinarily identify classical music, but this CD was one of her favorites. And the first track was her best-loved piece, Bach: Prelude for Unaccompanied Cello, Suite Number One in G Major, BWV 1007. She wasn't sure what the BWV stood for, but she knew the numbers went at least to 1012. She wondered if there were six before this prelude. Or maybe there were one thousand and six.

The car slowed and Anna heard the turn signal. Without opening her eyes she asked, "Why are we stopping?"

Neither James nor May answered. She looked and saw they were turning into the parking lot of a soft-serve ice cream place. Anna knew this would be a welcome stop for her friend. But her anger and depression stabbed at her heart. Next thing she knew, she had crossed her arms over her chest and blurted out: "Oh, just fantastic. Dairy and gluten. Enjoy your treat."

"I will," May said as she climbed from the car.

James opened his door and got out without a word. He popped the trunk and rummaged inside it as Anna slinked out and trudged to an unoccupied picnic table.

"For you," James said as he handed her some kind of ice cream bar wrapped in white.

"What is it?" She looked and read the label with its repetitive "So Delicious. Dairy Free." She looked up at him. "You keep frozen treats in your trunk?"

James smiled. "I have a cooler that plugs into the electrical outlet there. As for the treat, it's not ice cream. My sister swears by them."

"She's also dairy-free?"

"Her son is. Dairy-free and gluten-free. Therefore, she and the rest of the family nearly are. Easier to cook the same meal."

"He has Lyme too?"

James shook his head. "He's autistic."

"Oh. I'm sorry."

"No need to be sorry. It's mild. Asperger's is what they used to call it. Till the powers that be eliminated that more gentle diagnosis category. Now he likes to tell people he's autistic, even though you'd barely recognize it in him. My sister swears it's the diet that brought him back to her."

Anna opened the wrapper, bit into the creamy tan treat, and cooed in pleasure at the succulent coffee flavor. James laughed, as May returned with two twist cones and handed one to him. Anna eyed her. "You were in on this?"

"James told me about the treat. I suggested we leave the non-dairy ones for you and stop for the real thing on the way home."

That May and James had co-conspired added to Anna's earlier upset. But instead of saying anything, she focused on her dessert. She tried not to get further agitated as she listened to the two of them exchange small talk.

After they'd finished their treats, James excused himself and followed the signs to the restrooms.

"He's not that bad, you know." May stood and dropped her napkin in the waste bin. She returned and stood over Anna, hands on her hips. "What's wrong with you anyway? You never even said thank you, did you? You're acting like a spoiled brat, you know that?"

Anna looked up at May, instantly squinting since the sun was behind her. "I'm sorry. I'm having trouble controlling my feelings."

May sat next to her friend so she wasn't blinded. "How do you mean?"

"It's apparently another symptom of Lyme."

"You're not going to blame your behavior on your illness, are you?"

"Not entirely. But the rolling in and crashing down of depression—that's real. And the sudden feelings of rage—I have no idea where they come from. I honestly can't seem to control them."

"I'm sorry, Anna, but I'm not sure I'm buying this. I know how much you distrust him. It's poisoned you against him and everyone else—even me."

"No! That's not true. I promise."

"But you've been mad at me all day. You obviously don't like that I talk to him."

"I'm sorry."

"You should be." May stood and strode toward the car.

Anna felt awful as she trudged to the restrooms, nearly running into James as he ambled around the corner. "Oh. Sorry."

"No, please, excuse me." James swept his arm in a grand exaggerated gesture indicating she should pass.

Anna stepped past him, suddenly stopping and swiveling to face him. "Thank you."

James smiled. "You're welcome. I'll just go and wait by the car for you."

"I mean for the non-dairy treat."

"I thought you'd like that. They are so delicious, after all."

Anna nodded and made an attempt at a smile. She could feel the first crack give way in her icy demeanor.

Returning to the car, Anna saw that May had settled in the back seat and returned to her knitting. Anna reached for the rear door, but caught May's look of disapproval. Anna nodded. She knew May was right. Enough was enough. It was time to harness her distrust. As for her rage and depression, she would call her doctor later and ask him for advice. She opened the passenger door and climbed in. Glancing back at May she said, "Are you sure you want to sit back there?"

"Knitting needles and airbags. Not sure they'd mix well. And I'm on a deadline."

"Where are we going now?" Anna asked as she belted in.

"Uh, I was just thinking we were headed back to the estate," James said as he pulled onto the road. "Why? Where do you want to go?"

"I was just figuring the two of you made more secret plans together."

"Anna, behave yourself!"

Ann turned and looked at May. Pointedly, she said, "And I'm okay with that…as long as there are more treats in that magical dairy-free, gluten-free cooler of yours."

"I have three more bars."

"Really? Had I known, I might have eaten another one. Or two. Or all of them."

Anna was feeling better just being civil. She asked May what she was knitting so furiously. May told her it was a baby blanket for their next grandbaby due in a couple months. The shower was next weekend though. Anna had been invited and had accepted the invitation. "Did you forget?" May asked.

"I did. Sorry." She had forgotten everything: May's project, the shower, and even that May's youngest daughter was pregnant. It wasn't like Anna to forget so much. She was sure it was the Lyme, but even if it was, she was struggling to accept her new normal.

"I've told you what I'm knitting only about three or four times now."

"So I'm playing the role of your absent-minded mother now, am I?" Anna referred to the suspected early-onset Alzheimer's May's mother was experiencing.

"It's the Lyme. Or the co-infection," said James. "May even explain your earlier curtness."

"Curtness! Well if that isn't the understatement of the century," May said.

Anna had to agree with her. "Sorry," she said. She meant it, but she wished she could think of something more to say.

"It's okay," James said. "I think you might want to call your doctor though. See what he thinks."

"Who are you who is so wise in the ways of Lyme science?"

"My little sister, Beth, was diagnosed with it a few years back. She's been sick so long that she lives with my older sister now."

"The one with the autistic boy?"

"Yes. Esther's her name."

"And her son?"

"Jimmy." James saw Anna smile at him. "Well, yeah, James. But it gets confusing if we're both called that."

"That's a pretty big honor."

"Yes, I know. I'm blessed."

"So, back there, at the wake, I mean, what was all that about do you suppose?"

"The senator definitely does not like you."

"It's mutual. Believe me. But what of the widow's reaction? I thought she and Margaret were friends from way back. Do you think Frank really did something to ruin her husband's name?"

"I asked the sergeant. He didn't know, but he radioed back to the station. Apparently Frank worked for the New York State Department of Health's Office of Professional Medical Conduct as an attorney who prosecuted physicians."

"I thought he worked in the AG's office before he was elected into office."

"He interned there during law school."

"So he went after Dr. Brack?"

"Some would say he won too. The doctor didn't lose his license, but he was on probation for two years. News of that caused a ripple effect. Some of his regular patients fled and at least one hospital pulled his privileges."

"What did he do to deserve probation?"

"He was diagnosing and treating for chronic Lyme."

Anna took in a sharp breath. "Was Frank involved in the Joseph Cordon case too?" Dr. Cordon had treated Lyme patients at his New York City office. His probationary hearings were the stuff of legend in the Lyme community. The doctor was a godsend to many seriously ill patients, most of whom had been shuttled from one doctor to the next with a host of autoimmune or even psychiatric diagnoses. Dr. Cordon recognized the plethora of symptoms for what they were: a Borrelia burgdorferi infection.

"I think that was in the early 2000s," said May. "Maybe 2002 or 2003. I can't remember now. It was in that Lyme book you lent me—by the woman who lived in the same New York suburb as the Clinton's."

"Chappaqua?" James asked.

"Yes, that's the one," May said.

"Frank was already in Washington then." Anna thought she was beginning to see the significance of Frank's patient interviews. "Do you think he killed himself out of guilt?"

"I'm not sure I believe he killed himself at all," James said.

"You mean...?" But Anna couldn't say it. She'd never known anyone who had died that way.

"Murder. Yes." James looked dead ahead, concentrating on the winding road that led them up and over the hills.

***

Pamela Weintraub's nonfiction book, **Cure Unknown: Inside the Lyme Epidemic***, details her own path down the rabbit hole that is Lyme, and that of her family and of many patients. It also documents the history of Lyme disease through her extensive research, which includes numerous interviews with Lyme-literate physicians and researchers.*

For more information, visit Anna's "Lyme" board on Pinterest: https://www.pinterest.com/anna_mcgrory/lyme/

CHAPTER 27

"You don't think Senator Scary Pants had anything to do with it, do you?" Anna was still trying to wrap her head around the possibility that her boss had been murdered.

"He's too smart to have done it himself, but I'd bet he's behind it," James said.

"If that's true, are the three of us equipped to handle this on our own?" It was May. She was in the back seat knitting and trying not to panic. She had dropped two stitches worrying over the conversation in the front seat.

Anna didn't want to think about May's question. She raised a good point, but it was easier to ignore the dangers. Instead, she asked, "How do we exhume the bodies?"

"Bodies? Plural?" James asked.

"The burial for Dr. Brack is tomorrow. Unless you think we can get an injunction and stop it."

"I'm retired."

"Which is why I didn't think that was an option. Do you think we can get an order to exhume?"

"Maybe. It will take more evidence than just our conjecture."

Anna reached her hand out to May over the seat.

"You sure?" May asked.

"I think so."

May rummaged through her knitting bag, pulled out a small manila envelope, and handed it to Anna.

"What's that?" James asked.

"Before I answer that, do you think our conversation is being listened to?"

"It's a little late to ask that now," May said. Anna wondered when her best friend had become Captain Obvious. Had she just not noticed that about her before?

"I checked and double checked the car and all our devices. I think we're in the clear."

"May? You think we can trust we're in the clear?" Anna looked over at her.

May shook her head no.

"I'm suddenly starving," Anna said.

"Me too. Positively famished," May agreed. They shared a look and a huge grin.

"We're almost home, er, back at the estate," James said. He looked over at Anna who pointed to her ears. She added the same creepy crawly effect James had used earlier to indicate bugs. "But I'm not sure there's anything to eat. To a restaurant it is."

At the Water Street Grill in Williamstown, Massachusetts, the trio sat in the tavern studying the three documents in the envelope. Anna wasn't yet sure how much she was willing to trust James, so instead of telling him about the complete file they had found, she decided it was a good way to share the next round of patient files she and May had already identified as a second test to see if Senator Scary Pants knew everything going on at the estate. Now her experiment was also aimed at James. If the senator learned of the latest papers, it would mean that James was spying for him. She wondered if James had any idea what she was thinking.

The only hiccup in her newly hatched plan was that she had hesitated far too long when he asked where she and May had found these. The two women hadn't yet decided where they were going to plant them, though they had brainstormed. If James suspected that she had the entire file in her possession, she was sure that he would now know it given the awkwardness of her reply. She looked at May, who shook her head ever so slightly as her eyes grew wide. Perhaps James had perceived May's reaction as fright. Finally, Anna coughed up the location. "The car," she said.

"Which car?"

"Frank's."

"But it was searched thoroughly."

"Not thoroughly enough. Obviously," Anna said. And she proceeded to tell him about Frank's super-secret hiding spot inside the steering wheel.

"He'll know you lied," May said when the two of them entered the bathroom after ordering.

"But he really did have a hiding spot made there."

"How?"

"I don't know how. I just know that once I saw him access a folded piece of paper from there. Frank thought I was asleep."

"How folded?" May asked.

"Oh no. You're right!" The women were referring to the lack of more than one fold in the three papers.

"Let's say I ironed them so we could read them better."

"Why on earth would you do that? And why would he believe it?"

"You forget the note he gave you that night at MASS MoCA." May referred to the disappearing ink that she had found after applying a hot iron to the message.

"Okay. He might. So, do we have our game faces on?" Anna stood by the door, ready to return to their table.

"I think I have my 'I-have-to-pee-now!' face on, actually." May disappeared into a stall. "See you in a minute."

"Oh no, I'm not going back there alone." Anna took her own stall. "If you can't beat them...."

Over dinner, the trio decided it was too dangerous to reveal the latest papers to Senator Ponema. The three patients had each seen the same doctor who treated them for their chronic Lyme. If they were right, and the last doctor and Frank had been killed and staged to look like they had each committed suicide, they reasoned that the next doctor's blood would be on their hands if the scary senator learned of their find.

Instead, they talked about having James make a few calls from a burner phone to see if he could get some of his connections to help him obtain an order to have the two bodies exhumed. He stepped outside the restaurant and made a quick call to the sergeant who he'd met with earlier at the funeral home; James hoped he could convince him to arrange an autopsy tonight—before tomorrow's funeral and graveside service. The sergeant was reluctant, especially since James wasn't sure what it was he was looking for. Evidence of foul play wasn't quite enough detail. Yet somehow, James had convinced him to at least try.

By the time James returned, Anna was beaming. "We don't need a court order or whatever it is to exhume Frank's body."

"Because…?"

"He's buried on the estate."

"Of course," James said. "All we need are some shovels."

"Shovels? Plural?" It was May. She raised an accusatory eyebrow toward James.

"You women want your equal rights until shovels are involved."

"Yes, that sounds about right," May said. "Anna?"

"I'm with her," Anna said.

"And we should check with Margaret. See if it's okay with her," James said.

"Should we upset her before we know for sure?" Anna wasn't sure if she was playing devil's advocate or if she was just anxious to do this and get it over with. She figured it was a bit of both.

"Margaret would be pretty upset with you if you didn't at least ask her permission. How would you feel if someone dug up Tom without your knowing?" May's argument lost its steam as she and Anna bantered about the fact that Tom was still very much alive.

"At least I think he is," Anna said. She pulled her phone from her pocket and turned it on.

"Why do you keep it off?" James asked.

"So I can't be tracked. You know, NSA and scary spy stuff like that." Anna shook her head like "Duh!"

"Even when it's off they can track it."

"No way. How?"

"I don't know exactly. But I do have a couple extra military-grade Blackout Pockets. You can each have one, if you want."

Anna and May did want one. But as she thought about this new cell phone factoid, Anna grew irritated that her efforts had been of no use. She suspected Senator Ponema was tracking her every move. But if he had been doing so, wouldn't he have known they were headed toward the town where the wake was held? He seemed surprised to see them there earlier in the day. Maybe James was tracking her? Or the strange doctor? Anna tried to think of someone who could have been tracking her. She was in too deep to admit now that it was completely possible and likely probable that no one had been tracking her movements. Why was she disappointed by that sudden realization? Sometimes even Anna had to admit she could be overly dramatic, though she'd never say so.

As May and James ordered from the dessert cart, Anna scrolled through her missed texts. She hadn't turned her phone on since she'd been to the pharmacy to pick up her new medications. There was a message from her daughter wondering if Anna would be home for the weekend so the two of them could have a girl's day out getting their hair cut and doing lunch, as was their custom. One was from her Lyme doctor's office asking her to call if there were any severe side effects caused by the new medications. A thread started by a neighbor to all the houses on the block about her missing cat resulted in several back-and-forth messages, including two from Tom. And there was an automated message from her dentist's office reminding her of a cleaning appointment the following week.

Anna responded to them all, but her face couldn't mask her pain. James and May saw that she was bothered, and they shared a look.

"I'll be right back," James said as he stood and strode toward the exit.

"You okay?" May asked.

"There's no message from Tom."

"Maybe he called. Check your missed—"

"I already did. Nothing."

"Well, it's still early. Maybe he'll call later."

"I've had my phone off since Tuesday."

"Oh."

James returned with another of the incredible frozen treats that Anna could eat. He expected a more excited reaction when he handed it to her. Instead, Anna simply took it, whispered a thank you, and set it on her plate. She hung her head and willed herself to cry. "Stupid dry eyes. I can't even manage to conjure one tear."

"What's happened?" James was on instant high alert.

May held her napkin to her face and half whispered, "Tom hasn't been in touch all week."

"I could bring the entire box."

"Typical man," Anna said. "Divert to humor when the subject matter gets too thorny."

"Sorry. I meant no disrespect. What can I do?"

"Relax. I'm only kidding," Anna said.

The desserts appeared as a waitress delivered them to James and May. Seeing Anna's So Delicious bar, the waitress said, "Oh, I love those things! I keep telling my boss we need some dairy-free options on the menu, but he thinks I'm the only one who can't eat it." She bounced back into the kitchen, leaving the trio to look at their desserts. James and May were trying to gauge whether it was rude to eat when Anna was obviously so distressed.

"I don't know about your choices, but mine rocks!" Anna said as she picked up the wrapper and ripped into it.

"Oh, thank goodness," said May as she took a bite of her cheesecake.

"This is much better than talking about dead people," James said as he joined them.

Or my husband, Anna thought.

***

Anna can have her **cheesecake** *and eat it too, thanks to the numerous vegan recipes available online. All it takes are some savvy substitutions, such as using raw cashews, coconut cream, and vegan cream cheese.*

For more information, visit Anna's "Deliciousness" board on Pinterest: https://www.pinterest.com/anna_mcgrory/deliciousness/

CHAPTER 28

The next morning, Anna woke with the sun. Looking out her window, she saw Charlie running among the wilted daffodils, but no sign of Shep. She threw on her clothes, a light jacket, and boots, and joined the dog down by the pond. Together they played fetch for almost an hour. Charlie never tired of jumping into the pond to retrieve the stick Anna threw. Despite her best efforts to stay dry, Anna was as soaked as Charlie by the end of their game since he seemed to enjoy getting close to her before he shook himself off.

Still no sign of Shep, Anna decided to walk Charlie to the carriage house and check on his owners. The backdoor was wide open. Anna called out, "Shep? Sheila? You awake?"

"In here." Shep's voice was weak. Anna wondered if he was trying not to wake Sheila or if he was ill.

She closed the door behind her, keeping the wet dog outside on the porch to dry off, kicked off her boots, and wound her way into the living room where she found Shep reclined in his favorite chair, a blanket draped over him and a hat pulled down over his eyes.

"I wouldn't come any closer, if I were you," he said.

"Flu?"

"More than likely."

"Is Sheila sick too?"

"Not that I know of. She's at her sister's and doesn't know I'm sick. Prefer it that way."

"Understood. What can I do to help?"

"Feed Charlie his breakfast?"

"Of course." Anna headed for the pantry, measured out the food, and took the bowl out to the porch for Charlie. The dog was tired from their morning exercise, but bounded up as soon as he heard the food rustling in his dish.

Anna returned to the living room doorway, looking in on Shep but not daring to go any closer. "Anything else?"

"Can you take a look at the calendar hanging next to the phone for me? I think Charlie has an appointment at the vet today or tomorrow. Or maybe it was yesterday. What day is it anyway?"

"Friday." Anna looked. Sure enough, Charlie had an appointment in less than an hour.

"Maybe you can cancel it for me?"

"There's a fee for canceling with less than 24 hours notice."

"Not much I can do about that."

"I'll take him."

"I can do it next week when I'm feeling better."

"I know you can. But the number of times you've helped me, this won't even begin to even the score." Anna turned to leave. "Want anything while I'm out?"

"No. Thanks." Anna pulled on her boots and was just about to leave when she heard Shep add: "Wait. Would you grab me some ginger ale? And not that commercial crap. I like the real ginger and cane sugar."

"You got it." As Anna left, she grabbed Charlie's leash. "Come on, boy. Let's go for a ride in the car." Anna didn't have to ask the dog twice.

The cottage was quiet when Anna and Charlie entered. On the walk over, she realized she didn't have a car with her. She wondered if May would mind if Anna drove hers. She knew she could take Frank's car, but she was still afraid of it. Finding someone slumped over dead at the steering wheel tends to put a damper on driving the vehicle ever again. Apparently, it also put a damper on selling it. Margaret had done nothing to get rid of it. Anna would have taken Shep's truck, but it was an antique with a complicated stick shift. At least it seemed complicated to Anna. She could drive a standard, but she wasn't sure she could handle his truck.

"Morning." Anna looked up and saw James seated on the stairs petting Charlie.

"Hey." Anna wondered how long he'd been sitting there.

"You're wet."

"Yeah. Playing with the dog." She climbed the stairs past him. "I'm just gonna change real quick. Then..." She trailed off, not sure she should ask him for a ride.

"What do you need?"

She explained the situation. James didn't hesitate. "Of course I'll drive you. Gets me out of digging this morning."

"Margaret okayed it?"

"Not in so many words."

"You didn't call her?"

"No. You?" Anna shook her head as she climbed the stairs. That conversation would have to be tabled till later.

There wasn't enough time to make a new pot of coffee and drive to the vet, so after her quick change of clothes Anna poured the rest of the cold, day-old low-acid coffee into a cup for herself. James would grab a coffee on the way. There was an adorable little country store run by a young family within walking distance to Frank's estate. Anna always forgot about it in the morning since she was too cheap to buy coffee. She had convinced herself it was a matter of homebrewed coffee, not the pocketbook. Now it didn't matter, unless they had started selling her bladder-friendly brew.

They left Charlie in the car and went in together. The bell jingled as they entered. "Mmm," Anna said as she inhaled the aroma of coffee mixed with freshly baked muffins and pastries. "I wish I could eat gluten."

"There are some gluten-free pumpkin muffins this morning," the young woman who co-owned the store with her husband said as she passed behind Anna and James.

"Dairy-free too?" Anna cringed as she waited for the answer, realizing that might be too much to hope for.

"No. Sorry," she said. "Though we have vegan pomegranate muffins."

"With gluten?"

"Yes. Sorry."

"It's okay. I'm getting used to it." But Anna didn't do a good job of hiding her disappointment. Anna grabbed a four-pack of Shep's ginger ale that he liked and a fresh-baked dog treat for Charlie while James doctored his coffee and Anna paid.

In the car, Anna's stomach rumbled at a deep-pitched roar. She reached for the radio. "Mind if we listen to something other than my belly?" Yo Yo

Ma's cello picked up where it had left off the previous night.

"Much better," James said.

"Yeah. Sorry." Anna tried not to be embarrassed, but she didn't succeed.

"Mine does the same thing when it wakes up. It's just too early yet for me. How long you been up anyway?"

"A while." Off his look, Anna added: "Since sunrise."

She handed Charlie his treat and read through the ingredients list. "There's no dairy. And it's gluten free. I could have just had one of these." They laughed as her stomach objected again.

Charlie enjoyed the ride until James pulled into the parking lot. The dog's ears perked up and he let out a small whine that Anna had never heard from him. He lay down and it took both of them to coax him out of the vehicle. James pushed from one side of the car as Anna tugged the dog's collar from the other side.

Charlie nearly pulled Anna over with his determination not to enter the office. James took the dog, and Anna went inside to see if they had any treats or other ideas of ways they could coerce him inside. The receptionist apologized, saying it was their fault since the last time Charlie was there he had to have stitches. Anna didn't remember Charlie having an accident, but she was away for over a year and a half while her Lyme disease had knocked her on her back.

"Try this." The receptionist held out an organic hotdog.

"Bringing out the big guns, I see," Anna said.

"Sometimes it's the only way." The receptionist looked outside where Charlie pulled James across the lot to the other side and sat down. She chuckled. "Your husband has his hands full."

"Oh! No! That's not—he's not—"

"Sorry. Didn't mean to presume."

"No. Of course not." Anna grabbed the hotdog and headed for the door. She grabbed the handle, but before she turned it, she tried to steady her nerves, fearful of the small butterflies that danced in her stomach at the idea that she and James were something more than colleagues.

She took a deep breath and walked outside. James looked up and they locked eyes. Again, Anna tried to put the butterflies to rest. As she approached, she held up the hotdog. "Look what I have, Charlie." She broke off a small piece for the dog, who gobbled it down.

"What does it say about me that I think that actually looks good?" James asked.

"You're finally as hungry as I am?"

Anna broke off pieces and set them in intervals leading to the door. Before he knew what he was doing, Charlie had entered the building chewing contentedly.

"Nice job," James said. Anna smiled at the compliment, though she worried over her sudden realization that she could get used to James complimenting her more.

On the way home from the veterinarian's office, James offered to buy Anna breakfast at the small diner they had passed earlier. Anna had to admit she was hoping they might stop there. She loved their eggs and hash browns. She also knew they carried Abigail's Bakery bread, a New England-produced gluten-free, dairy-free bread that was her favorite.

While Charlie sat in the car gnawing on a new bone she'd bought him at the vet's, Anna and James discussed the visit. "I still don't understand why the dog can get vaccinated, but you and I can't," Anna said.

"You've heard about the drug trials?"

Anna had. "I guess there were so many lawsuits that the pharmaceutical company dropped the vaccine," she said.

"Yes, and the other company with a promising vaccine dropped theirs before attempting to roll it out."

"Do you think it really caused problems for people?"

"I don't know. But people thought it caused their Lyme arthritis," James said.

"Is that it? I thought there were more serious health problems than that." Anna had read somewhere—she couldn't recall where now—that some people in the early vaccination phase were hospitalized.

"I don't know enough about it either."

"Do dogs have the same side effects?"

"I only know what you do."

Anna took out her phone and typed. "Luckily for us, Google knows."

"You sure you want to use your phone for this?"

"I'm sure the senator already knows we took Charlie to the vet. And he knows I have Lyme disease. Might as well use this opportunity to make it look like I don't know the phone is bugged or whatever it is they do to know what I search for." Anna found a few articles on dog side effects. All of them listed lethargy with possible warmth of the skin or sensitivity at the injection site.

"That sounds like a possible side effect for any vaccination," James said.

"I agree." Anna scrolled through a site. "Wait. It lists less-common side effects: anaphylactic shock and possible immune disorders."

"You mean the dog catches Lyme disease from the vaccination?"

"It doesn't state that outright, but it sure sounds like it. Harm can be done to the dog's blood cells, eyes, or kidneys." Anna pulled the curtain aside to look at Charlie inside the car. He wasn't sitting up, so she couldn't see him through the darkened windows that were cracked a bit for fresh air. "Maybe I should just go check on him."

She started to scoot out of the booth as James took out his keys. "Let's try this first." Anna watched as the windows went all the way down. A moment later Charlie poked his head out and looked around. Anna waved at him. He wagged his tail. "Do you think he can get out? Should I close the windows a bit?"

"Maybe just a few inches." Anna watched Charlie pull his head back inside the car as the windows went up a bit. "He's such a good dog."

"They all are," James said.

"Ah, yes. No such thing as a bad dog—"

"Just a bad dog owner." James finished the sentiment for her.

The food arrived, prompting Anna to put her phone away. The toast looked the same as what was on James' plate. Sure enough, when Anna asked if it was gluten free, the waitress realized her mistake. As she went to fetch a new batch of toast, Anna wrapped the mistake in a napkin. She looked up and saw James watching her. "Oh, sorry. Do you want it?"

"No. I think Charlie will appreciate it more."

"Just trying to be a good dog...well, not exactly owner...friend, I suppose."

"Have you ever had a dog?"

"Just one?" Anna explained that she grew up on a small farm that had a reputation for taking in strays and unwanted pets. "At one point we had a baker's dozen of dogs."

"That's crazy."

"We also had goats, chickens, sheep, rabbits, cats, horses, and cows," Anna said.

"Is that all?" Anna smiled big at the question. She enjoyed telling people about her unusual upbringing. "How did you come by all those different animals?" James wanted to know.

"The local farmers knew if a mother rejected her baby, I was willing to nurse it to health. We got a few that way. Some we bought—like the time my mom wanted an azalea for Mother's Day, but my dad bought her a goat and named it Azalea."

They shared a laugh. "Did she like it?"

"I don't recall what her exact reaction was, though I do remember her buying her own azalea and planting it."

"Do you have any animals now?"

"Good grief no. As the oldest, all the barn chores fell to me. Before I could take a shower, get ready for school, or eat breakfast, I had to traipse back and forth to the barn lugging five-gallon pails of water. I hardly ever finished my chores with dry pants. Then in the afternoon, I had to do it all over again."

"Sounds like a lot of work."

"It was. But I also learned a ton from them. Besides two male dogs that didn't get along and a few too many roosters at one point, we never had a problem with the animals being unfriendly toward each other. The sheep would sleep with the horses. A crippled cat we had slept with our German shepherd. There was even an owl who returned every year to our barn. He would fly down to a post near the food bins and eat a handful of feed I'd leave there for him—or her—while I finished with the rest of the animals."

"Sounds kind of magical."

"I didn't appreciate the chores and all the animal hair on my clothing as a teen. But now I can see that you're right—it was kind of magical." Anna smiled as her thoughts took her back to that time and place in her life. She drifted off recalling the friendly bull who liked it when Anna entered his paddock and scratched his neck. That reminded her of the time they thought her pony was pregnant, which prompted her dad to build a special oversized birthing stall. Near the due date, Anna slept in the barn next to a cutout opening overlooking the stall. She was determined to be ready when the moment arrived. Unfortunately for her pony, it turned out to be a false pregnancy, complete with all the physical signs that she was with foal. Anna now wondered if she was making that part up—remembering things incorrectly—or if a phenomenon such as false pregnancy existed at all.

Anna looked up and saw James studying her. When she met his eyes, he smiled big.

"Sorry. I kind of got lost in my nostalgia." Anna looked away, feeling those butterflies return to her stomach, and upset with herself for having the sensation.

"No need to apologize."

Anna appreciated his undivided attention as she told him tales of her life on the farm. She wondered if she had dismissed such a life too easily.

***

*Anna surprised herself with her happy memories of **farm life** and how much she missed the animals. While it was hard work, she was happy she had experienced such a life when she was growing up.*

For snapshots into life on a farm, visit Anna's "Farm Life" board on Pinterest:

https://www.pinterest.com/anna_mcgrory/farm-life/

Chapter 29

Back at the estate, Anna confided in May. "I feel like such an idiot. I'm married and yet..." Anna couldn't finish her thought.

"You're married. Doesn't mean you can just shut off the part of you that enjoys someone's company. Especially when he pays such close attention to you."

"I feel like simply entertaining any improper thoughts is as good as cheating."

"You feel guilty. That's normal. But you didn't do anything wrong, so don't beat yourself up." May stood and padded over to her knitting bag. She pulled out a small book and handed it to Anna.

"*The Pocket Pema Chodron*?"

"I've been reading this and one of her longer books. This is just excerpts from her other works, but it's helped me to explore and accept my feelings. She actually advises that we not hide what we've been taught to think of as our negative emotions. Instead, we need to meditate on what we're experiencing so we can get to the heart of what we really think and feel. From there, we can accept ourselves—foibles and all—as we grow in our self discovery."

"You sound like you should have your own book."

"I'm learning. I think."

"I've been meditating daily, or nearly so," Anna said. "Quieting my mind. Focusing on my breathing."

"So now just be in your feelings, whatever they are, without judgment."

"I don't know if I can do that."

They sat a moment in silence. May had a thought. "What if it were me who confided in you that I had such thoughts about someone."

"Do you?"

"Not now. But once, a few years back, I couldn't help fantasizing a bit about what it might be like with someone I'd just met," May said. "I didn't act on those thoughts, but I still felt guilty."

"You can't blame yourself for runaway thoughts," Anna said. "Our minds and emotions so often just run amuck up there."

May looked directly at Anna. Anna smiled. May smiled.

"Thank you," Anna said.

"My pleasure."

She and May decided to meditate together. Anna sat and tried to quiet her mind, focusing on her breathing and simply acknowledging her thoughts as they appeared, but not dwelling on them. It felt good to meditate with her friend. She thought she could feel their energies swirling together and combining. It made her feel stronger. Like she could face any challenge in her life, even unwelcome thoughts and feelings.

When they finished, Anna stayed behind to reach out to Tom. "Are you coming home this weekend?" she texted, wishing it was a message she had received from him.

"Ha. Very funny. So, are you?"

"Do you have time for a chat?" Anna's stomach twisted in agony as she waited a full two minutes. Just as she was about to text him again, her phone rang in her hand.

"Tom. Thanks for calling."

"I literally only have thirty seconds. Maybe a minute. Client meeting."

"Oh, okay. Well, if this is a bad time..."

"No. Just tell me: you're not coming home this weekend, right?"

"Right, I'm afraid."

"Why not?"

"I was sick again at the beginning of the week—a bad reaction to the meds—so I'm behind."

"You're feeling better now, though?"

Anna smiled. He cared. She knew it, but she wanted to hear him say it. "Yes, I am. Thank you."

"Nice of you to take Charlie to the vet this morning."

"It was nothing. I certainly owe Sheila and Shep plenty." Anna realized something. "Wait. How did you know that?"

"Talked to Sheila today. She told me Shep was ill."

"Oh. Right. Of course."

"So, next weekend then?"

"Yes. Lola's shower is Sunday. And Joanie and I made plans Saturday."

"Girl's day out?"

"Exactly. It's been a while."

"What if I make reservations for the two of us at Angelina's for dinner that night?"

Anna loved that Tom remembered it was her favorite place. It was the only Italian restaurant she'd ever eaten at that reminded her of the food her grandmother used to make. "That sounds like a scrumptious idea."

"Consider it done. I have to go now. You take care."

"Yes. Right. You too." Anna heard the line go dead before she got a chance to say it, but she said it anyway: "I love you." Her shoulders slumped. When had they stopped saying I love you to each other? The ache in her stomach grew as she recalled a conversation they had shortly before Anna got sick. It was a one-way conversation mostly: Tom telling her he wanted out of the marriage. That he wasn't in love with her anymore. Anna was shocked and heartbroken. She hadn't seen it coming. She slept in their son's old room that night, and the next day, while Tom was downstairs at his office, she packed a suitcase and went to stay with May and Jim. After only a week, Tom asked her to come back home. He wanted to talk things through.

Anna returned just in time to get swept up in the last details of Joanie's wedding. She and Tom pretended so well, Anna actually began to think she'd imagined his confession. When she got sick, nothing more was said about it. Anna only now realized that Tom had probably just tabled the discussion until she was feeling better. Maybe he was ready to again move on. But if that were true, why propose a romantic dinner for two at her favorite restaurant?

Anna joined James and May in the main house of the estate. They had returned to the chore of dividing the inventory while they pondered whether or not to ask Margaret before they dug, or to talk to her about it afterward. James continued to check each item for hidden patient notes while Anna and May tried not to reveal the truth with their facial reactions. A knock at the front door saved the two women from laughing at the sight of James turning over a lamp and removing the felt bottom; it was too much seeing him work so hard only to come up empty handed again and again.

Anna and May both headed to the door. "Do you think we should tell him?" May asked.

"I don't know. I feel guilty, but I'm still not sure what he might do."

"Not sure what we'd do for amusement if he found out," May said, prompting both women to laugh.

Anna's laughter stopped when she pulled back the curtain next to the door. "It's him."

"Him who? The weird doctor?"

"No. But now you say that, I guess it could be worse." Anna opened the door. "Senator Ponema. What brings you here?"

"May I come in?"

Anna saw James enter and nod almost imperceptibly. She stepped aside to allow him in. As he crossed the threshold, Charlie bounded in almost knocking the senator down. "Charlie! Say you're sorry." Anna enjoyed seeing the senator flustered. "Sorry," she said on the dog's behalf, though everyone knew she didn't mean it.

"Perhaps I may be permitted to sit?"

They walked into the chaotic living room.

"You've been busy," Senator Ponema said as he sat in the only chair not filled with various art pieces.

"Trying to finish up so the estate can finally be settled," Anna said. "Fortunately, I have great help."

"I'll go put the kettle on," May said, wanting to be of help in another part of the house.

James cleared a space on the sofa so Anna could sit. He stood next to her, alert and ready for anything except what the senator said next.

"I want to apologize for the commotion at the wake."

"Really?" Anna couldn't believe it. She wondered what the senator's real end game was.

"Yes. Really," he said. "I'm not sure how you and I got off on the wrong foot, but I'd like to propose a truce."

"We've been at war so long, I'm not sure I could adjust to us being allies."

"I think we could be friends."

"Let's take it in baby steps, shall we?" Anna thought back to the first time the senator had hurled nasty rhetoric in Frank's direction. It was during Frank's original campaign for U.S. Senate. The then-junior Senator Ponema backed his party's opponent, which was understandable. But the lies he spun were unconscionable. Frank and his team never trusted the senator after that, always keeping him at arm's length or further away when possible.

James nudged Anna's shoulder, waking her from her remembrance. She looked at Senator Ponema's outstretched hand and took it reluctantly. He shook so hard, Anna thought her arm might detach. "Allies," the senator said. "I can live with that. Thank you, Anna."

May called from the next room, announcing the coffee was ready. Senator Ponema let Anna's hand go and headed toward the kitchen. "Coffee! That sounds perfect," he said as he left the room.

Anna stood and faced James. She wasn't sure what to say. She wondered if she was being punked, though to say so seemed too cliché. "Do you trust him?"

"Not in a million years," James said.

"I wonder what his endgame is."

"Do you trust me yet?"

Anna was surprised by his blunt question. "More than I trust the senator."

"That's not saying much."

"Nope. Sorry." Anna locked eyes with James. She wanted to trust him. She thought she might even actually trust him completely. But this business with the senator had put her off. She couldn't be sure what she felt. She wondered if James knew her inner struggle. Or her attraction to him. Maybe it wasn't even him she didn't trust, but herself when around him. She looked away, suddenly ashamed.

"I see." James turned and headed in the direction of the coffee, leaving Anna to once again appreciate her lack of tears. She was sure her frustration and confusion would ordinarily produce a flood right now.

The next morning, Anna woke to soaking wet sheets and the shaking chills. Her head felt like she was suffering from a hangover, and her ears buzzed with the sound of a thousand cicadas. Uncertain where she was, she scanned the room for clues. Seeing the antique dresser she had always not-so-secretly coveted, she realized she was at the cottage. She threw off the soaked covers and sat up, making her head ache in a way she had never felt before. It was both a sharp stabbing pain and a dull constant ache. Her ears refused to let up, and she panicked when she realized she was gasping to get a deep breath. She stood, but teetered unbalanced. Finally she called out a pitiful "May?"

She sat again, too dizzy and out of breath to take a step. She lay down and rolled to the other side of the queen bed where she found the covers were dry. She had hoped they might be. She tried to get a large enough breath to call out to May again, though she wasn't sure what her friend could actually do for her. Finally, Anna simply did the only thing she could manage: she closed her eyes and returned to sleep.

Anna dreamt she was on a spaceship being poked and prodded by alien beings. A bright light shone in her eyes, making her squint in pain. When the light abated, Anna awoke and opened her eyes for real.

"Good morning." It was Dr. Rory Matthews, her urologist in the Berkshires.

"Am I in the hospital?"

"No. Tom called. Asked if I would look in on you."

"After I called Tom." Anna turned and saw May standing nearby. Through the half-open door beyond, she could see James pacing. May turned in the direction of Anna's gaze. "We were worried about you."

"Is Tom here too?"

"No, hon. Said he had a client meeting he couldn't cancel." May looked sad as she answered. Anna wondered if May saw the hurt in her own eyes too.

"Ouch." Anna looked down at her arm where a needle had been inserted.

"Sorry," said Dr. Matthews. "Know how much you hate needles. Thought I could sneak it in while you were chatting with May."

"Blood tests?"

"Just to confirm. Or as much as I can, at any rate."

"Confirm what?"

"Babesia." Off Anna's confused look, Dr. Matthews said, "It's a protozoan spread by ticks. You'll need a new medicine. I'll call it in before I leave." He pulled out the needle. "There. That didn't hurt that much, did it?"

"I guess not." Anna tried to look away from the needle and her blood within it. She was known to pass out upon seeing blood and needles. She wanted to remain conscious until she understood what was going on.

The doctor had a list of questions regarding symptoms for Anna, all of which confirmed for him his suspicion of Babesia—the dizziness, night sweats, ear buzzing, and air hunger. "Once you've eaten something, you can take ibuprofen for your headache and fever. You should also take the new medicine with food."

"More antibiotics?"

"Nope. This time it's a drug used to treat and prevent malaria. Generic version of Malarone. Designed to kill the parasite that's making you so ill."

"How could she have gotten this?" James was too agitated to wait in the hallway any longer.

"As I said," Dr. Matthews said, "we're seeing it quite frequently from a tick bite."

"But why now? She's been treated for Lyme for so long, how could this have been missed before?"

"It may have been incubating in her system all this time. Or, chances are she was bitten again. The ticks are so small—"

"Yes, I know. The size of a sesame seed," James said. Anna appreciated how aggravated he was on her behalf. She felt like she had her own personal Lyme advocate. She wondered if there was such a profession. Maybe she could do that after Frank's estate was settled. And once she was well again.

"In their nymph stage, yes," Dr. Matthews said.

"Could she have gotten this any other way?" James asked.

"There are some who postulate that Lyme and its co-infections are now being transferred via other pests such as mosquitoes and horse flies."

"I mean could she have been poisoned by someone?" The question hung in the air a moment. Anna wondered what James could be thinking.

"I've never heard of such a thing," the doctor said.

"But is it possible?" James pressed for an answer, sure he was onto a solid theory.

"I suppose so, yes, since it is also transmitted via blood transfusion and in utero."

"You're thinking the coffee?" May asked.

"I'm not sure," James said.

"He couldn't have known which cup I'd drink from," Anna said.

"He knew you're the only one who uses the cashew milk," said May.

"He also shook my hand so hard so that I thought it would fall off. I thought it was just that he squeezed it extra tight, but maybe he had a small needle in his palm?" Anna looked at her hand for any sign of a pinprick or rash, though she couldn't find one.

Dr. Matthews examined Anna's hand. "I don't see any sign of a pinprick, but then again, I probably wouldn't be able to find it without magnification."

Anna appreciated that he had looked, or had pretended to, but she suspected that Dr. Matthews thought she and her companions were being more than a bit paranoid right now. The doctor concluded his examination, called in the prescription, and left with instructions to call him should Anna get any worse, or if she didn't begin to improve within 48 hours.

As James drove to the pharmacy, May ran a bath for Anna and helped her into it. "It will be good to feel human again," Anna said. "Thank you."

"No need to thank me. It was James who drove me crazy asking when you'd come downstairs and shouldn't I check on you. I figured you'd gone out for a walk, but he was sure you were still in your room."

"He didn't check himself?"

"Didn't think it was proper." Anna smiled and thought that perhaps she could trust him after all. "When I finally checked in on you, I felt awful for having waited so long. He was right the whole time."

"Don't beat yourself up. I would have thought I was on a walkabout too."

"You do like your morning strolls."

"Especially with Charlie."

"Roger that. I'll see if Shep would mind if his dog visits you this afternoon."

"And for the night?"

"Whatever you need."

May left Anna to her bath, and to her meandering thoughts of whatever she needed. This time, she didn't stop herself imagining who she would most like to wake up to in the morning. And it wasn't Charlie.

***

Anna and May each found that **meditating** *alone, together, or with a group helped them feel less stressed and more joyful. They also discovered a number of books on meditation by Pema Chodron, a Buddhist nun and resident teacher at Gampo Abbey, Cape Breton, Nova Scotia, Canada.*

To learn more, visit Anna's "Meditation" board on Pinterest:
https://www.pinterest.com/anna_mcgrory/meditation/

Chapter 30

By the afternoon, Anna's headache had subsided and her temperature had returned to normal. She still had some mild imbalance episodes, but they only lasted a few seconds when she stood. Her air hunger persisted, however, and the ringing in her ears was deafening. She knew she was in for a ride yet again, but she was determined to work despite her symptoms. Charlie had come and gone, and, after napping most of the morning into the afternoon, Anna was ready to join the living. As she sat on the edge of her bed, she heard the front door bang shut below.

She stood and walked to her window. She saw James carrying a spade and walking in the direction of the family burial plot. She pulled on her jeans and a sweater, and headed down the stairs. She held tightly to the rail to keep her balance, but managed just fine considering her weakened state. She pulled on her boots and coat and grabbed a walking stick that she had considered ornamentation since it had never been used before. That she knew of, anyway.

Anna's pace was slower than she liked, but she was glad she could walk at all. By the time she caught up to James, he had already produced a small pile of dirt.

"What are you doing here?"

"Good to see you too," Anna said.

"I mean it. You should be in bed."

"I'll go crazy if I stay there any longer."

James resumed his digging. "At least sit down," he said as he plunged the spade into the dirt.

Anna hobbled over and sat on the granite bench—a memorial to Frank's grandfather, placed there by his grandmother so she could visit his grave every day, which she did till the day she died according to Frank.

"Any luck with the doctor's autopsy?" she asked.

James apparently didn't hear her as he grunted through his work. He was an unrelenting machine, moving several shovelfuls of dirt per minute. Anna felt bad for him, watching him work so hard. She wished she could help. Or that she had at least thought to bring him something to drink.

They both heard it at the same time: the echo of the shovel hitting the coffin. James quickly worked his way around the wood, clearing the last shovelfuls until he could open the lid. He handed the shovel up to Anna as she stood over the grave watching. Reaching, he unclasped the lid and opened. Anna screamed. She couldn't help it. Instinct and fear prompted her visceral reaction. She covered her mouth and quieted herself. Staring in disbelief, she asked the obvious: "Where's the body?"

James didn't have any more idea than she did. Though he did share with her the news he'd just received: the doctor's body had gone missing too. He had just taken the call, which is what prompted him to finally dig up Frank's grave without asking Margaret's permission.

"Maybe we should tell her now," Anna said, though she couldn't think how they would manage that conversation.

James closed the coffin and walked back to the estate to get the tarp, spikes, and rope while Anna waited. When he returned he saw her eyes were red. "You managed to cry?"

Anna nodded. "A few tears. Not nearly as much as I wish I could."

She watched James seal up the hole, and accepted his arm when he offered it, appreciative of his help as they plodded back to the estate.

May had brewed a fresh pot of afternoon coffee. The three of them were joined by Shep, who brought fresh pizzas from their favorite place—including a gluten-free, cheeseless vegetable pizza for Anna. It was Shep who had given the supplies to James so he could cover the grave. He was in on the odd happenings now, whether he wanted to be or not.

None of them cared to consider how best to tell Margaret they had opened Frank's grave or what they found there. Or didn't find. They knew they shouldn't be discussing it in the kitchen, so they had adopted a simple code—easily understood by anyone who might know what they were discussing. Yet still they chatted about whether or not to tell Margaret that the jar of bread and butter pickles Sheila had put up for her was actually empty, and that they had no idea how that could have happened since the lid was still sealed.

"I'm glad you're feeling better," Anna said to Shep during a lull in the conversation.

"I'm sorry you're not."

"Will Sheila be joining us?"

"She's still visiting her sister," Shep said.

"I thought she would have come home soon as she heard you were sick."

"You didn't tell her, did you?"

"No, I thought you did. Tom said he talked to Sheila."

"You told Tom, and he told her?"

"No, he told me she told him."

"I'm so confused," May said.

"That makes two of us," said James.

"So how did Sheila know?" Anna wondered out loud.

"She didn't. Or she would have come home by now," Shep said.

Anna agreed with Shep. His wife was the doting type who took excellent care of her family and friends—especially her husband. Anna set down her pizza and left the room. An idea was forming in her mind. And it wasn't good. She had to be certain before she shared her thoughts with the others. In her bedroom, Anna grabbed her phone off the charger and dialed. The ringing phone sounded over her speaker. "Hello. This is Tom McGrory. Sorry I missed your call. Please leave a message and I will get back to you."

After the beep Anna said, "Tom, it's me. Call when you get a moment, please. Thank you. Love you." She closed the phone and realized if what she thought might be true, she wasn't sure if she could love him anymore. And if what she thought were true, she was sure he hadn't loved her in a very long time.

"Knock, knock." May stood at Anna's open bedroom door and watched her sit, eyes and fists clenched tight. Anna exhaled a primal cry. "Oh my heavens," May said as she hurried to her best friend's side. "What is it?"

Anna jumped up, spooked by her friend. She signaled one moment as she opened her phone and synced it with a wireless Bluetooth speaker she rarely used. She turned up the music and said, "We've been worried about trusting the wrong man."

"Shep?"

"No. Tom."

May gasped. She sat on the bed. "If that's true, then I think the time has definitely come to trust James. You need his help on this."

"I wish Frank had said something about him, or left me a note that proved he trusted him."

"You mean beyond that?" May nodded to the Keep This Coupon laminated ticket.

"Maybe it is the original, after all."

"I think it'd be harder to fake than you think. Especially if Frank never showed it to other people."

"I'm not sure if he did or not."

May sat and thought a moment. She realized, "Margaret trusts James!"

"Margaret trusts Tom."

"Touché."

May turned off the speaker and said to Anna, "I'm sorry you're feeling so exhausted and depressed. I think the best medicine is a little walk around the pond. Come on." May helped Anna up as if she really needed the extra hand. She usually did, but her adrenaline had kicked in and was masking her Lyme, Bartonella, and Babesia symptoms.

James was waiting at the bottom of the stairs. "You okay?" He asked Anna as May continued to hold her friend's elbow.

Anna nodded and pointed to the door. James looked confused.

"Nothing a walk outside can't cure," May said. "Perhaps you'd be so kind as to join her? I'm tuckered."

"Of course," James said.

As James pulled on his shoes and his jacket, Anna mouthed the word "tuckered?" to her friend. May shrugged. Mugging for the microphone could be tricky. An occasional lapse into some preconceived notion of what she might say if she spoke the truth was to be expected. Wasn't it?

James held Anna's jacket open for her, helping her into it. May remained behind to clear any dinner mess, though she didn't need to since James and Shep had cleaned the kitchen already. Instead, she grabbed her knitting, turned on the gas fireplace, and settled in to continue her project.

Outside on the path, James reached for Anna's hand.

"I'm okay," Anna said. "Feeling better in the fresh air already."

They walked to the pond and stopped near a large rock at the shore. "Tom and I used to bring a blanket here so we could sit and watch the stars."

"Sounds like a nice way to spend an evening."

"It is."

James followed Anna's gaze over the surface of the pond where the half moon danced on the dark water.

"I think Tom's been spying on me. On all of us."

"Why do you think that?"

"He knew you and I took Charlie to the vet today."

"You mean yesterday."

"Oh, right." Anna had a fleeting thought, wondering if she'd ever be clear headed again.

"Shep didn't tell him?" James asked.

Anna shook her head no. "He said Sheila told him, but…" She trailed off, unable to find her words since the hurt ran so deep.

"Sheila doesn't know that Shep was sick. That's what the conversation was about earlier."

"He must have bugged the cottage and the estate, or know who did."

James was suddenly concerned. "Do you have your phone?"

"Not on me. Why?"

"No. That's good. They can be rigged to listen in on conversations."

"I told May that. Or maybe she told me. I don't remember now. But it's part of the reason we started using burner phones."

"When you thought I was spying on you."

"Before that. When we noticed the creepy senator showing up every time we found something of Frank's that he wanted."

"Have you told Tom about finding the file?"

"What file?"

"I know you and May have it. I'm not as stupid as I look."

"I don't think you look stupid."

"I know you didn't trust me before, but telling me about Tom seems to indicate maybe you trust me now."

"I'm still trying to decide if I really do." Anna said. She grew quiet, and

James didn't interrupt her thoughts. She felt like she should trust him, but she couldn't think of a reason why beyond the raffle coupon. She thought about the look on his face when he opened up Frank's grave and realized she might finally have her proof. "You seemed genuinely surprised that Frank's casket was empty."

"I was. But I wasn't. Since I had heard from the sergeant in New York about the missing doctor's body."

"Oh my gosh." Anna put her hands over her mouth as she let out another of her primal screams. She fell to her knees and yelled, "No!" And for the first time in weeks she cried heaving sobs.

James knelt down and tried to hold her, but she couldn't be touched. She shook him off and continued to sob. He sat on the damp, dew-covered grass and let her get it out of her system. Finally she reached the stage of deep, stuttering, breaths. She wiped her face with her sleeve and murmured, "Do you think Tom could have...killed Frank?"

"I'd be lying if I said the thought hadn't crossed my mind."

"We were here, returning the presidential china we'd borrowed for Joanie's wedding."

"Meaning he had opportunity," James said.

"And, if I'm right about him, he may have had motive too."

"An autopsy would have helped," James said. Seeing Anna's pain, he added, "It still might have been suicide."

"Do you really think so? After all the strange things that have been going on?"

"No. But if it looks like a penguin and waddles like a penguin..."

Anna smiled. She loved that he had changed the cliché to include her favorite animal. But how did James know that about her? She watched him as he stared across the water, still uncertain how much she was willing to trust him. After all, she had been married to Tom for more than a quarter century and she had only just tonight realized she couldn't trust him. James turned and looked at her, causing her to look away.

"Still don't trust me, I see."

"I'm afraid to," Anna said. "How did you know about penguins?"

"They were my mom's favorite animals. It was her saying. Why?"

"They're my favorite too. The Adelie penguins in particular."

"The little Arctic ones that waddle like this?" He stood and did his best impersonation of an Adelie penguin, with his hands out at his sides like flippers.

Anna couldn't hold her smile. "Yes, that's it."

"That was my mom's favorite kind too! What are the odds?"

"I thought you knew that from spying on me."

James stopped his silly waddling. "I don't spy on you. I keep an eye on you. There's a difference. Why not take the coincidence as a sign you can trust me? I mean, how many people even know about that particular breed of penguin, much less call it their favorite animal?"

"Probably more than you think," Anna said.

"Really?" He stood, contemplating.

"They're so darned cute."

"But I hear their colonies stink. Guano, or something like that. Is it called guano for birds?"

Anna wasn't sure, nor did she want to think about the realities of life among the Adelies. She'd probably never get to visit them in the Arctic, so it was enough for her to just enjoy photographs and videos of them.

As James sat again, Anna wondered why she couldn't just trust him completely. She wanted to. She needed to, if only to trust somebody—anybody—but especially someone who was in a position to actually help her navigate all the weirdness she now faced. Finally, in an instant, she decided she would trust him. "My dad's favorite animal was a—"

"Walrus?" James finished for her.

"No," Anna laughed. "A turtle. Who has a walrus as their favorite animal?"

"You mean besides me?"

"That's exactly what I meant," said Anna, who hadn't meant that at all.

***

*What is your **favorite animal**? Has it always been your favorite, or is this a recent development? The Adelie Penguin has been Anna's favorite animal for as long as she can remember.*

To see some of the favorite animals of Anna's friends and family, visit Anna's "Favorite Animals" board on Pinterest:

https://www.pinterest.com/anna_mcgrory/favorite-animals/

CHAPTER 31

Though it was late, James and Anna convinced May to join them for a nightcap out at the diner where the two women had tried to eat the night James had slipped them the secret note. It was more crowded than Anna or May liked, but that was to be expected on a Saturday night. They got lucky and found an empty booth in an alcove. As James went to hang up their coats, Anna took out the file and spread it out on the table.

"What are you doing?" May sounded genuinely surprised.

"He's suspected we had this all along. I think he can help us," Anna said.

"So you do trust him."

"Let's just say I've decided to take a gamble on him. Like you said, we need his help."

May reached into the bottom of her knitting bag and pulled out her own photocopies of the file, along with the notes she and Anna had pulled together.

"The infamous file." James said as he sat and started reading. "It's a cover up?" He looked up at Anna and May.

"That's what we've determined. The Lyme controversy has been going on for some forty years and doesn't seem to be letting up," Anna said.

"What proof do you have?"

Anna frowned. "Only speculation. But why else would Frank and the Lyme doctor have to die?"

"Maybe it has nothing to do with Lyme," James said.

"But Senator Ponema wants this file on Lyme patients badly enough to keep pestering us," Anna said.

"And to poison her," May said.

"Again, speculation," James said. "Though I suspect you're right." He told them about having the jelly jar tested that the senator had brought Anna as a gift. James was surprised when the results turned out to be negative. "The technician thanked me for the delicious jelly though."

"Oh no! I actually enjoy his wife's homemade jelly," Anna said.

"I'll make you some," May said. Anna and May shared a knowing smile. Years ago, May had tried to teach Anna how to can vegetables and fruit, and to make jellies and jams. Anna was a horrible pupil, but she did enjoy sampling May's work. Now every fall May set aside a couple jars of nearly everything she canned to give to Anna. For her part, Anna made sure to supply May with plenty of fruit and vegetables and fresh lids. It was one of the many symbiotic qualities of their friendship.

"I see all the correlations you've made to doctors, places, and dates, but I don't understand why these particular patients are so unique. I mean, any one of these doctors must have seen hundreds of patients. Why focus on this small group? Have you done any digging to see if you can find information on any of them?"

Anna and May told James how they had conducted oblique searches from different library computers in the county. "We didn't want to start searching each patient's name for fear of tipping someone off that we were looking for these particular patients," Anna said.

"You both watch a lot of detective shows, don't you?"

"You mean we could have searched each patient's name?" May asked.

"More than likely," James said. He stared at his glass a thoughtful moment and added: "Though, I must admit if someone knew who was listed in the file, the names could have triggered an alert."

"Better safe than sorry," May said.

"What did you search for if you didn't type in patient names?"

"We typed in a few names. Just not more than one from a particular doctor or from the same town," May said.

"And?"

May flipped over one of the sheets of data to a chart and pointed. James read.

"Wait." It was Anna. She realized something as she pored over the patient interviews. "The dates they got sick." She rifled through pages of interviews, skimming the interviews, looking, pointing, and circling the information.

May grabbed a couple of the sheets with Anna's circles; James grabbed a few others.

"They were diagnosed at different times, but—"

James cut May off, finishing for her. "They each trace their illness back to about the same time. Late summer, early autumn 2005 here, September or October 2005 on this one, and September 2005."

"This one is specific to the date: September 23 to 25, 2005. And this one is the last week or weekend in September," May read aloud.

"Another September 23 to 25 here. Something about being away at a retreat and coming back feeling awful," Anna said. They grabbed the remaining interviews, including the copies of the ones Senator Ponema now had.

"They're all at the beginning of autumn or September 2005 in this pile."

"This one too," May said. "How did we miss this?"

"And listen to this," Anna said. " 'Sure it was the weekend we were at the camp on Old Stone House Lake in Southern Berkshire County.' "

"They were poisoned?" May asked.

"It sure looks like that," James said.

"It's like the Tuskegee study all over again," Anna said as May excused herself and left the table. Anna was comparing the CDC's refusal to acknowledge the existence of Chronic Lyme to the 1932 Tuskegee Study by the Public Health Service, working with the Tuskegee Institute, which studied 600 black men—399 with syphilis and 201 who did not have the disease. The study was questionable at best in the early days, but crossed an ethical line when sick patients were not offered penicillin when it became the drug of choice for treating syphilis in 1947. Instead, patients were offered free medical exams, free meals, and burial insurance as the conditions of the worsening illness were studied.

According to the research Anna had done some years earlier while helping one of Frank's younger constituents with a report she was writing, in 1969 the CDC reaffirmed the need for the study to continue and had the support of the local medical societies. It wasn't until the first news articles appeared in 1972 condemning the studies that it was finally shut down. Afterward, the U.S. government settled a $10 million out-of-court agreement and promised lifetime medical benefits and burial services to all participants, which was eventually expanded to include wives, widows, and offspring.

"Do you really think the government is knowingly putting so many people at risk?" May asked, returning to her seat a minute later.

"I'm not sure how else to explain things like the faulty tests that miss more occurrences of Lyme than they catch," said Anna. "And when doctors do treat for Lyme, they're chastised by colleagues or sued until they can no longer help their patients."

"We learned that one the hard way," May said, referring to the nightmare at the wake.

"I'm beginning to think that if we were to follow the money trail, we'd find that lobbyists for the pharmaceutical and insurance companies are buying the silence of our U.S. Senators and members of Congress," Anna said.

"There's little doubt lobbyists hold an unnatural sway on our political system," May agreed.

"It's an awfully cynical view of our government," James said.

"Says the government worker," May said.

"I can't help thinking the entire government system is stacked against the ordinary citizen," Anna said.

"That's a pretty broad accusation to throw around," James said.

"You mean as a retired secret service agent you're offended that I would even postulate such a theory?"

"No, I'm not saying that at all. I'm just pointing out that we are rather slim on evidence and generous on speculation."

"There are the two missing corpses to account for," Anna said. "That's evidence."

"But evidence of what? Foul play?" said May.

"I'm just pointing out that it's something we have that's not pure speculation. As is the number of people who were infected on or near the same date."

"It was a peace rally," May said, reading from the smart phone she had been holding just under the lip of the table.

"You're using your phone?" Anna was suddenly scared for all of them.

"Relax. I borrowed it from the waiter."

"What excuse did you use?"

"My battery died. And we needed to settle a bet."

"Are there any photos?" James asked.

"Tons. What are you looking for?" May handed the phone to James to scroll through.

"I don't know. I suppose it's too much to hope we'd spot a familiar face there."

"The senator would have sent someone to do his bidding," Anna said.

"Like him?" James held up the phone to Anna so she could see the familiar face staring back at her. She couldn't believe her eyes. It couldn't be. Could it?

James showed May. "I don't understand," said May. "Why would—"

"So, who won the bet?" The waiter delivered their late-night snack of potato wedges and ranch dressing, with a modified dressing made especially for Anna's dairy-free, pepper-free diet.

James deftly closed the window and cleared the history before handing the phone back. "Looks like we all lost this one."

"Hmm." The waiter eyed them as he grabbed his phone.

"Thank you, though," May said. "Really appreciate it."

The waiter turned to leave and turned back to the table again. "Were all your batteries dead?"

"Excuse me?" Anna said.

"Everyone has a smart phone these days. Except your table. What gives?"

"Busted." It was James. Anna and May looked at him in alarm. "We agreed no phones on our outing tonight. Imagine our surprise when all three of us actually lived up to that agreement and left them at home."

"So, you all lost the bet since you used my phone."

"Exactly."

It seemed it was enough to pacify the waiter as he headed for the next table.

"Now what do we do?" May asked.

It was the three-million-dollar question. Anna opened her mouth to say something. James and May looked her way. She closed her mouth again and shook her head no. A full thought had yet to form. She was still too stunned by the face looking back at her, with an arm around an apparent new friend, Patient Number Seventeen, or Two, or whatever number that person represented.

"Well, I don't know about you two, but I'm going to eat. These look amazing," James said, helping himself to a small plate and filling it with potatoes.

Anna had to agree that they looked delicious. She was happy they'd decided to go out, even though it was long after her normal bedtime. Luckily, she had thought to grab her newest medication—the generic version of Malarone, the medicine commonly taken by travelers to countries where malaria is a known problem. Because Babesia is a malaria-like parasite, Malarone had apparently been found effective in fighting it as well.

She'd meant to take her second daily dose at dinner, but her Lyme fog struck again and she forgot. She knew she was supposed to take the medicine at about the same time each day, but figured this once she'd be okay on a different schedule. She wondered out loud if any of the patients in the file had been dealt any co-infections on top of their Lyme. Her question sent the three of them sifting through the file again to see if they could find an answer.

***

*How do you help yourself **feel better** when you're sick? From gluten-free, vegan chicken-noodle soup to taking a warm bath, Anna is still searching for that perfect therapy.*

For more information, visit Anna's "Feel Better" board on Pinterest: https://www.pinterest.com/anna_mcgrory/feel-better/

Chapter 32

The next day, the trio completed their work at the estate. It was about time the rest of the items were properly sorted, stowed, and otherwise accounted for. Now that James knew where the file was, he no longer searched every painting. Thus, the moving of the rest of the items in the estate took less than a day to complete. Though Anna was certain Tom knew exactly when they completed their task since he must be the one listening in on them, she called his office and left a message with his practice manager that the estate was complete and the next move was his. Once his stiletto-heeled colleague had finished all the appraising work, Margaret could finalize the conveyance to the Trustees.

While it had been decided a local white glove service would move most of the items Margaret wanted with her in Boston, James and Anna wrapped up a couple paintings, including the artwork by Anna's son, and packed them in the trunk of James' car. James followed May and Anna in May's car as they headed out of town, up toward the hairpin turn, where they stopped for lunch and to discuss next steps. Jo and Glen were expecting them since Anna had phoned ahead on her last burner phone.

At the restaurant, Jo met the trio and ushered them up to their apartment where they would be away from any curious ears as two separate private parties dined on each floor. The table was already set for them. In almost no time, a waitress brought in their food and water. "I'm going to help Glen, but if you need anything, just poke your head out and give a holler," Jo said before she left them.

James was impressed with the service, friendship, and privacy, and said so.

"Wait till you taste the food!" May was an enthusiastic supporter of everything Glen and Jo created.

Anna loved that her best friend enjoyed herself here. As she watched May settle in her seat, though, Anna struggled with setting down her bag with the file. She had so many questions that she wasn't sure where to start. "Should we work and eat?" Anna asked.

"Oh please," May said. "Let's eat first. Then work. I mean, look at this! It'd be a crime not to give it our full attention."

How could Anna refute that logic? She sat and enjoyed her meal—all gluten-free, dairy-free, soy-free, bladder-friendly foods that tasted so much more fantastic than she ever thought possible when she first began her restrictive diet. "I feel like we should photograph this meal and share it with the world. I wonder how many others are suffering like I am?"

"We're not suffering now," said May. "This is incredible."

Anna laughed. She enjoyed her friend's fervor over the coconut rice with fresh shallots and garlic, and the authentic Cuban black beans, which was one of Glen's signature dishes even before his wife got sick and had to alter her diet. But the piece de resistance was the gluten-free, dairy-free yeast bread. "I think I could eat this entire loaf on my own!"

"You'll have to fight me for it," May said.

"Me too," James said. "I'm not sure I can stop eating, everything's so good."

"Why thank you," said Glen as he stepped into the room carrying a pie.

May clapped her hands. She was positively giddy. "What is it?"

"Coconut cream. My own secret recipe." Glen reached to remove the breadbasket to make room for the pie.

May grabbed the basket before he could touch it. "I'll keep this safe right here. Thank you very much." She made room next to her plate.

Glen laughed heartily. "I love that you're all enjoying my cooking so much!" As the trio peppered him with compliments, Glen ducked out again, explaining that he was needed in the kitchen to finish serving the second of the two parties. He hoped that he and Jo would be able to join them once the food service was finished. He'd called in an extra hand to help with clean up today. Anna appreciated his support, but felt guilty, wondering if it was right of her to include the culinary couple in their discussion. She wasn't yet sure what they were facing. It was bad enough she'd put May in harm's way. "We should have gone to the cabin," Anna said, leaving out all her thoughts about her worry.

"Are you kidding? And miss this meal?"

"I was thinking the same thing," James said.

"That we should have gone to the cabin or that you wouldn't want to miss this meal?" May asked.

"A bit of both, maybe," James said to May. He turned to Anna. "Though they already know enough to be at risk."

Anna knew it was true. If there was someone who wanted to harm her and her friends for what they knew, it was already too late. Anna pushed away from the table, suddenly anxious to get started. She grabbed her bag and carried it to the sofa, where she opened the file on the coffee table. They had made a quick stop for another two burner phones, pads of paper, tape, markers, and pens. She pulled the office supplies out, opened a new pad of paper, tore open the pens, and tapped a green one against the empty paper. "Okay. What do we know? What do we think we know? What do we need to know? What do we guess? And why in heaven's name would anyone even care about this stupid file?"

"Do you want a piece of pie? It's delicious."

Anna glanced at her friend annoyed. Her mood softened, however, when she saw May's look of bliss. "In a few minutes. Thanks."

Anna stood and paced. "Why would anyone want the file?"

"Yes, that's a good place to start," said James. "It must be tied with the date and place the patients became ill."

Anna flipped a page and wrote, "How was the Lyme disease transmitted?" She tore out the page and set it on the coffee table. James stood and read it aloud as Anna resumed her pacing, dropping the pen once and the pad of paper twice in the process.

"Tell you what," May said. She was moving her plate aside and clearing an opening on the table. "I'll take notes. You two talk."

"I'll gladly let you take notes," said Anna, handing over the pad of paper and pen, "but I want to hear what you have to say too."

"Don't worry. I won't be shy."

James handed May the loose sheet as he joined Anna in the pacing. Because it was such a tiny room, they frequently had to stop and allow the other to pass in front of them. "We might owe Jo and Glen a new carpet at the end of all this," May said, nodding at the footpath they were wearing into the rug.

"They don't want us to know that they poisoned the patients," said Anna.

"Did they poison them?" May asked. "At Tuskegee they didn't cause the syphilis."

"Another question then: Did they poison the patients? Or did the patients somehow contract Lyme at an alarming rate? Maybe other peace rally attendees were fine?"

"We should see if we can learn whether there were other incidents of Lyme traced back to the camp from people who attended at different times."

"If it was an accident, why the need for the file?"

"It wasn't an accident," Anna said. She was starting to see some of the pieces come together. "Frank interviewed those people for a reason. Maybe he felt guilty. Maybe he was the one who poisoned them. He had opportunity, after all." Anna referred to the photo they had found of Frank standing with a camper and smiling for the camera.

"Frank might have been an inadvertent carrier of the Lyme disease bacteria," James said. "They—whoever 'they' is—could have planted it on him knowing he was going to meet with them."

"That's another bunch of questions that needs to be asked: Was that group targeted for a specific reason? If so, why? Who is behind this? What did Frank know at the time? What did Frank later learn if he wasn't in on it from the beginning? How did he know to interview these people, unless he was in on it from the beginning, or learned of the experiment, if that's what it was?" Anna sat. "We have more questions than answers. And I don't know which ones are the most important."

"Should we just give the file to Senator Scary Pants?" James and Anna looked at May. "I mean, Senator Ponema."

"I know who you mean," James said. "I'm surprised we haven't asked that yet."

"Would he kill other doctors?" Anna asked.

"If he killed anyone. It's still possible there were two suicides," James said.

"Then where are the bodies?" Anna asked.

"Oh yes, good question! Deserves a page of its own." May wrote it at the top of a blank piece of paper and tore the page off.

Nearly an hour later, Anna and James weren't sure how much progress they had made. But May smiled at the transformation of the three doors and two of the windows in the small space where she had hung all the sheets of paper with their questions, grouping them together by subject matter. She placed pens at intervals to encourage the others to add questions and notes to them.

"Now what should we do?!" Anna sat on the sofa, frustrated and tired.

"I can do some of the computer research," May offered.

"I can contact a buddy of mine who's still in the service. He might be able to get us some answers to things that might be classified."

"Isn't that dangerous?" Anna asked. "Can we trust anyone else?"

"You trusted May and your friends here at the restaurant," James countered. "I've known him my entire adult life. We were roommates freshman year at university."

"Not trying to be a pain. Just asking."

"Sorry. Didn't mean to get so defensive."

"You guys can kiss and make up later," May said, causing Anna to turn crimson. "We need to hatch a plan and get back on the road. I would rather not drive at night."

James walked around the room, reading all the signs. Anna did the same, staying well away from him as she moved. May served herself another piece of pie and sat and enjoyed it, waiting till Anna and James had a plan.

James grabbed a pen and initialed a sheet: JRS. "I'll take this one."

Anna looked and nodded. "Yes. Good."

From the sofa, May pointed at the door that led to the restaurant. "I can take all those about the patients and doctors," she said.

"I'll initial them for you then, shall I?" Anna said as she did so. "And I can take all the ones on the disease itself. I have a doctor's appointment next week. I won't leave until he answers every last one."

Two of the sheets with the Lyme questions were on the door next to James. Anna pointed. "Oh, sure. I'll initial them for you. A. And what's your middle initial?"

"A is good. With your red pen, it looks like I got As on my papers."

"Playing the overachiever card now, are we?" May asked.

"Enjoying that third piece of pie now, are we?" Anna said.

"Absolutely! And if you knew what was good for you, you would at least finish your first."

Anna wasn't hungry, but she had to admit the pie was delicious. She took one more bite. But while she enjoyed the taste and the texture, she just didn't have the appetite to finish it. Ordinarily she'd be pleased to be able to walk away from a scrumptious snack. Not this time, though. Who knew when she'd get a chance to taste Glen and Jo's cooking again.

They pulled down the sheets of questions and handed them to each person. Glen and Jo hadn't even had a chance to join them. Anna felt better knowing that her two friends wouldn't know more than they had already learned during their earlier visit.

The trio decided not to accidentally-on-purpose find any more pages of the file in contrived hiding places for now. Not until they had a few more answers to their questions. They hoped their digging really would be secret and that they could trust everyone they approached in their search for answers.

It was decided that May would drive home from the restaurant and start in on one of her questions at a random library in the morning. She'd always wanted to visit every town in New Hampshire. This would give her a good excuse to see some of the ones still not crossed off her list as she traveled to various libraries to use their computers. Anna and James were heading to Margaret's. Somehow they had to tell her about digging up Frank's grave and his missing body. They owed her an apology, and agreed it had to be tonight. And in person.

Once that was taken care of, Anna would take the bus home where she would keep an eye on Tom and try to discover what he knew, who he worked for, and what he was up to. They still didn't know for certain whether or not Tom was listening in on them, but Anna had no other explanation for his knowing that she and James had taken Charlie to the vet and having lied about how he knew. Anna also had her list of questions for her doctor. Hopefully the answers would help the trio determine how the Lyme bacteria might have been transmitted to those patients.

James planned to drive to D.C. first thing in the morning. He intended to accidentally-on-purpose run into his friend. It wouldn't be too difficult.

James knew which senator his friend was assigned to. He also knew the senator's schedule was posted on his website. Once James found a public computer, he could memorize the itinerary, and make sure he just happened to be at one of the events.

"I feel like we should have a Super Triplets Powers fist bump or something," May said as they picked up the last of their things and headed for the door. Anna smiled. Her nerves would have been shattered long ago without her quirky friend. Anna held up a fist. May reached hers toward Anna's hand. James chuckled, but did the same. "Wonder Triplet Powers activated!" May said.

After carrying their dishes to the kitchen and saying farewell and thank you to Glen and Jo, the trio left, hopeful that they were on their way to gaining more answers than questions.

***

*Anna has discovered a whole world of **dairy-free, gluten-free, sugar-free** treats. They may not all be as sweet as some more traditional desserts, but since she's given up sugar, she has found that she only needs a small dose of sweetness now. Sometimes, she prefers no sweeteners at all. It's a good thing since her body can't tolerate any of the artificial sweeteners, either.*

For more ideas, visit Anna's "No Sugar, Gluten, or Dairy" board on Pinterest:

https://www.pinterest.com/anna_mcgrory/no-sugar-gluten-or-dairy/

Chapter 33

After driving tandem down the winding two-lane road of the Mohawk Trail, the cars exchanged honks in Greenfield, Massachusetts, as May drove north up Interstate 91 and James and Anna drove east across Route 2 toward Boston. Anna had tried to re-read their questions to herself, but found that doing so made her nauseous as the car navigated the curves. While they would have loved to debate Frank's role in all this and postulate what was going on, they talked instead about benign things, in case someone was listening in. The latest topic was fueled by the discovery that the patients interviewed in Frank's file had all gotten sick while staying off-season at a traditional lakeside summer camp.

"I went to summer camp on a lake once when I was a kid. What about you?" Anna asked.

"No. I was lucky just to grow up," James said.

Anna waited for him to expand on that comment. She watched him as he drove. His jaw tightened. So, too, did his grip on the steering wheel. Finally, she couldn't take it anymore. "Are you going to tell me more?"

"I'd rather not."

"Then why'd you say anything at all?"

"I don't know." James breathed deep. He glanced at her, and back to the road. "Sorry. Tell me about your camp experience."

Anna got lost in her memories as she shared with him her first ferry ride to a 4-H camp on Kelly Island in the middle of Lake Erie. She confessed that she had cried the first day and night there, but that after a week she didn't want to return home. Even now, she sometimes fantasized about living away at camp. She often thought about opening her own camp, though she wasn't exactly sure how she'd do something like that. Still, she enjoyed the daydream of running a camp for kids and teens.

"I'm surprised you'd consider doing something like that," James said. "Given your illnesses. And the ticks that cause them, I mean."

"But in my case, has it been ticks causing me to get sick or Senator Scary Pants?" They still weren't sure if it was possible to poison someone with Lyme disease and the various co-infections that Anna was now fighting. But they thought it seemed awfully suspicious that she always became more ill after the senator visited her. "Hear that, Senator? I know you had something to do with this!"

James laughed. Anna laughed. The two of them enjoyed the notion of Anna speaking directly to the senator via the bugs they suspected might still be in the car or embedded in their cell phones.

After a few minutes of thinking, Anna said, "Maybe I'll have a city camp. A concrete jungle—but in a good way—where kids can play, explore, and let their imaginations soar. Without the threat of ticks." Anna listed what she'd love to have in a camp: a theatre, art room, gymnasium and climbing wall, plus a huge kitchen to cook and bake in, and a library with tons of books and plenty of computers to write on that aren't hooked up to the constant distraction of the internet.

At Margaret's, Anna let the long climb up the seven flights slow her naturally. She was not anxious to face her. Nor was James, who matched Anna's slow pace. The doorman had buzzed ahead to alert Margaret that she had visitors. He also took their things up to Margaret's in the elevator for them. At the top of the stairs, Margaret's door was open and the delicious scent of homemade cookies greeted them.

"After dinner?" Anna asked James as they approached.

"Agreed." James said.

"Knock! Knock!" Anna said as she stepped into the foyer. Laughter greeted their ears. It sounded like a party was in progress. "I didn't even consider that she might have company," Anna said.

"Me, either."

"I hope we're dressed okay."

"You are. You look great today."

"Thank you," Anna said. She was appreciative of the enthusiastic compliment, but also wary. If she looked great today, did that mean she didn't usually look great? And should she be bothered or flattered that he noticed? Self consciously, Anna looked down at her left ring finger where her engagement and wedding rings had been fastened for more than two decades.

At the end of the hall, Anna stopped. She made sure her shirt hung just right, that she stood straighter, and she painted on a smile. She took a deep breath and turned the corner, ready to join the others. Except no one was there. Instead, she found Margaret sitting on the sofa and dabbing at her eyes as she watched a party on the TV, which was broadcast in surround sound. The delicious scent turned out to be a couple candles. "Margaret?"

Margaret patted the seat next to her. Anna joined her as James followed. Margaret grabbed Anna's hand and squeezed it tight. In her other hand, she held a handkerchief, which was obviously damp with tears. Anna watched a few moments and realized Margaret was watching footage of the surprise party on their 40th wedding anniversary. Anna and Tom had worked with Frank's D.C. team to pull off the event. Anna shot James a worried expression; this apology was going to be more difficult than either of them had imagined.

"There you are!" Margaret squeezed Anna's hand again, as a slightly younger Anna waved and smiled at the camera. Margaret's younger self stepped into the frame and put an arm around her. Frank stepped into the frame from the opposite side and slipped an arm around Anna too. Frank and Margaret each kissed Anna's cheek.

"I remember that," said James. Anna had almost forgotten he was there as she was transported back to that moment. As she watched the party, she wondered why she and Tom hadn't videotaped more events with their children as they were growing up.

The camera swooped past Frank to a mirror-backed bar where James stood ramrod straight and alert. Anna felt relieved to see him in the video. "There you are."

"I told you I worked detail for Frank."

"I never doubted you," Anna said.

James shot Anna a look. Anna flashed him a "Who me?" smile. James just shook his head. Anna hoped he was amused, but guessed he might be more frustrated that it had taken her so long to trust him.

The TV went off. Margaret held the remote. But Anna thought she had seen something. "Wait. Let it play a little longer."

"You saw it too?" James asked.

The television clicked back on and the video resumed. Sure enough, as the camera panned, it captured three men disappearing through a door: Senator Ponema, the weird doctor, and Tom. "It could just be the men's room," Anna said, knowing somewhere in her gut that it wasn't. "But men don't go the bathroom together, do they?"

"I remember the layout of the ballroom. It was not the men's room. Though it was, in a way."

Margaret paused the video. "How do you mean?" she asked.

"It's quite literally the backroom where all the deals were made. Our service swept it before the event and again after. But during, we weren't permitted in there. We were specifically warned by the director that night even though it was a commonplace standing order."

"Maybe we can fast-forward. See if the video captured when Tom emerged again. And who he was with when he left," Anna said.

"What do you hope to find?" Margaret asked.

"It might not reveal anything," James said.

"Or it might, since it already has." Anna reached for the remote. "May I?" Margaret handed it over and Anna fast-forwarded. The cameraman walked amongst the guests, prompting individuals to say a few words to the couple. It took a few minutes even at fast speed, but finally Anna was rewarded as another mirror in the hall captured an image of the strange doctor emerging from the room, followed by the senator.

"Is that the strange man who was so rude at Frank's wake?"

Anna confirmed that it was. "Do you know who he is?"

Margaret shook her head no. "I don't remember seeing him at our party. I wonder who invited him."

"The invitation list! That's brilliant. Finally, we'll be able to put a name to the face." Anna let the video continue to play as she told Margaret what little she did know about the odd doctor. The door opened again, and this time Tom stuck his head out, looked around, and stepped out. Anna froze the image. "He look guilty to you?"

"I don't know," Margaret said. "Maybe he's just looking to avoid having to talk to the doctor again."

"I remember that," James said. "I knew I recognized him from somewhere. My partner ran a check on him to make sure he wasn't flagged."

"And you're just recalling this now?" Anna asked.

"He was clean. People look suspicious for a variety of reasons. Maybe there were hookers in the room and he didn't want his wife—uh, I mean you—to see. Or perhaps he wanted to avoid a specific guest. Once they're checked, they're forgotten—unless they come up hot, of course."

Anna let the video play the few more minutes to the end, but none of them saw anything more that intrigued them. "Do you think I can make a copy to watch later?"

Margaret wasn't sure what Anna's suspicions were, but she thought that might be Anna's business and didn't want to intrude. "Of course."

They sat a moment in the quiet, with only an occasional distant car horn to remind them they were in the heart of Boston. James cleared his throat. "Margaret, there's something I need to tell you."

"We need to tell you," Anna corrected.

"I was the one who made the decision to proceed."

"I would have too, if I hadn't been so sick."

"Just tell me already!"

"We dug up Frank's grave. I'm sorry. We should have asked you first," James said.

Margaret eyed them both. James sat tall and proud, but Anna withered in Margaret's gaze. She was too much like a second mother to her. Anna felt horrible for having betrayed her. "I know you wouldn't have done so without a solid reason. So, what is it?"

They told her about their suspicions that Frank and the New York doctor, whose wife Margaret had gone to camp with as a young girl, might have been killed and staged to look like suicide. Margaret gasped and reached again for Anna's hand. It was painful to think that her husband may have been murdered. Yet, somehow that was more comforting than imagining him taking his own life.

"And what did you find? Or what did the coroner discover?"

"That's just it," said Anna. She swallowed and tried to find the words. "The casket was empty." Anna felt Margaret's grip weaken as the widow fainted into the sofa pillows behind her.

"Well, that went better than expected."

Anna looked at James in alarm. "Shouldn't we do something?"

"I think you two have done quite enough, don't you?" a male voice said.

***

Anna enjoyed her time away at **summer camp**, *learning to sail, swim, canoe, and make lanyards. She'll be looking for a new job now that her position as assistant to a U.S. senator and his widow is winding down. Perhaps running a summer camp is something she can do.*

To learn more, visit Anna's "Summer Camp" board on Pinterest: https://www.pinterest.com/anna_mcgrory/summer-camp/

Chapter 34

Tom entered Margaret's condo. "What were you thinking, digging up Frank's grave?"

Anna stood. "Tom. What are you doing here?"

"Answer the question."

James instinctively moved to protect Anna, positioning himself between her and her husband.

"What are you doing? It's not like I'm going to shoot her."

"You've been spying on us," Anna said.

"It's 'us' now, is it?"

"No, not in the way you're insinuating. I mean all of us. Including May and Shep and Sheila and probably Margaret, for crying out loud."

"I haven't been spying. I've been watching out for you."

"That line's already been taken," Anna said.

As Tom talked, he walked around the sofa, prompting James to move so he was always between Tom and Anna. His instincts were well honed after years of training and practice. James had only been shot once, taking a bullet in the shoulder for a visiting dignitary—the result of a domestic squabble not entirely unlike the one he thought he sensed growing now. Anna appreciated his help on the one hand, but was also frustrated when she couldn't meet Tom's eyes since James kept blocking her view.

"Why would you dig up the coffin?"

"You didn't say body," Anna said. "Why didn't you say body? You knew, didn't you?"

Tom's jaw visibly tightened. James reflexively prepared for an attack.

"Maybe we can talk this through in private."

"I don't think that's a good idea." It was Margaret. She had awakened and unbeknownst to anyone had dialed her phone, which was resting on the sofa cushion near her. "I've called security. They'll escort you out."

"It's not like that! I'm not the bad guy here! I was told to watch and listen and to report any suspicious activity to..." Tom trailed off, realizing he'd just said too much.

"Who?" James asked. "Someone I know?"

"I wouldn't know who you know."

"CIA? FBI?"

"I can't say."

"Are you working with Senator Ponema and that weird doctor?"

"Doctor Hale? No."

"Is there a problem here, ma'am?" One of two security guards announced himself with his question as he strode into the room.

"I'm not sure yet," Margaret said. "Stay a few minutes, please." The guards stood, on alert and ready. They were more than the typical rent-a-cop. Not that Anna had any disdain for rent-a-cops. She had been one in college. It was a good way to pay the bills. She had worked the weekend shift, assigned to an office building. Since she only had to do rounds once every hour, she had plenty of time to do her homework. One of her roommates hated that she got paid to do her homework and complained to Anna almost every day for a week—until Anna brought her an application so she could try her luck at landing a similar gig. She did, and ended up liking it so much that, last Anna knew, she had started her own security agency.

"There isn't going to be any problem, is there, Thomas?" Margaret asked. Anna loved that she used his formal name. Margaret only ever did that with anyone when she was truly upset with them.

Tom sat and hung his head. All eyes were on him. No one moved a muscle. Finally, Tom took a deep breath and said, "I'm famished. Let me take you all to dinner." He looked at the guards. "You can join us if you want." Tom looked from each set of eyes to the next, unable to rest on any one pair. There was too much accusation in any of them.

"We can talk in my neighbor's condo."

"No. We can't. Not after the last time we met there," Tom said.

"I'm feeling like dim sum," Anna said.

"Margaret? That okay with you?" Tom asked.

"Can you even eat that?" James asked Anna.

"Probably not. But I've been craving it for weeks now. Ever since May reminded me about our book group's discussion last summer. We were hoping to find a book we could read that had dim sum in it just so we'd have an excuse to drive into Boston and eat in Chinatown." Everyone looked at Anna. "What? So my mind meanders. May understands this." She looked pointedly at Tom. "And she accepts that about me."

"That's because her mind wanders too," Tom said. Anna wasn't sure whether Tom meant the remark to be a slight or to make her feel better. She was out of her depth with him. She wondered when he had started down the path that led to his new identity. He definitely did not seem like the man she had married.

"Dim sum it is," Tom said. He turned to the guards. "Boys? Care to join us?"

The guards looked at Margaret. "That would be highly irregular," she said.

"We'll bring you back some then," Tom said. Anna wondered why he seemed to be feeling jolly all of a sudden.

"Yes, we can do that, right, Joseph?" Margaret asked.

"Yes, ma'am. Thank you." The other guard cleared his throat. Joey took the hint and added, "Finn would love some too, I imagine."

"The more the merrier!" Tom said, following the guards to the door.

"What are we doing?" Anna whispered to Margaret and James when Tom disappeared around the corner.

"Getting answers," James said. Margaret said nothing, but her look seemed to convey that she agreed with James, though Anna couldn't be certain.

Anna stopped and popped the DVD out of the player. She slipped it into its protective cover and into her shoulder bag, which she grabbed from where the doorman had left it near the entrance.

In the hallway, Tom held the elevator door open. The two guards were still with him. "It's a tight fit, but I think we can get everyone and still be within the load limits." Margaret joined him, but Anna stopped at the top of the stairs. "Ah yes, my wife doesn't like cramped spaces."

"Or boxes held up by a few flimsy wires braided together in a cable," Anna said. "I'll meet you downstairs."

"They're not flimsy wires," Tom said.

Anna headed down the stairs. James followed her.

Tom snarled. It was subtle, but both Margaret and Joseph noticed. "It's good you're jealous," Margaret said as the doors closed. "I was beginning to think you no longer had any feelings for Anna."

Tom just stared ahead, watching Anna's feet descend the stairs through the small window in the ancient elevator door.

"You okay?" James asked as he followed Anna down the stairs.

Anna stopped and turned toward him, but the action was too fast for James to copy. He stepped right into her, and the two went tumbling down the last two steps to the next landing. Their feet were tangled, but otherwise they managed to land side by side, facing each other. Anna felt tears spring to her eyes, but instead of crying in pain or frustration, she started laughing.

"Sorry," James said, as he joined her in the laughter. He helped her up. "Okay now?"

"Nothing's broken. Physically anyway. Mentally I feel like my entire world is falling apart."

"It does look that way."

"Well, you're no help," Anna said as she started down the stairs again.

"Don't say that."

"Relax. I was only kidding."

"Okay. Good. Because the one thing I want to be is helpful to you."

"You are. You have been. Without you and May, I would never have gotten through all this so far. And there's no way I'd be able to face whatever is next."

They continued down the rest of the floors without talking. Anna wished her mind had been as quiet as the two of them were. She had a million questions that she knew should have been about Frank and the doctor and their missing bodies, and the list that she, James, and May had brainstormed at the restaurant. Instead, Anna obsessed over whether Tom still loved her anymore. And whether she still loved him.

***

*If there's one thing Anna loves, it's **dim sum**. While she's not sure she can eat much of that sort of thing any longer, she might be willing to try.*

To see other restaurants Anna enjoys, visit her "Restaurants" board on Pinterest:

https://www.pinterest.com/anna_mcgrory/restaurants/

CHAPTER 35

The first restaurant they tried was mobbed, as was the second, and the third. It seemed every tourist in the world had swung through Boston's Chinatown that evening. They decided to do dim sum another time. Tonight they needed to find a quiet spot to eat where they could hear each other speak. Anna was disappointed, but also figured it was a blessing in disguise since she wasn't sure there was anything she could eat in any of the restaurants without paying for it the next day.

They took a cab to the Parker House where Margaret had called ahead and was able to secure Frank's favorite table. It sat in the back corner and provided a reasonable amount of privacy so he could mix business with pleasure. Anna was surprised Margaret was able to get any table so easily on a Thursday night—and especially Frank's old table. Anna wondered if Tom had called them earlier in the day, or if Margaret was in on whatever it was Tom was up to. Her head hurt. She didn't like questioning the motives or loyalties of everyone she knew.

Anna desperately wanted to order something to calm her nerves. While to some that might entail alcohol, Anna craved chocolate. And not just any chocolate, but chocolate ice cream with chocolate chips and hot fudge sauce. When they walked in, she realized she was underdressed. Even if she did look great tonight, which she doubted since she was never a fan of her own reflection—a trait she hoped she hadn't passed onto her children—she wasn't dressed for the primarily business-casual crowd.

Meanwhile, Tom wore a tie like most of the gentlemen seated. It was unlike him to wear one except when he had a court appearance. Such was the luxury of being your own boss. Anna wondered why he had worn one now, again questioning whether he or Margaret had known they'd all be eating here tonight.

Anna ordered off the gluten-free menu, thankful she could at least still eat fish and meat. Her options were limited, but the chef was a friend of Margaret's and was someone Anna had worked with more than once to cater a private dinner at Frank's request. He conveyed through the waiter that he was happy to adjust the salmon dish so Anna could eat it without worry. As soon as everyone had ordered, Tom got down to business. "I want to tell you everything."

"Good. Please do," said Anna, unable to wait out the long, dramatic pause that followed his statement.

Tom explained how he had been approached by the ranking member on the U.S. House Committee on Oversight and Government Reform to serve as eyes and ears to any improprieties on the U.S. Senate Committee on Health, Education, Labor and Pensions since the Senate committee was thought to be improperly investigating the Centers for Disease Control.

"So you *were* spying on Frank. And on me. You were hoping I'd find that file. Or that before he died, Frank would reveal its whereabouts." Anna was angry. It was making eating near impossible, though the salad was too delicious to ignore.

"I didn't consider it spying, per se," Tom said.

"And what else would you call it, per se?" Anna countered.

"I suppose it was spying."

"Because of you, Senator Ponema has shown up each and every time we happen to find a patient interview."

"That's not me. He's on the committee I'm meant to report *on*, not to."

"Maybe so, but isn't it quite the coincidence that every time we've found something, the scary senator or his underling has shown up?"

"We also think he's been deliberately making Anna sick," James said.

"Is that possible?" Margaret asked.

"From what little I've learned through my contact, it is," Tom said.

"You knew he's been making me sick?!"

"I suspected. So I asked."

"Before or after my latest diagnosis?"

"I, uh—" Tom faltered, uncertain what he could possibly say.

"Did you know that now that I have Babesia, I can never ever for the rest of my life donate blood?"

"You've never donated blood. I would think it'd be a blessing." Tom cringed as he said the words.

Anna just stared at him. She couldn't believe how crass he'd become. While it was true that her fear of blood and needles kept her from donating in the past, she was still struggling to wrap her head around this latest diagnosis and its lifelong effects.

"Do we actually know if it's possible the senator has somehow been making you sick on purpose?" Margaret asked again, trying to quell the storm between Anna and Tom.

"I'll verify with my Lyme doctor this week," Anna told Margaret, as she glared across the table at Tom.

"My source wasn't sure if it's possible or not," Tom said.

"And does your source know if I'll ever get well again?"

"I don't know."

"You really don't care what happens to me anymore, do you?" It was almost whispered, but even people at the next table picked up on the desperation in her voice.

"No, that's not true. I just...do you really think we should continue to do this here?"

"I'm not anxious to be alone with the spy who's reported on me these past...how long have you been spying on us?"

"It began about the time Frank started interviewing patients. Apparently, that alerted someone high up that a senate member of the committee was doing something outside his job scope."

"He was only trying to get answers to a hideous illness that the government refuses to acknowledge," Anna said.

"Do you know that for certain?" It was Margaret. She seemed genuinely concerned that her husband might have been up to no good.

Anna looked at James, who nodded his agreement.

"From what we've found so far, it seems Frank discovered a group of people who were all poisoned with the bacteria that causes Lyme disease, and who suffered needlessly when treatment was denied them," Anna said, careful not to reveal that they had the file.

"Like the Tuskegee Study?" Tom asked.

"Even worse. Unless it's never been revealed that those poor men were infected with syphilis on purpose."

"I don't know if that question was ever asked," said Tom.

"You think my Frank was killed so he couldn't reveal what he found in those interviews?" Now Margaret was the one who sounded desperate.

"He seemed to think they had all been poisoned at the same place and time," James said.

"All of them? How do you know that? Unless you have the file," Tom said.

"We're inferring from his notations on the few patient interviews that have turned up," Anna said.

"Are you still reporting to your source?" James asked Tom.

"I'm not sure."

"What does that mean?" Anna asked. She was beyond frustrated with him and tempted to throw the elegant crystal water goblet that sat on the table in front of her at his head.

"It means I'm not sure if I should continue to do so since I'm trying to evaluate what is actually going on here."

"What's actually going on is you're spying on your wife and likely going to get her—me!—killed in the process," Anna said. She wondered if her shift into talking about herself in the third person meant anything dire. She worried it might mean she would soon be dead.

"Did you know about the bodies?" James asked.

"I knew Frank's wasn't in the casket when it was lowered into the ground, but only by accident." As they stared at him, Tom explained how he had offered a hand in moving the casket from the car to the gravesite. There were two fewer pallbearers than had been in attendance at the wake, and Tom figured he would help. When he reached for the extra handle, he was nearly pushed off his feet by the funeral director's son. The only thing that kept him from falling was that he had somehow managed to get a grip on the casket's handle before the shove. He knew the gesture was rude, and focused his attention on that. But something niggled at the back of his brain. When Shep called him to let him know about the empty casket, Tom realized it had felt light in his brief touch. And it didn't take a rocket scientist to work out why only four pallbearers were needed that day.

"Shep was helping you?" Anna was even angrier.

"He was my eyes and ears outside the cottage and the cars. We couldn't bug every surface of the estate property."

"Who else?" Anna asked.

Margaret raised her hand.

Anna closed her eyes and hung her head. "I wondered how you got this table so easily at the last minute." She turned and looked at James. He shook his head no. "Great. So the only one I thought was spying on me, wasn't. And May? Is she in on it too?"

"What? No. Of course not." Tom had no idea why Anna would even ask. Anna suddenly wished her best friend was here. She wished there was a Super Triplet Power ESP she could invoke. Anna felt a toe tap from beneath the table and looked at James, who she knew must have done it. He looked down to his thigh where his phone was on. The screen indicated May was listening in. Anna smiled despite herself.

"It's good to see you smile," Tom said.

"I'm not smiling for you." Anna pushed her chair away from the table and stood. James moved to stand too, but Anna stopped him. "Stay. Please. Sort this out. See if there's a way we can work together somehow, or decide what we do from here. I'm exhausted. I'm going home."

"Home? Where is that? You're never home," Tom said.

"I meant to May's. She's the only one I want to be with right now." Anna glanced at James, feeling guilty for saying that since she didn't feel angry toward him too. But he did confuse her. And right now, anything beyond pure friendship from her one true friend was too much for her Lyme-and-co-infected mind and body to handle. She simply wanted to sleep. And maybe cheat on her diet by eating a little—or tons of—chocolate.

On her way out, Anna stopped and bought the Parker House signature dessert: a Boston cream pie. She knew it had chocolate, gluten, corn syrup, and sugar—none of which she could eat, but she was going to have a piece or two anyway. She was sick of being sick, and if this made her even more ill, that was life. The staff person triple wrapped it with a bag of ice so it would keep cool till she could get it home to share with May and her husband.

She wasn't yet sure how she was getting home. She didn't have her car and she hadn't memorized the bus schedule. She recalled an Uber driver who had offered to drive her for a reasonable rate before, but she didn't know if she still had her phone number.

As she strode toward the front door, she was surprised to hear a man call her name from one of the plush chairs. She turned her head in his direction, but before she could respond a hand covered her mouth as another grabbed her arm and whisked her into a hallway and into an elevator. In a mirror, she saw the face of her assailant just before she passed out from the ether-soaked rag.

***

*Anna never was good at **giving blood**. The one time she tried to donate, she fainted before she even reached the tables. She felt so guilty that she donated her time instead, registering people who stopped in to donate a pint. While she fainted a few more times while helping out, at least she felt useful in the environment that was completely alien to her.*

To learn more, visit Anna's "Selfless Donations" board on Pinterest: https://www.pinterest.com/anna_mcgrory/selfless-donations/

Chapter 36

Anna shivered uncontrollably. As part of her mind teased out whether one could shiver controllably, another part of her mind took her on a visual journey of faces plastered on random animals running around together in a lively circus-style event in a large field. May was a rabbit, hopping about collecting beautiful flowers. Shep was a sheep dog chasing Charlie as the actual dog he was in real life. Sheila was a hen sitting on a nest next to Margaret, who was an owl on a high branch watching over everyone. James was a kangaroo, looking like he was searching for a fight. Tom was a lizard, climbing the tree where Margaret sat. The odd doctor was a grasshopper and Senator Scary Pants was a mole who kept popping up next to Anna. With no mirror to peer into, Anna looked down at her hands. They were the soft paws of a feline, possibly even a small wild cat like a lynx or a bobcat. She pounced and almost caught the Senator Scary Pants mole.

Odd voices penetrated her weird dream. Anna knew somewhere inside herself that she needed to wake up, but she was enjoying chasing the animals who had betrayed her in life. And she enjoyed watching May the rabbit as she now attempted to knit a giant afghan. Anna was so cold that she hoped May would finish the blanket soon and give it to her. Anna wondered if she was making it for one of her grand bunnies. Finally, it was the smell of chocolate that caused Anna to open her eyes.

"She's awake! Ask her." It was the odd doctor. What did Tom say his name was? She'd think of it eventually.

Martin, Senator Ponema's assistant, crouched near Anna's head holding a plate with a slice of the Boston cream pie by her nose. "It's good. You want some?"

Anna tried to answer, but her tongue felt like it was the size of her fist and her mouth was dry. She tried to sit up, but she couldn't move her hands to help herself. She realized she was lying on the floor. She could feel a strong breeze and knew she was near an air conditioning vent. Was she still in the upper floors of the Parker House Hotel above the restaurant where she made her grand exit? Did it matter? Would she die and her body disappear like the others? What did these men want from her? And how was she going to escape? If only she hadn't made James stay behind. She wondered if he or May knew she was missing. If so, they'd be looking for her. But what if Tom knew she was gone? Would he go looking for her? She honestly wasn't sure.

"Why isn't she talking?"

"For a doctor, you really are stupid sometimes, you know?"

"Don't call me stupid! No one calls me stupid!" Anna wondered if Martin knew he was hitting a nerve with the odd doctor or if it was just a lucky shot.

"The ether needs to wear off," Martin said.

"Now what are you doing?" The doctor was objecting as Martin cut the bands that held Anna's wrists behind her back.

"It's not like she's going to be able to use them yet." It was true. Try as she might, Anna could not move her arms. She wondered if it was a permanent effect, or if it would pass. Maybe if she did regain their use, she could pretend not to be able to and somehow escape. She wasn't sure if she could manage to pull that off, but she tried to concentrate on it so she wouldn't forget and accidentally move her arms in the meantime.

Martin reached and tried to help Anna sit up. "You're cold," he said. Anna nodded. Or at least she thought she did. She wasn't sure if any of her nerves were firing. "Help me pick her up and put her on the bed."

"I'm not touching that."

What? Had Anna just heard the strange doctor correctly? Had he really just called her a 'that'? What was wrong with him? And what was his name? Not that it much mattered. She didn't see herself escaping just to Google him anytime soon.

Martin struggled to lift Anna by himself. She reminded herself that his grunts and groans weren't because she was particularly heavy—she had actually lost all the middle-age weight she'd gained slowly over the years. She could thank her most recent bout with Babesia for that. Instead, she realized that because she couldn't move, she was effectively dead weight. The thought of that frightened her. She wasn't ready to think of herself as being dead. Not that she feared death; she was just determined to be around for the day when Joanie called to tell Anna she'd soon be a grandmother.

He dropped her only once, but Anna knew she'd have a headache from the loud thump her head made when it landed. She figured she'd have a headache anyway from being drugged. Had they really used ether on her? Anna wondered how much more it would have taken to kill her. Was that how Frank and the doctor in New York state had been killed? Did ether remain in the blood stream or in the lungs to be easily found during an autopsy? Was that why their bodies were taken?

Anna was frustrated by all her unanswered questions. She wished she'd gone into teaching or astrophysics or anything other than government work. Hadn't Frank once kidded, "This job'll kill you if you let it"? It was during the particularly grueling election process that ended up first taking Frank to Washington. Anna and most of Frank's staff had pulled several all nighters. They occasionally slept on cots in a storeroom. But the 24/7 slog paid off. Now Anna desperately wished Frank had lost that election. She wondered if Frank had ever wished he'd lost it too. In her mind she called out to him. "Frank? Can you hear me? If so, please send help!" It was her last complete thought as she passed out beneath the layers of covers Martin had wrapped her in on the bed.

When Anna next woke, she found herself tangled in the mass of blankets and sweating so profusely that she was soaking wet. She kicked off her covers and rolled to the side of the king bed. In the darkened room, a clock glowed 3:17. She hated the three o'clock a.m. hour ever since Joanie's friend had told her that it was the time ghosts could haunt you. Or was it take over your soul? Anna couldn't recall now. Nor did she believe any of it. Yet it still made her skin crawl.

Her stomach growled. She was starving, which surprised her since she had just eaten a huge dinner exquisitely prepared by the chef at the Parker House. Or had she? Now that she thought about it, she had left during the salad course. How could anyone leave before finishing a meal at the Parker House? Wait. Anna now remembered where she was, or where she thought she was, and how she got here. She strained to listen, wondering if Martin or that odd doctor was in the room with her. Doctor Hale! She smiled as she remembered his name. She frowned again recalling Tom's spying on her and the doctor's refusal to touch "that" and not "her."

Hearing nothing but the rumble of her stomach, she sat up. The lights clicked on. Motion detectors, Anna realized. She wished there were also bugs so someone would know she was here. Double doors opened as Martin entered.

"Good morning, sunshine!" He said.

"Why did you grab me?"

"Oh, good. The effects have worn off." Martin reached for her, but she instinctively pulled away. "Cooperate or I'll have to duct tape your wrists behind your back again." He touched her arm, and pulled his hand away. "You're soaking wet. Come on. I'll get you a robe. You can shower. The good doctor's sleeping anyway."

"I don't want to shower!" Anna said, immediately opposed to anything her captor offered. Her stomach growled.

"I suppose you don't want any of that delicious Boston cream pie either?" Martin helped her up and guided her to the bathroom. He pulled the door closed behind her, waiting outside.

"You're going to let me do this alone?"

"I'm not a pervert," he said. Anna could hear him rustling around outside the bathroom. He knocked on the door. "You still decent in there?"

"Yes, I haven't changed in the eight seconds since you left me," she said. The door opened a crack and he handed her a robe. "Why are you being nice to me?"

"It's not you I'm being nice to. I'm being nice to my nose. You stink." Anna slammed the door closed, almost catching his fingers.

"You're lucky you didn't get me! Try something like that again and I'll eat all that pie—or is it actually cake?—myself."

Anna looked in the mirror. "How am I going to get out alive?" She thought it rather than speak it. She was afraid Martin might hear her and answer that she wasn't. She didn't want to hear that yet. She looked at her eyes and worried anew. They were more bloodshot than normal. She wondered if she was already dying. How much could one body take? Ether, whatever it might have been mixed with, four prescriptions, two kinds of bacteria, and a parasite—she was not in great shape, and she had the low white blood cell count to show for it. What had it been? Below three. She didn't know what was normal, but she knew her GP and her Lyme doctor were not happy about the results of her recent blood test.

Her stomach rumbled. Anna was starving. And she suddenly had an idea. A wonderful idea. She hoped it wasn't awful too—like the Grinch. She shook her head, wondering how she could possibly think of the quote from her favorite Christmas tale at a time like this. "Martin?" She called.

"Yeah, I'm still here."

"Any chance I can have a piece of cake now? I'm starving."

She held her breath, waiting for him to answer. She heard him grunt and stand. His footfalls took him out of the room. She wondered if it was a multi-bedroom suite, or if this was the only bedroom. More importantly, was there another bathroom? She hoped so, and that Martin and the doctor would stay out of hers. She knew her life might depend on it.

She opened the door a crack when she heard Martin approach. "Thank you," she said, taking the cake from him. He had brought her what was left of it—about two thirds had disappeared. She was so hungry she could probably have eaten the entire thing. She knew she would definitely finish this much. "Sorry for taking so long; my head's so foggy, I feel like I'm moving through soup."

"It's okay. No one else is up anyway." She closed the door and heard him sit again. She wondered who the no one else included. He hadn't said the doctor wasn't up. Instead, he made it sound like there were others. Or maybe just one other—Senator Scary Pants. She thought that's who called to her in the lobby just before.... But she didn't want to think about that now.

If she was going to survive—and Anna had just decided that she was going to—she knew she must determine where the best place to leave a note might be. It had to be hidden from her captors if they used the bathroom, but found by staff if they were even permitted inside to clean it. She opened the cabinet beneath the sink and found extra rolls of toilet paper and boxes of tissues. There was already a back-up roll of toilet paper in the basket on the back of the toilet. Anna pulled out a box of tissues and set it on the shelf where the towels rested, figuring that this way no one would have cause to open the cabinet except the cleaning staff.

Now what to write? She thought about her message, trying to make it short. She still wasn't even sure it would work to use cotton swabs dipped in chocolate icing to communicate her needs. It took her a moment, but she finally settled on, "Help. Anna McGrory hostage. Call May Beale, Concord, NH." She wished she'd memorized May's phone number instead of relying on Siri to "Call May, home," or "Call May, mobile."

It took less time than she thought. It was so effective that after her shower Anna decided to dry off the wall and leave another message, closing the curtain and hoping no one else would need to use this stall. The last decision to make before she left the bathroom was should she brush her teeth after she ate the final piece of Boston cream pie or before so she could allow the taste of chocolate to linger.

***

Anna enjoys chocolate, especially when it's baked up in the Parker Restaurant's **Boston cream pie**. *That's one recipe she and May will have to try to recreate under Anna's dairy-free, gluten-free, and sugar-free regime.*

Anna loves her board "Deliciousness" and invites you to visit it on Pinterest:

https://www.pinterest.com/anna_mcgrory/deliciousness/

Chapter 37

"Tell me where it is now!" Senator Ponema bellowed. His face was so red, Anna hoped a cardiac event might be imminent. It was difficult for her not to laugh at him. He should have hired someone to interrogate her. Anna had never been interrogated before, but it seemed to her that he didn't have a clue what he was doing.

Martin, on the other hand, gave the distinct impression that he'd had some training. He was certainly an expert at taping her up. He had quickly taped her ankles to the legs of the chair where she sat, and just as briskly bound her hands behind her back. He had a velvet pouch unrolled on the table next to where he sat and divided his time watching the senator's questioning and playing an electronic game on his phone. Anna couldn't quite see what was in the fabric, but the glint of silver hinted at dental instruments. She wondered if he'd seen the movie *Marathon Man*. She desperately wished she hadn't since she couldn't shake the awful scenes of the Nazi dentist from her mind.

Doctor Hale—Stanley, she had discovered was his first name— disappeared into the next room. She wondered if it was another connecting bedroom or a bathroom. She still didn't know exactly where she was within the Omni Parker House, though she guessed it was the Harvey Parker Suite, which she'd only seen in pictures on the hotel's website. At least it was a classy place to be interrogated. Anna pictured others who had stayed in the suite named for the inn's founder. How different their experience must have been from hers—unless Mohammed Ali, the Grateful Dead, Ted Williams, Margaret Thatcher, and the ten unnamed presidents who had stayed here had duct taped guests to the custom cherry wood furnishings too?

Stanley returned with a syringe. He was pushing the liquid up and out the tip. Anna hated needles and had to turn away. "You don't like what my colleague has, do you?" Senator Ponema asked. "Tell me where the file is and I'll make him back off."

"What kind of doctor *makes* patients sick?"

"What kind of hostage refuses to answer questions?" the senator answered.

"You're probably not even a real doctor anyway," Anna said as Stanley approached her.

He stopped and blinked. Anna wondered if he was offended, or if he was a robot processing what she had just said, which is what he looked like. "I am a rheumatologist."

"I rest my case," Anna said. Her mean-spirited remark was based on her having read that it was a rheumatologist at Yale who was the cause of Lyme disease not being properly categorized, studied, and treated. She couldn't remember the details, but knew it was something many in the Lyme community believed to be true. She'd read about it in the book her Lyme-literate doctor had recommended she read.

Martin chuckled at Anna's comment as he continued playing his game. Stanley turned and looked at Martin. Once again, Anna wasn't sure if Stanley was offended by her statement and Martin's laugh, or if he was even capable of emotion. Stanley strode to Martin and thrust the needle in front of his face. "Careful!" Martin said as he sat up.

"You do it," Stanley said.

Martin took the needle and placed it on his velvet roll. He went back to his gaming. Stanley looked back and forth between Martin and the senator.

"It's okay, Stanley. If we need it, we'll use it." The senator turned to Anna. "All you have to do is tell us where it is and we won't need it."

"All I do is tell you where it is—if I even had the file—and I'd be dead," Anna corrected.

"Nonsense! No one here's going to kill you," the senator said. Anna caught Martin's pause in his gaming and his quick glance at her. Their eyes locked for a split second, but it was enough to tell her that her suspicions were accurate: they had no intentions of allowing her to get out of this alive.

"What about Frank and the doctor from upstate New York?" Anna asked.

"What about them?"

"Someone obviously killed them."

"As I recall, both were ruled suicides."

"What about the missing bodies?"

"What missing bodies?"

"Both bodies went missing. Tell me you didn't have anything to do with that?"

"Martin. The syringe, please."

"No. Please."

"Where is the file?"

"All I can tell you are the next places we were going to search," Anna said.

"We? You mean you and your friend May?" Senator Ponema asked.

"I didn't mean May. She was just helping me with my illnesses. All thanks to you, no doubt." The senator just smiled at the implication. "You did poison me with Lyme and the co-infections, right?" Anna hoped this time she could steer the conversation in a new direction and get some answers. Didn't the bad guys always divulge their super-secret sinister plots before killing the hero? Was she the hero? She wasn't sure what she was, but she was pretty sure hero was not exactly it.

"Such an imagination." The senator turned to the two men. "She really thinks we infected her with BB, Babesia, and Bart."

"We did." Stanley said it so matter of factly that Anna wondered if he was capable of telling a lie. That was it! She recalled the senator telling her the odd doctor was on the spectrum. He must have Asperger's, which wasn't what the medical community was calling it any longer, but which Anna thought was a much better name for what he had than autism. She had read that some Aspies couldn't tell lies, while others couldn't tell them convincingly. She wondered if she could use that to her advantage.

"I don't understand how you could do that to me."

"It's simple," Stanley said. "The bacteria and protozoa live in bodily fluids."

"I thought it was only transmitted via ticks."

"Borrelia burgdorferi, Bartonella, and the Babesia parasite can live in test tubes, flies, gnats, mosquitoes, and, of course, the guts of their mammal hosts such as deer and rodents. The infected liquid doesn't even have to be transferred into your blood stream. Just a splash of infected bodily fluids can transfer the organism to a new host," Stanley said.

"Why doesn't everyone know that?" Anna was flabbergasted.

"What if patients start thinking they can get Lyme disease from urine?" Senator Ponema said. "We'd have mass hysteria."

"People would be more careful, like when they have AIDS or syphilis," Anna said.

"We don't want people to be more careful," said Dr. Stanley Hale. "We want more people becoming ill."

Anna stared at him. She couldn't believe he was saying these things. "Why aren't you sick?" Anna asked as her mind grappled with the horror that these men were doing this to people *on purpose*.

"Naturally, we take precautions."

"How?"

The doctor just smiled. Apparently he wasn't willing to spill every secret.

"You devised an inoculation that protects you from the bacteria?"

"Of course," the doctor said. "We wouldn't unleash something we couldn't control to a reliable extent."

"Why aren't you sharing the antidote?"

"That's different from an inoculation."

"Whatever!" Anna was furious and frustrated. She hardly noticed Martin disappear into her room. "Why isn't the vaccine available to everyone?"

"It is a business as well as a philosophy," Stanley said. "Senator Ponema and I are members of the American Eugenics Society."

The senator stamped his foot in protest, but Anna pushed on. "Lyme disease is an elaborate eugenics experiment?"

"Not experiment. Phase. It was designed not only to improve the human genetic code, but to reduce the population."

"Then why obsess over one missing file?"

"I do not obsess."

"Your grumpy partner does." Anna and the doctor regarded Senator Ponema who was turning a brilliant shade of red. If he'd been a cartoon, smoke would be streaming from his nostrils. "What you're doing is evil."

"It's not evil. It's simply advanced evolution," the creepy doctor said.

"Gene manipulation is not evolution," Anna said, as Martin slunk back into the room and to his seat.

"Borrelia burgdorferi does not manipulate genes. It activates genetic mutations and inefficiencies, causing the weakest among us to get sick and to eventually die off."

Anna took stock of her own body, noticing that it was aching and she was exhausted. "Why not just kill us? Why make us so sick?"

"Dead people don't buy medicine." Dr. Stanley Hale turned and marched toward the door where he had disappeared before. Anna stared at him, too horrified to speak.

"Where are you going?" Senator Ponema asked.

"I'm going to take my nap." He closed the door behind him.

The senator nodded to Martin, who grabbed the needle and walked toward Anna. "Okay, okay," Anna said. "I'll tell you what I know—or think I know." Martin stopped and waited. "Given the not-so-random pattern that emerged from Frank's clever hiding spaces, I developed a list of next spots to check. It might be better if I write them down."

"Just tell me!"

"Okay, okay. Good grief, you're impatient."

"And you've been stalling for far too long."

"Forgive me if I don't really want to die yet."

"We'll keep you alive till we have what we want." That was exactly what Anna figured, which is why the last thing she was going to do was divulge the whereabouts of the file. Instead, she told them about the cabin in Western Massachusetts and she listed a couple places in Washington, D.C., that Frank frequented—the Smithsonian Museum of American History's National Quilt Collection, which he used to visit when he needed to clear his head. It reminded him of his grandmother and her sisters—happy memories of growing up. There was also his favorite seat at the Lansburgh Theatre, which was one of two venues where the Shakespeare Theatre Company performed.

She added in a Bed and Breakfast in the Pennsylvania hills—an out-of-the-way haven for the road-weary traveler, about halfway between D.C. and Frank's Berkshires estate. Frank used to enjoy sneaking in an overnight or even a weekend stay in the Naturescape Room of Santosha On the Ridge in East Stroudsburg. Anna could almost picture Frank really hiding a few of the patient interviews at the peaceful inn he loved so much.

At the end of her ramblings, the doctor emerged. Apparently a nap meant twenty minutes on the dot. No less. No more. Dr. Stanley Hale wondered why everyone didn't do it. He and the senator left on their mission to track down the final pages of the file.

Martin removed Anna's wrist bandages and unbound her ankles. "Don't try anything," he said.

"I don't understand why they even need the file." Anna looked at Martin, but he was silent. "Are they going to kill everyone who talked to Frank? Isn't it bad enough they infected them? Did Frank know that was what was happening when he went to that camp?"

"You ask too many questions," Martin said as he grabbed the room service menu off the desk.

"Did you know about the missing bodies?"

Martin handed her the menu. "Just tell me what you want to eat."

"Okay. But did you?"

"I can't talk about any of this with you."

"So you did?" Anna tried to read through the menu, but her mind was churning. "Did you kill them?"

Martin snatched the menu away. "I didn't kill anyone!"

"But you made sure the bodies disappeared."

"Enough already!" Martin grabbed her and led her into her bedroom where the bed had been made. He thrust her inside her bathroom. "Get cleaned up. I'll order you a burger and fries."

"On a gluten-free bun."

"Anything else, your highness?"

"I'll split a Boston Cream Pie with you."

"That's not gluten free."

"No, but it's worth the cheat."

Martin shook his head in exasperation and closed the door on her.

She listened at the door and heard his muffled call to room service. Her optimism spiked, having just seen that house cleaning had somehow managed to tidy up her room. While Martin settled in outside her bathroom door to wait for their order to arrive, Anna opened the cabinet beneath the sink. The chocolate note had been cleaned off. So was the one she left in the shower. Anna hoped that meant someone had figured out how to reach May.

Anna also realized that she hadn't seen the maid enter the living room area of the suite. That meant there must be a door to her bedroom that led to the hallway. How had she not noticed it before? She reminded herself she'd been drugged pretty heavily. She knew now what she had to do. She hoped Martin would leave her arms free so she could escape. If not, she'd need something sharp to cut her ties with later, which is why she slipped the complimentary sewing kit into her waistband.

Martin made Anna promise to ask no questions during lunch, threatening to throw her lunch away if she didn't comply. Anna was too hungry to ignore his request, so she remained quiet. After eating, Martin let Anna visit the bathroom one more time, and tucked her into bed. "You're not going to bind my wrists again?" Anna was surprised when Martin headed for the double doors without doing so.

"No need," he said. "You'll sleep well."

"You drugged me?"

"Be thankful I poured the contents of the syringe into your drink and didn't use the needle." He left, closing the doors behind him, though Anna was fast asleep before he did so.

***

*While Anna was pleased with herself for making up so many possible hiding spots that **Frank** might have used, the exercise made her realize just how much she missed him.*

Anna invites you to visit "Frank's Fave Places" on Pinterest: https://www.pinterest.com/anna_mcgrory/franks-fave-places/

CHAPTER 38

"Anna, Anna. Wake up."

Anna tried to open her eyelids, but they felt like they'd been sewn shut. Finally, she managed to open one. She saw Tom and wondered if she was dreaming.

"We don't have much time," Tom said.

Anna wasn't sure what there wasn't much time for, figuring that if it meant she didn't have much time for sleep, she should just close her eyes and eke out every last second she could of the activity.

"Anna! Come on, help me out here." Anna felt her body being pushed and prodded. She opened her one cooperative eye and saw she was sitting up on the edge of the bed. Tom was wrapping one of her arms around his neck, but Anna was falling forward.

Suddenly another hand had her other shoulder: James. "She's been drugged," he said.

"Really? What gave it away?"

"Sarcasm isn't going to help." Anna could feel her body being lifted and her feet dragging. "Stop. I have a better idea," James said. Anna felt like she was a sack of flour as she was hoisted up and carried. She liked this much better than having her feet dragged beneath her. At least now she could sleep again. She hoped she was imagining the almost-imperceptible grunts and groans as James hauled her to safety.

Anna's sleep took her to the jungle where she bushwhacked her way through a million mosquitoes dive-bombing her as she tried to get away. "I can't find a vein," one mosquito said. "She's dehydrated," another said. "You have to try again," yet another mosquito said. "I'll get a butterfly," the first mosquito said. Anna liked butterflies. Butterflies were calming. They were nice. They didn't bite people. But ouch! This one did. Anna tried to swat at it, but her arm was stuck.

"Anna! Anna! It's okay," a mosquito with the face of James said.

"Hold her still," the original mosquito said.

Finally the butterfly was done and flew away, but the sting of its bite was left behind. Anna just wanted to get out of the jungle. How she wished she were home. She imagined she had ruby slippers, and clicked her heels together. "There's no place like home," she said.

"She's really out of it," one of the mosquitoes said as it flew away.

"Yes, but at least she's with us. Even if only in her dreams," the other said as it joined its friend.

Huh, Anna thought. So, I'm dreaming now? In that case, I'll have a giant chocolate milkshake and fries. Oversize it, please, she said to no one since she couldn't manage to actually conjure up an imaginative chocolate milkshake and French fry store.

The next time Anna woke, she was in a new place. She blinked as the light from the window blinded her. Once her sight adjusted, she noticed worn and tired nautical ephemera, likely picked up beach combing or purchased at a tag sale. She looked around at the sparse furnishings: a dresser, a side table, and a lamp. She turned away from the window and saw a twin bed. Someone was asleep on it, their back to her. "May?"

The body turned. Anna tensed as she realized it wasn't her best friend. Was it Martin? Is this where she would meet her demise? "Hi, sleepy head," James said.

"You're not Martin." Her relief was evident in her tone.

"No. You're safe now."

Anna felt tears well up in her eyes. "Where's Tom? Or was I imagining that he was helping earlier?"

"He's here. It was my turn to watch you."

"How long have I been asleep?"

James looked at his watch. "Twenty-two hours and seven minutes, not counting however long you were out before we found you. Your chocolate note worked. Good thinking."

Anna smiled, grateful that her ingenuity had saved her. James told her that the maid had found the note under the sink first and, not being able to read it as she looked at it upside down, mistook it for a mess left by a toddler. She wiped it away and went about her task of cleaning and replacing toiletries until she saw the note in the shower. She wondered if it was real or a practical joke, but she took a picture of it before scrubbing it off. On her break she showed it to her boss, who was the one who tracked down May.

He also told her how he and Tom had sprung her from her room.

"There was a motion detector," Anna said. It was almost a question.

"I knew they'd have some system in place to make sure you couldn't escape," James said. "The maid must have triggered it when she went in to clean."

"Yes, I recall Martin going in to check. He said it was nothing."

"He also disabled the detector."

"Was he still there with me, in the next room?"

"We found no trace of him or of anyone."

"Senator Ponema and that creepy Doctor Stanley Hale were both there too. Until I sent them on a wild goose chase." Anna told James the places she sent them to look for pages from the mysterious file. As Anna became animated, she tried to sit up. "That creepy doctor admitted they made me sick." A sharp pain stabbed at her right front forehead, piercing through to the base of the left side of her skull. She pictured an ice pick puncturing her skull as she grabbed her head and moaned in pain.

James was up off the bed and at her side. He had water and some pills on the bedside table. "Take these," he said. "You'll feel better soon. It's the after effects of the morphine-ether cocktail they gave you to make you sleep."

Anna wasn't sure she'd ever feel better, but she took the medicine. A moment after handing James the glass back, she doubled over in pain. This time it was her lower abdomen. James helped Anna walk into the hall and to the bathroom. She caught a glimpse of the ferry as it passed by the window. "Are we on Cliff Island?"

"Great Diamond."

"What? Who's idea was that?"

"Your husband's."

"But I hate Great Diamond Island."

"All the better to hide you."

Anna smiled, realizing that Tom really did know her. He wasn't crazy about the posh Casco Bay island, either, since it catered to a crowd that made them both feel uneasy. At least Tom had brought her to the old side of the island with its traditional cottages from another era. They both liked this area much better. It was a more authentic Casco Bay experience in their opinion. Those who stayed at the Diamond Cove Resort were probably just as happy not to have Anna and Tom there, either. To each his or her own, Anna realized.

Anna was famished. Her last meal had been with Martin as his captive. Fortunately for her, Tom had put together a plate of some of her favorite things from her restrictive diet for her to enjoy when she awoke. She sat in the sunny window seat, a blanket across her lap, and nibbled at the plate of fresh vegetables, fruit, and a piece of gluten-free bread with cashew butter as Tom and James discussed what the next steps should be. Tom wanted to go guns blazing and take out the three kidnappers. James wanted to expose them for their conspiracy since they were obviously colluding with drug companies or someone high up in government to make so many people ill. Anna hoped a compromise might be reached where they could do some version of both, though she also hoped it meant that only the proper law enforcement officials would be armed.

"Who do you think the creepy doctor and Senator Scary Pants are working with?" Anna asked.

"Or for," Tom added. "And don't forget Martin. He's obviously working right along with them in this—whatever this is."

"I'm not so sure he wants to," James said, noting how the motion detector was disabled and that he'd left Anna alone. "I'm also guessing he's the reason Anna was knocked out but not killed by the drugs."

"I agree," Anna said. "I got the sense he was the hired henchman in the kidnapping, but not buying into what they were doing." She relayed how Martin seemed upset when she asked if he'd killed Frank and the doctor. "And the doctor didn't include him when he told me that he and the senator were members of the American Eugenics Society."

"Is eugenics still a thing?" Tom asked. It was mostly rhetorical. Anna just shrugged.

"I'd believe anything at this point," James said.

"Think we can manage to get a list of the members?" Tom asked.

"I'm hoping my contact in the service will be able to help us with that."

"I won't be surprised if we discover one or two big names," Anna said. "Probably deep-pocket corporate donors to the political corruption that is our system."

"Let's hope it tips us off to any members who might hold the reins of journalism outlets. Difficult to expose a conspiracy if the conspirators control the news," Tom said.

"So you do think it's an all-out conspiracy? Not just a few greedy people out to make a fast buck?" Anna was still trying to wrap her head around the possibility that her captors were part of a much larger network.

"The Eugenics Society must reach further than just a few greedy people," Tom said.

"I agree," James said.

"I'd like to get that senator and doctor alone, though," Tom said.

"I don't think they'd tell you anything," Anna said.

"I don't want them to talk," Tom said. "I'm just out for revenge."

"Thank you." It was weird, she knew, but in a way Anna was touched. She thought that maybe Tom did still care about her. But they had a mission, so she continued on without missing a beat. "You know that someone you were reporting to was sharing the information with Senator Scary Pants, don't you?"

"Yes, you already made that clear. Maybe James and his contact can uncover who it is."

"And if they can't?" Anna asked.

"We distribute the file and what you've told us as far and as wide as possible—every journalist you've ever dealt with on Frank's behalf, WikiLeaks, bloggers, Freedom of the Press Foundation, the works," James said.

"I can write a press release to accompany it," Anna said.

"Good idea," Tom said. "You're a great writer."

Anna smiled. "Thank you."

"You're welcome."

Anna and Tom held each other's eyes for a long moment before Anna got back to business. "So, what are we going to do first?"

"You're going to stay here and get better," May said as she traipsed into the room.

"May!" Anna said. She made a move to stand, but she was too wrapped up in her blankets and too exhausted to move.

"Stay there," May said as she approached and hugged her.

"I'm so glad you're here," Anna said.

"I'm so glad you're here too," May said. She choked up, too upset to say that she worried she might never again see her friend.

"Here's what we're going to do," James said, taking charge. "Anna, You're going to write that release, outlining your kidnapping experience and the information you learned from your captors. May and Tom, you're going to make as many photocopies as you can for general post and scan in documents to later email, adding it to Anna's narrative. I've bought an air-gap computer and—"

"Air gap?" May asked.

"It's not connected to the internet," James said. "I also have a printer and all the supplies. Tom, you need to list everyone you know on that committee you've been reporting to, and who's been helping you on the ground. We have to be prepared for one of them to betray us before we know who they are. Being ready is going to be our best defense."

"Be ready for what?" Anna asked.

"For the worst-case scenario," James said.

"They finish what they started," Tom said. "You told us yourself that you knew you weren't supposed to get out of there alive."

"I'm going to meet with my friend. See if I can get a probable list of the senator's criminal associates. And try to find Martin. His help saved Anna's life. Maybe he'll be willing to help us discover how deep this thing runs and who the players are."

"Will I be in hiding forever?" Anna asked.

"Only until we expose whatever's going on here," James said. "I think they kill to keep their secrets."

"What if it's not a conspiracy," May said. All eyes turned to her. "I mean, what if it was just a few greedy men out to earn some money by making many people sick?"

"Exactly," Anna said. "I said the same thing just a few minutes ago." Anna loved that she and May were so simpatico.

"Then hopefully we'll uncover that truth," James said. He grabbed his jacket and headed toward the door.

"You're just leaving? I thought you were supposed to protect me?"

James and Tom shared a look. "Tom is prepared to do that."

"Tom?" Anna wasn't so sure that was true.

"I've had some training."

"He's a better shot than me," James said.

Anna felt like she was meeting her husband for the first time. "When did you learn to shoot a gun?"

"It was part of my undercover training to work for the government. A just-in-case scenario."

"And have you had to use your just-in-case training yet?"

"This will be my first time," Tom said.

"You sure he's a better shot than you?"

"Well, that may be a bit of an exaggeration," James said. "But he can disable a target."

"And I suppose you're a black belt, May?"

May laughed, and everyone joined her, but it was a decidedly nervous laughter.

***

*The **Casco Bay Islands** offer an escape that feels like a world away, yet are easily accessible via the Casco Bay Ferry Lines, which links the rural islands to the bustling city of Portland, Maine.*

To learn more, visit Anna's "Casco Bay Islands" board on Pinterest: https://www.pinterest.com/anna_mcgrory/casco-bay-islands/

Chapter 39

"May is that you?" Anna was sure someone was standing inside her room. Had she just imagined it? She reached to click on the light, but it didn't work. "Tom? Are you here?" She tried holding her breath so she could hear better. Maybe the fan going off when the electricity went out was what woke her. Squeak! She did not imagine that sound. The floorboards creaked as someone walked across them. "Who's there?!"

Anna rolled off her bed between the twin beds and reached toward the new burner phone Tom had given her where it was plugged in on the bedside table. She grabbed it and in one quick move turned on the flashlight and shined it in the general direction of the squeaky floorboard.

"Ahh, too bright! Turn it off!"

Anna screamed at the sight of Doctor Stanley Hale as he shielded his eyes, holding a loaded syringe. What had he done to May and Tom, she wondered, but only for a split second as she tried to decide what her next move should be. The creepy doctor stood between her and the door. Somehow she'd have to coax him in closer so she could escape. Or she could jump out the window and risk breaking a leg or two. Anna stood and kept the light shining on him.

"You're not going to get away this time," the creepy doctor said.

Anna saw that she was able to keep him off his guard with the blinding flashlight app. She wasn't sure how to get him to move though. She needed a distraction. "Something's been bothering me about your little eugenics experiment."

"I told you, it's a phase, not an experiment."

"Phase, experiment...you say po-tay-to, I say po-tah-to," Anna said.

"That makes no sense."

As she tried to get in a better position, she took a step toward him. He recoiled, stepping to his left. Anna wasn't sure if her conversation was helping to distract him, but she also realized she could manipulate him simply by making it look like she was going to touch him. "No. What makes no sense is allowing those who are unaffected by the gene manipulation of Lyme disease—"

"It's not gene manipulation—"

"You know what I mean. Ultimately you'll end up with better genes from those who naturally survive the Lyme disease purge." She took a step toward him, but he was beginning to adjust to the glare.

He took a step toward her. "And co-infections."

"Those too. But by inoculating yourself and the senator and who knows who else, aren't you perverting the intention of the phase?"

He stopped, suddenly angered. "No! It is you and all the ill people who are the perversions to the genetic code of the human race."

Anna was getting frustrated. She couldn't seem to distract the doctor enough to get him to move out of her way so she could make a dash for the door. She changed tactics. "You're so obviously in control of things, why do you even care about the stupid file?"

"No one was supposed to know about our experiment. But your boss couldn't help himself. Felt guilty, he said."

"That's why he was at that camp. He infected all those people."

"It was necessary."

"Why?"

"To prove we could do it," the doctor said.

Anna was connecting the dots. "To threaten people who don't want to pay for an inoculation? I suppose you charge an exorbitant fee."

"That was an unexpected business benefit."

"I don't understand."

"We needed to prove to our silent partners that we could control the bacteria and who became infected, thus increasing their profits."

"Big pharma."

"And now that you know, you must die."

But Anna wasn't willing to die. Instead, knowing his aversion to being touched, she lunged at him. It worked. Finally, the doctor scurried to the far wall.

Anna raced out the door and to the top of the stairs. She held tightly to the banister as she hurried down, trying to be just careful enough not to slip in her socks. Uncertain who might be with the doctor, she shone the light ahead of her. The front door was wide open revealing that the electricity was cut on this side of the island. Anna turned off the flashlight, afraid of attracting the senator or Martin or whoever else was here, and not wanting to reveal to the doctor where she was. She grabbed a jacket, which was hanging beside the door, and donned it as she ran out. She wished she could grab her shoes too, but she wasn't sure where they were.

Anna felt her way down the front stairs of the porch to the grass as her eyes adjusted to the waxing crescent moon. It wasn't much light, but it was enough. And maybe it was just dark enough to help her disappear in the shadows.

Anna knew the tide was low. It was her custom to write out the tidal chart whenever they visited the islands. Over the past few days she had been in the cottage, Anna noted the approximate times of the tidal change. Based on her observations, she had written out the next week's tide schedule. All times were a best guess, but she knew that the next high tide wasn't due till nearly first light. That gave her time to run to the spit that connected the island she was on to the summer community of Little Diamond Island. Once there, she could hide and call for a water taxi. If it weren't so cold, she might even consider swimming across to the more populated Peaks Island. She wondered now at the wisdom of hiding out on an island that was mostly deserted except in summer. How she wished she could simply run into the police station on the year-round island across the waters of Diamond Pass.

Anna's feet were sopping wet after she crossed. The sandbar was accessible, but the tide was already washing over it as she raced across. She stopped briefly, sheltering behind the first outbuilding she found to listen for approaching footsteps. Where were May and Tom? She wondered. Were they dead? Captured? How many others were after them? Hearing nothing, she continued on her way. She decided to head for the community building near the ferry dock—she thought the islanders referred to it as the casino, though she wasn't sure since she and Tom had only been here as day hikers years ago when the kids were young. She thought it was an odd name for the building. It made her mind wander as she wondered why anyone would want to gamble while vacationing in paradise.

Anna felt her feet going numb. Though the temperatures weren't quite below freezing, Anna wondered if she should worry about frostbite. She stopped and removed the soaked socks. She balled them up, realizing she shouldn't just leave them for someone to track her. She checked the pockets of the coat and was relieved to find hand-knitted mittens. This was May's coat. She pulled the mittens over her feet, and walked as carefully as she could. The last thing she needed now was pneumonia. Though, if the doctor caught up with her, it might be her best-case scenario. Thinking about the syringe he carried spurred her forward faster.

It was only about a half mile from one end of the island to the other. Anna was motivated by her determination to survive. She wished she had some sort of weapon besides a super-bright phone flashlight. She tried to remember the lessons from the self-defense classes she'd taken with her daughter and May. She had some moves if someone grabbed her from behind, which made her feel better. However, she also realized the moves hadn't worked when she was knocked out so easily with the ether. Recalling that moment caused her to lose hope. "Mustn't lose hope. Mustn't lose hope. Mustn't lose hope," she thought. By making it a mantra, she aspired to force herself to remain positive.

At the casino, which was connected by decking to the island's main dock, Anna walked the wrap-around porch until she was out of the wind. She opened her phone to dial a water taxi, but the brightness of the screen startled her and she closed it again. She listened for a count of thirty and, after not hearing anyone approach, she again opened the disposable phone and dialed information. The loudness of the recorded voice scared her, causing her to panic and close the phone yet again. She turned the volume down and tried once more. This time, she was able to get the number of a water taxi and connect to the service. However, this early in the morning— it was almost three—her only option was leaving a message to arrange for a future ride. She needed a ride now, but left a message anyway, just in case she'd still need one when the manager checked in around six. She wondered if the media would play the sound bite as her last words.

She shook the thought off, reminded herself of her "mustn't lose hope" mantra, and dialed emergency services. She needed someone to get her.

Someone she could trust. And though she'd been warned by both James and Tom not to trust any authority, she hoped calling the local police would be safe. Surely there wouldn't be a mole in the department here.

"Nine-one-one, what's the nature of your emergency?"

"Someone's trying to kill me. I ran away. I'm on Little Diamond Island at the Casino hiding on the porch. Please help me!"

Though she was urged to stay on the line, Anna again panicked and closed the phone, afraid the sound or light would attract the doctor, the senator, Martin, or whoever they had brought with them. She made sure, however, that the dispatcher understood that she was really on the closed-up island, explaining that she'd crossed the spit that appears during low tide. She pleaded with her to hurry. Anna was exhausted and cold. Adrenaline could mask those things only just so long.

Anna listened harder, willing the police boat to hurry to her. She wondered if they'd send the Coast Guard instead. Or the fire department. Did they play a quick round of rock, paper, scissors to see who answered the prank call she was sure the dispatcher thought this was? She still heard no footsteps following her. Finally, she gave into her exhaustion, sitting on the floor of the porch and pulling her legs up into the almost cape-like coat. She shivered and her teeth chattered, though she tried to hold her jaw tight so she could continue to listen for any would-be attackers.

She saw a search light at the same time she heard the engine of the boat as it approached. It arrived from the northeast instead of the southwest, where she had anticipated it would have been docked in the city. Perhaps it was already on patrol and had been diverted to her location. Police cars patrolled the streets during their shifts. Wouldn't police boats do the same? Many of the islands belonged to the city of Portland, after all.

As the boat docked, a patrolman identified it as belonging to the Portland Police. Anna pulled her legs free and stood. She took a shaky and tentative step to the corner of the building and, sucking in a deep breath, looked around the side. Almost immediately, she was caught in the spotlight. She ducked back into the shadows and listened as the patrolman radioed in that they had spotted her. She said a small prayer, apologizing for not praying more often—like when times are good—and asked for strength. She purposely avoided saying Amen, figuring that this way she would keep the direct line of communication open in case she needed to reach out again soon.

Finding courage in her prayer, she strode around the corner and headed for the dock just as one of the patrolmen marched toward her. "Ma'am, are you alone?"

"Yes, it's just me."

"Are you hurt?"

"No, just frightened and exhausted."

"Cold too, I imagine," said the officer, who couldn't have been much older than her children. He offered her a hand, slipping a comforting arm around her shoulders. "Right this way. We have a warm blanket for you and some low-acid coffee."

Anna stopped as a shiver ran up her spine. "Low acid? How do you know that about me?"

"It's all the rage among millennials now. Easier on the digestive system."

"Yes it is," Anna said, dubious that this was just an odd coincidence. She decided to test him. "I forgot to grab my phone." She tried to roll away from him and retreat, but it was as she feared: his grip tightened on her shoulder.

"You won't be needing your phone, ma'am," the officer said. "Not where you're going."

The next sequence of events occurred in the span of only seconds, yet time slowed to an eternity for Anna as she realized she'd made a huge mistake. Anna heard another boat approaching from the direction she had presumed it would. Its floodlight was on and hit her and her would-be kidnapper. She heard a woman scream at the same time a light in the docked boat's cabin snapped on and Anna saw Senator Ponema and Doctor Hale.

The senator strode to the back of the boat. "It's over now, Anna. Come with the good gentleman."

From behind her a voice called out. "Anna, goose!" It was Tom. She knew immediately what he meant by the odd command. While most people would shout "Duck!" Anna and Tom realized years ago when their kids were preschool age that in the popular game Duck, Duck, Goose, duck meant sit still, while goose meant run.

Anna's three weekend workshops and several weeks of Wednesday Warriors Women's Self-Defense classes kicked in. She threw her elbow into the young man's solar plexus, causing him to double over. She rolled away, and started to run, but heard a gunshot. She dropped to the wooden deck. She knew that while the tide was coming in, it still wasn't deep enough to cushion her fall below, but she had no choice. She rolled beneath the three-rail fence that lined the dock and, cradling her head as best she could, she fell to the rocks and water below. As gunfire exploded above her, she did a quick body scan. She would be bruised, but she didn't think anything was broken.

Though she knew she couldn't remain in the cold water for long, she also knew the beach was exposed. If a spotlight caught her, a bullet would surely follow. So, seeing the glint of a dinghy tied up below the dock, she crawled to it and tried to use it as shelter. She considered tipping it over and huddling beneath it, but she didn't want to give away her location with unnecessary noise or motion. As it was, she hoped the senator and his creepy ally would presume she'd been hurt. Maybe they'd leave her for dead.

The second boat approached, announcing itself as Portland Police and ordering the guns dropped. In the ceasefire, Anna listened to the second boat moor alongside the first. At least six boots hit the deck above her. "Body down. He's dead," one officer said.

Anna heard boots walking on the first boat. "Two dead," an officer said.

"Where's the woman?" Another voice asked.

Anna held her breath, uncertain if this boat was trustworthy. She sent up another silent prayer, asking that Tom be all right, and for a sign that she might be able to trust these men.

"Anna?" It was May.

"Ma'am, please stay on the boat."

Anna couldn't believe it. It was May! That must be her sign. She was safe at last. She made a move to stand, trying to will herself to call out, but she was so cold and exhausted, only a weak "May?" resulted.

"Anna, you're safe now." It was Tom. He put a hand on her shoulder. She turned and buried her head in his embrace.

"You're alright," Anna said, full of relief.

"Are you?"

"I might have gotten a bit bruised up, but nothing seems broken." Anna paused, worrying over how to phrase her question. Finally she just blurted it out. "Did you kill the senator and the doctor?"

"I was shooting to wound and disarm, not to kill."

"That is who's dead, though—right?"

"Yes, it is."

"If you didn't kill them, who did?"

"My guess is the man who was impersonating an officer," Tom said. "But only a thorough investigation will tell for sure."

"And what happened to him?"

"I wounded him."

"I'm glad to hear it wasn't you who killed them," Anna said.

"Who's there?" An officer asked as he pointed his light below the dock.

"It's okay, officer," Tom said. "I have my wife. We're coming out."

Tom guided Anna to the beach area where an officer with a warming blanket met them. Anna heard running on the dock above, and saw May racing toward her as the officer and Tom led her up to the decking.

"Anna! You're alright!"

"May! I thought you were dead."

"I thought you were."

"How did you get to Portland and back here?"

"We have some catching up to do," May said. "Let's just say that you were right about Martin."

On the boat, May and a female officer helped Anna remove her wet clothes. They wrapped her up in an oversized police jacket and another warming blanket. Anna appreciated being dry as they waited for the water ambulance to join them. While Tom walked the scene with the detectives, talking like he was the senior officer in charge, May described how she had been ambushed. Anna had gone to bed early, or more accurately, at what had become her customary eight o'clock bedtime. May sat on the porch drinking ginger tea and knitting, while Tom rode his bike to the other side of the island to pick up supplies that were waiting with the Diamond Cove staff. When the lights went out, May was grabbed, gagged, and bound in a flash.

May didn't recognize the assailant's voice. He told her to keep quiet or she'd have her throat cut. The gag was so far down her throat, she could hardly breathe, never mind make a noise to wake Anna. May was walked to an awaiting boat where Martin sat at the wheel. The assailant left her with him and returned to the house. Martin fired up the boat and left. He told May they needed to get the police, but they couldn't call it in. The emergency call service had been subverted and would go directly to Senator Ponema and the pilot of his boat. He removed her gag, unbound her, and drove her to shore. The two of them raced to the police station where it took some serious convincing that the police should get a patrol boat out there, but refrain from using the radio. Martin and May had no proof. Why should the police believe them? But they couldn't ignore the threat, either. So they kept Martin at the station while May accompanied the boat.

They were headed for the ferry dock on Great Diamond Island, but noticed the boat and the spotlight on the Little Diamond Island dock. When gunshots sounded, the police made May duck for cover in the cabin as they approached.

In the water ambulance, Tom shared his experience. The lights were fine on his side of the island, so he had no reason to hurry back. He and the staff member broke down the groceries and supplies into smaller packages so they could be stowed in the bike's front basket and in the milk crate on the back, as well as in Tom's backpack. Still, some supplies had to go in two bags. They tried to distribute the weight evenly so he could hold the bags as he steered the handlebars. It took much longer than he had anticipated. Tom was kicking himself for not bringing the golf cart. But he had wanted the small bit of exercise.

When he returned to the cottage side of the island, the lights were out. He knew immediately that their hiding place had been compromised. He hid the bike behind a bush and, gun pointed ahead, quietly snuck up to the house, which he found was empty. In the kitchen, he saw Anna's tide chart and instinctively knew where she would go to try to escape—the opposite direction that anyone other than her husband would have thought.

Tom tracked her, but realized someone else had too. He was able to knock out the would-be assassin with a blow to the head. His next action occurred when he arrived at the casino and told Anna to goose.

Anna's cuts and bruises were tended to in the hospital in Portland and she was released. Jim had driven up to be with May. None of them could leave yet since their formal statements had to be made at the police department the next day, so they stayed at a local hotel.

In their hotel room, Tom held Anna as she tried to quiet her mind enough to sleep. "I never wanted to leave you," he said. "A few years ago. When I said that, I didn't mean it."

"Then why did you say it?"

"It was my lame attempt to get out of watching and listening in on you and the senator. I thought if we were separated, they'd have to find someone else. Once they did, I could apologize profusely, beg your forgiveness, and try to patch up the damage I'd caused."

"They wouldn't let you out of their service?"

"Worse. They hinted that if I didn't do this, the next person they recruited might be unsavory."

"Oh." Anna was quiet as she imagined someone creepy listening in on her every conversation. "I think I'm glad you stuck with it."

"I am too," Tom said. "I love you."

Tears sprang to Anna's eyes. "It's been so long since I've heard you say that. I've missed you. I've missed us."

"I have too."

"I love you too," Anna said. Silently she sent up another prayer—this time of thanks.

***

Their marriage would survive the unbelievable ordeal of the past several months. Anna was so relieved and happy that she made a special **Love and Marriage** *board on Pinterest.*

To learn more, visit Anna's "Love and Marriage" board on Pinterest: https://www.pinterest.com/anna_mcgrory/love-and-marriage/

Epilogue

Anna and May sat on the porch of the Cliff Island Library, one of two hotspots on the island. It was a key reason the women loved their visits here—that they had to purposely set out to find Wi-Fi. Otherwise, their days were unfettered by the constant interruptions of the outside world via email and social media.

"I don't see it yet," May said, looking at her computer screen.

"That's because I haven't sent it yet." Anna typed on her laptop.

"I thought you were done."

"With the main story, yes. Now I'm stuck trying to think of what to write in the epilogue."

"Does it need an epilogue?"

"I don't know. Maybe that's the problem. But I thought I'd leave on sort of a high note."

"That we all got away with our lives isn't a high enough note for you?"

"That *they* all got away with their lives," Anna said, correcting May. "You mean the characters in my book. They are not us."

"Whatever you say. You're the writer."

Anna had been working on her book since the week after being attacked. She was determined to get the word out about the conspiracy surrounding Lyme disease since it seemed that all the press outlets must have been owned or managed by members of the American Eugenics Society. They were everywhere, like Hydra in Marvel Comics. And, like Hydra, they seemed to be super secretive and elusive.

Only a handful of outlets had picked up the story of Frank's missing file and Anna's kidnapping, mostly on the internet. For conspiracy theorists, it was enough proof that a conspiracy existed. For many members of Lyme disease support groups, the evidence confirmed that Lyme was real, that tests were inadequate at best, and that recommended lengthy treatments of antibiotics were correct. However, the evidence did nothing to persuade the changing of the CDC or NIH language and guidelines, which frustrated Anna. Therefore, she decided she'd take the quote "Fiction is the lie through which we tell the truth" from Albert Camus to heart and write a novel about her ordeal.

"Hang on," Anna said. "I have an email from—I mean, it can't be from him—but it's from his account."

"James?"

"No. He hasn't been in touch since he got reassigned." James had been successful in locating about two-dozen names on the American Eugenics Society's membership—all of them deceased. He, Tom, and Anna realized that the names he found were only people the secret society members were willing to share, such as the dead Doctor Hale and Senator Ponema. Frank was also on the list. They guessed that it really was his guilty conscience that led him to interview the Lyme patients.

"You miss him?" Anna shook her head no. "Oh, come on, not even just a little?" May asked. "All that attention could be easy to get used to."

"Jim pays you loads of attention."

"We're not talking about me though, are we?" May watched her friend for signs her cheeks were turning crimson, but they weren't. "Really? Not at all?"

"I was his assignment. He was hired to pay attention to me. It isn't the same as being actually interested," Anna said. Following Frank Barber's mysterious death, James had been hired by the CIA to investigate the suspicious circumstances and was eventually assigned to protect Anna. "Besides," Anna said, "Tom's been fantastic. He's explained his distance. Now that he's no longer reporting to the committee, I feel like we have our marriage back."

May held up her clipboard. "If I have anything to do with it, you sure will!" May was referring to her role as stage manager for Tom and Anna's vow renewal ceremony, which was happening in two days, and was the reason they were on the island now. It was to be a near recreation of Joanie's wedding day, with far fewer in attendance.

Most notably missing would be Margaret, who had double crossed Anna and Tom. She had been so helpful in arranging the hideout cottage on Great Diamond Island. Then she gave Senator Ponema the location. The authorities had found Margaret's text in the senator's phone records. And though there was no evidence to support the theory that Frank was murdered, it was suspected Margaret may have killed him and staged it to look like a suicide. As far as Tom knew through his sources, Margaret had yet to be interviewed since she was currently hiding out in the small nation of Andorra, situated in the Pyrenees between France and Spain—a country without a formal extradition agreement with the U.S. Anna wondered if Margaret was bored in the tiny country that catered to a winter ski crowd. She certainly hoped so.

May watched as her friend inserted her ear buds and her eyes went wide. May glided to Anna's side and pulled one of her ear buds out, placing it in her own ear. Anna didn't object. Instead, she backed up and began the video at the beginning. It was Senator Ponema. He was sitting at his home office desk, staring into the camera. "If you're seeing this, it means I'm dead," he said. "And no doubt you think you've won. But let me tell you something, Anna McGrory, you have no idea what you've interfered in. This is bigger than me or you or Doctor Hale or Frank Barber. This is bigger than the United States citizenry. This is worldwide.

"You can't stop the spread of Lyme disease and its many co-infections any more than we can. You think this was just a simple eugenics experiment gone wrong? A xenophobic attempt to improve the human population by controlling the desirable heritable characteristics through eradicating the weak from our population?

"Look around. What do you see? Wall to wall people. That's what's killing this planet. Not some climate change propaganda talking point. There are simply too many human beings. Those of us in the American Eugenics Society saw that. As did people from around the globe. We had the courage to team up and do something about it.

"And now you want to unravel that. Well, consider this: if Lyme disease is eradicated, many other diseases will be too—Alzheimer's, MS, ALS, Lupus, fill-in-the-blanks—since their core cause is the bacteria that causes Lyme. You know this from your own experience, don't you? You're welcome, by the way.

"You think our population growth is out of control now? When these diseases are eliminated, then where will everyone live? And how will humans survive with only our planet's limited resources to sustain them?

"You aren't part of the solution. You're part of the reason we needed to launch this mission. But it's not my problem anymore since I'm dead. I hope you're happy now."

The screen faded out. Anna and May removed their ear buds and were quiet a minute. Finally May said, "I think you've found your epilogue."

"Seems a bit heavy," Anna said. "I was hoping to end on a high note, remember?"

"How did he set the message up to arrive now?" May asked. "He's been dead for months."

Anna was wondering the same thing. "Unless someone else sent it for him."

"From his email?"

"Wouldn't that be easy for a hacker?" Anna asked. Anna started typing. "Maybe James can get some answers."

"See? You do think of him," May said.

"Only when it comes to the case." Anna was not deceiving herself on this issue. In fact, because of the bugs in the cottage and the estate, Tom knew that Anna had been attracted to James. They talked about it, about Anna's jealousy over the woman she still referred to as Miss Stilettos, and about the distance that had grown between the long-married couple. Their gulf was not solely caused by Tom's having been forced to spy upon Anna. That was something the two of them had come to terms with and were currently working on as they created a loving and trusting marriage again.

After Anna forwarded the email, she and May sat and quietly contemplated the message and it's meaning. As they pondered it, a familiar freshly groomed black and brown dog—a rescued hound mix—raced onto the porch. He flopped at Anna's feet and presented his belly for scratching. Anna and May laughed, enjoying his enthusiasm. "Where's your mommy?" Anna asked as she pet the dog.

"Right here," Joanie replied, stepping onto the porch.

Anna set aside her laptop and stood to catch her daughter in an embrace. When she pulled back to look at Joanie, something worried Anna about her appearance. "Are you feeling okay?"

"Yeah, Mom," said Joanie. "I'm fine. You?"

"I'm good." Off May's look, Anna amended her answer. "I'm better than I was." Anna looked at Joanie again and squinted, trying to identify what it was that was off about her daughter's appearance. "You don't have Lyme, do you?"

"No, Mom. It's not Lyme. Though I did catch something you've had before."

May giggled as she figured it out. Anna glared at her friend. "What are you laughing at?"

"Relax. It's all good," May said.

Anna looked at Joanie again. She noticed the color in her cheeks. She looked down at her belly. "Are you...?"

"We wanted to wait and tell you and Dad at dinner tonight," Joanie said. Anna waited. She wanted to hear it in no uncertain terms. She raised her eyebrows in question. "Alright, alright, I'll say it. You're going to be a grandma!"

"Yay! Welcome to the grandmother's club," May said. "Congratulations, Joanie!"

Tears sprang to Anna's eyes as she hugged her daughter. "That's fantastic news! I love you, kiddo."

"I love you too, Mom."

Anna turned to May. "Think maybe it's about time I learned to knit, don't you agree?" Of course, Anna knew May absolutely agreed with her on this matter.

***

Anna hoped she would find as much pleasure in **knitting** *baby items as her best friend May did. She certainly enjoyed the images of knitted baby blankets, sweaters, and booties that she found on Pinterest. It was easy to imagine herself knitting now that her grandbaby was on the way.*

To learn more, visit Anna's "Crafts & More" board on Pinterest: https://www.pinterest.com/anna_mcgrory/crafts-more/

The End

ABOUT THE AUTHOR

After surviving several bouts of Lyme and related co-infections, award-winning screenwriter and Emmy-nominated producer Dana Biscotti Myskowski has found that her illness has introduced her to what's most important in life: family, friends, reading, writing, and meditation. A mom to two fabulous young adults, and married to her true love for 30-plus years, Dana finds herself caring for retired loved ones who now live with her and her husband, herding three dogs, writing, and cooking. (Photo by JP Myskowski)

READ WHAT OTHERS ARE SAYING:

"When her beloved senator boss winds up dead, even Lyme Disease can't stop Anna McGrory from becoming a self-proclaimed Nancy Drew. With more twists and turns than the Mohawk Trail, *I Cannot Play With You* is suspenseful, surprising, and a total page-turner."
—Hilary Weisman Graham, TV writer *Orange is the New Black & Bones*, and author of *Reunited* (Simon & Schuster)

"As a writer and songwriter, I was always taught to 'show, don't tell,' and to engage the audience with a twist on something familiar. Dana Biscotti Myskowski does a perfect job of both, weaving together a murder mystery and Lyme! Who knew it could be done, and who knew it could be so much fun to read? I love that she educates through fiction, too. It makes learning much more memorable. Highly recommended!"
—Dana Parish, singer/songwriter *Not My Problem, Thankful, Always be Your Girl, Someday I'll Fly, Broken Ones*, & more (Sony/ATV), and champion for those suffering with Lyme and other tick-borne diseases

Thank you so much for reading one of our **Crime Fiction** novels.
If you enjoyed the experience, please check out our recommended title for
your next great read!

Caught in a Web by Joseph Lewis

"This important, nail-biting crime thriller about MS-13 sets the bar very high.
One of the year's best thrillers." *—BEST THRILLERS*

BLACK ROSE
writing™

SCOOBY-DOO! PICTURE CLUE BOOK

DINOSAUR DIG

by Erin Soderberg

Illustrated by Duendes del Sur

Hello Reader — Level 1

ISBN 0-439-20231-0

12 11 10 9 8 7 6 5 4   1 2 3 4 5 6/0

Designed by Mary Hall

Printed in the U.S.A.

First Scholastic printing, September 2000

SCHOLASTIC INC.

New York Toronto London Auckland Sydney
Mexico City New Delhi Hong Kong

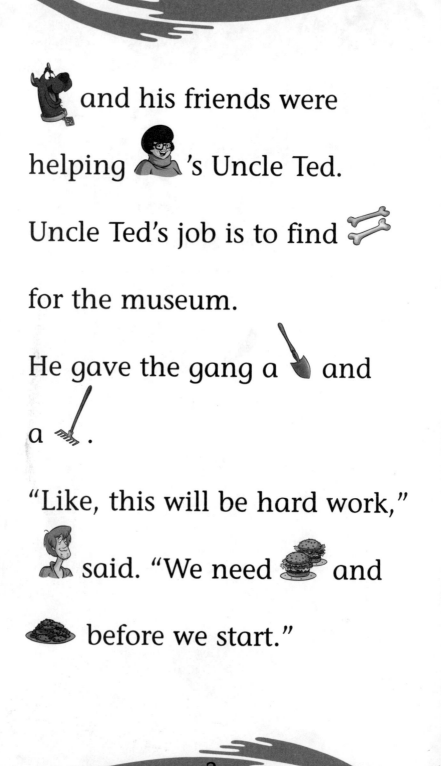

and his friends were

helping 's Uncle Ted.

Uncle Ted's job is to find

for the museum.

He gave the gang a and

a .

"Like, this will be hard work,"

said. "We need and

before we start."

"Have you found any 🦴 yet?"
🧑‍🦱 asked.

"Look in that 📦," Uncle Ted said.

 looked. The 📦 was empty.

"Oh, no!" Uncle Ted shouted.

"All the 🦴 are gone."

"Maybe there's a  ghost hiding all the ⦿ !" 🧑 said.

"Roh, no!" said 🐕 .

"We have to help Uncle Ted find the missing ⦿ ," 👩 said.

"He needs the ⦿ for the museum," 👩 said.

"Let's look for clues, gang!" said 👱 .

and looked for clues.

They found a food .

"Let's check the ,"

Shaggy said.

They found some and .

But they did not find the

missing .

"Jinkies!"  said.

She found a big ⬤ in a ⬤ .

But there were no 🦴 .

👤 and 👤 found a 🪣 .

But they did not find the 🦴 .

"Well, gang," Uncle Ted said.

"Let's make a . We can look for the in the morning."

Uncle Ted made .

Then the gang roasted over the .

"Like, I hope the ghost does not like ," said.

"Did you hear that noise?" asked.

" , let's go check it out,"  said.

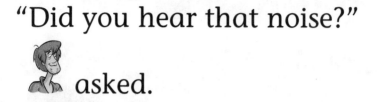 jumped into the 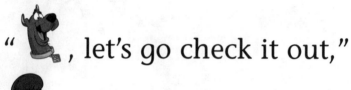 .

"Would you do it for a 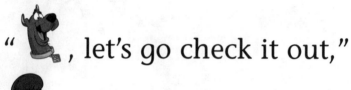 ?" asked.

Oh, no! All the 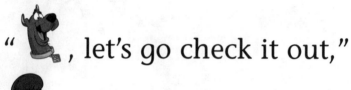 were gone!

Did the ghost take the ?

wanted to find the .

"Come on, gang," said.

Maybe they would find the .

Hopefully they would not find the ghost!

The  helped 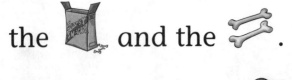 and the

gang to see in the dark.

 used his nose to search for

the 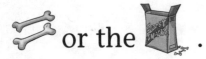 and the 🦴 .

They looked in a 🛏️ .

They found Uncle Ted's 🐕 .

But they did not find the missing

🦴 or the 📦 .

smelled and wagged

his 2 .

dug a giant in the dirt

with his paws.

Uncle Ted's jumped into the

and pulled out some .

There was no ghost!

"You found the , !"

said.

"You saved the museum's ,"

Uncle Ted said. "You are a hero!"

threw a .

"Scooby-Dooby-Doo!" barked.

Did you spot all the picture clues in this Scooby-Doo mystery?

Each picture clue is on a flash card. Ask a grown-up to cut out the flash cards. Then try reading the words on the back of the cards. The pictures will be your clue.

Reading is fun with Scooby-Doo!

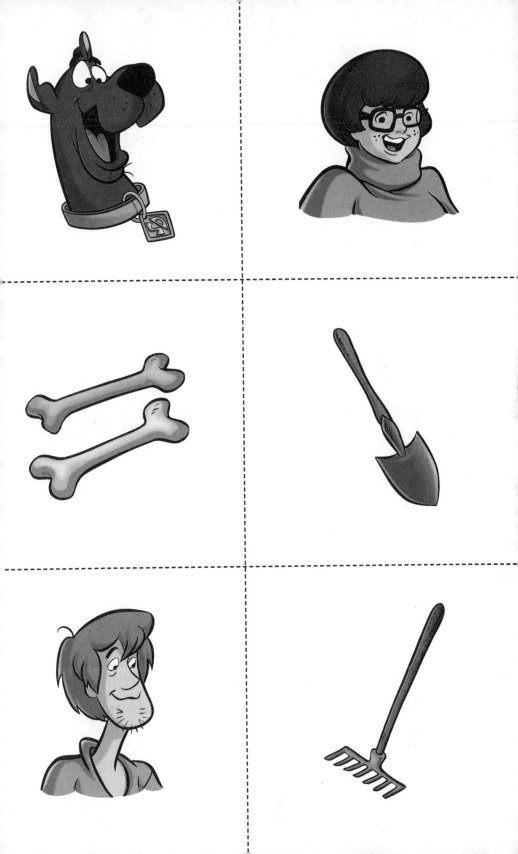

Velma	Scooby-Doo
shovel	bones
rake	Shaggy

cookies	burgers
dinosaur	box
truck	Daphne

rock	apples
Fred	hole
pail	campfire

sleeping bag	marshmallow.
moon	Scooby Snacks
tail	dog